PETER C
THIS MAN IS DANGEROUS

REGINALD Evelyn Peter Southouse Cheyney (1896-1951) was born in Whitechapel in the East End of London. After serving as a lieutenant during the First World War, he worked as a police reporter and freelance investigator until he found success with his first Lemmy Caution novel. In his lifetime Cheyney was a prolific and wildly successful author, selling, in 1946 alone, over 1.5 million copies of his books. His work was also enormously popular in France, and inspired Jean-Luc Godard's character of the same name in his dystopian sci-fi film *Alphaville*. The master of British noir, in Lemmy Caution Peter Cheyney created the blueprint for the tough-talking, hard-drinking pulp fiction detective.

PETER CHEYNEY

THIS MAN IS DANGEROUS

DEAN STREET PRESS

Published by Dean Street Press 2022

All Rights Reserved

First published in 1936

Cover by DSP

ISBN 978 1 914150 85 2

www.deanstreetpress.co.uk

CHAPTER ONE
THE PICK-UP

EVEN Miranda Van Zelden couldn't spoil the pipe-dream I had on the corner of Piccadilly and Haymarket.

It was one of those nights. You know what I mean. Everything was O.K., and you feelin' that you're a go-getter and that you got 'em all beat to the game. I felt on top of the world an' I don't often get that way.

Take a look at me. My name's Lemmy Caution by rights but I got so many *aliases* that sometimes I don't know if I'm John Doe or it's Thursday. In Chicago—the place that smart guys call Chi just so's you'll know they've read a detective book written by some punk who always says he nearly got shot by one of Capone's cannoneers but didn't quite make the grade—they used to call me "Two-Time" because they said it always took two slugs to stop me, an' in the other place where coppers go funny colours when they think of me they call me Toledo.

I'm tellin' you I'm a big-shot an' if you don't believe me just take a look at any dump where they got a police record and a finger-printin' apparatus an' you're mine for keeps.

All of which is very fine but it don't get you no place an' it don't do anything about that smart jane Miranda Van Zelden who is a baby who has caused me a whole lot of trouble an' I don't mean maybe.

But Haymarket was lookin' fine to me. You see I ain't never been in London any before an' I'm tickled the way I made it gettin' here. Somebody out in New York was tellin' me that these English coppers is so smart that they even arrest each other for practice; they told me that I got as much chance of bustin' the passport check-up as a nice blonde had of stayin' that way in Ma Licovat's love parlour at Greek Alley an' Twelfth . . . well, they was wrong.

I made it. I slipped over via Marseilles where some old punk who takes a keen pride in twicin' Customs' guys sold me a first-class American passport for four hundred dollars with a real guy's name on it an' a picture that looked like me after I'd had a smack in the puss an' everything complete.

I'm walking down Haymarket an' it's eleven o'clock, an' I've had a swell dinner an' I am wearing a tuxedo an' a black fedora. If you must know more then I'm goin' to tell you that I weigh two hundred pounds an' I got that sorta mug that dames fall for in a big way because it is a relief from the guys in the Russian ballet. I have also got brains an' some girl in Toledo nearly drunk herself to cinders on bad hooch because I gave her the air, which, they musta told you, means sex-appeal, so now you know.

I said it was a nice night. I was meanderin' down Haymarket just thinking things over quietly to myself, because I do not want you to think that I am a guy who takes a whole lot of chances that ain't indicated. This Miranda Van Zelden business wasn't no baby's play-time hour I'm tellin' you, an' I knew that there was one or two guys would iron me out just as soon as take a look at me if they had known what the real schedule was.

Maybe you folks have heard of the snatch racket. You pinch some guy or some dame, or maybe a kid—they gotta be classy of course, an' you just take 'em away to some hideout until their folks cough up plenty dough. Some of the nicest guys I ever knew was in the snatch racket. It's a classy game an' pays if the Feds don't get their hooks on you.

Which brings me back to where I was just before I turned off, don't it. Feds. . . . Special Agents of the Federal Department of Justice—G men—the little fellers who can do no wrong. Well, I sorta had an idea that one of these palookas was on the boat comin' over from Marseilles . . . still, I guess we can come back to G men a little later on.

Presenting Miranda Van Zelden—glorifying pulchritude. Ladies an' gentlemen give the little girl a hand. Now you know each other I'll wise you up about Miranda. This dame is an heiress to about seventeen million dollars—does it make you gasp some? She is also as wild as they make 'em, an' she is about the swellest looker that ever a tired business man dreamt about while he was bein' kept late at the office.

The first time I ever spoke to Miranda was at the Honeysuckle an' Jasmine Inn which is out on the main Toledo Road. This was the night when Frenchy Squills decides that he will have a little argument with the Lacassar mob that is runnin' the dump. You can take it from me that the amount of jasmine an' honeysuckle operatin' that night would have stuck in your eye. It mighta been called Lead Alley because the amount of hot iron that is flyin' about that Inn is nobody's business.

It was about one o'clock in the morning an' I am leanin' up against one of the ornamental pillars in the dance room, waitin' for something nice an' hot to pop. I have also got an eyeful of Miranda who is dancin' with some gorilla of Lacassar's—she was interested in mobsters at that time—an' I am thinkin' that Miranda is easy to look at. She is lithe like a panther with a figure that could bust up a diamond wedding an' she dances like a fairy. I was just thinkin' that it was durn silly for a swell dame like she was to go hangin' around that sorta place just for the sake of gettin' a thrill outa rubbin' shoulders with a lot of punk that wasn't fit to clean her car sump.

Before I go any further I guess I'd better wise you up as to what the position was in Toledo with these boys. What I was doing up there is just nobody's business. I sorta go around looking for trouble any time there's anything good hanging on the end of it, and I'd gone there from Oklahoma where things was gettin' a bit hot for me at that time, also I'd heard about Miranda.

Nobody wasn't quite certain as to who was chasing who. Mr. Roosevelt, President of the United States, and a guy called J. Edgar Hoover, of the U.S. Department of Justice, had said they was goin' to run mobsters out of America. The Police Department heard 'em and said so too. But at this time whether the mobsters was chasing the police or the other way round nobody knew by rights. Repeal never stopped a thing. There was more skullduggery an' a bigger rake-off after repeal than there ever was before.

Frenchy Squills reckoned that he was running Toledo. He was a king high bootlegger, highjacker, racketeer, an' what will you, in those parts up to the time Tony Lacassar showed up. Tony blew out of Chicago after some argument in a garage where four coppers, three G men and a travelling salesman who was so drunk that he thought he was in Oshkosh, all got filled up so full of lead that they just didn't know.

Tony got the tip to push out for a bit, so he went up to Toledo, and he took up there with him the finest bundle of go-getters that was ever in a racket. I've seen some bad guys but the Lacassar mob was just pure poison.

Tony starts to muscle in, an' when he muscles in on a dump he don't mean maybe. Frenchy tries to put up a show but after they find one of his muscle men nailed up on a tree near Maumee Bay with 4-inch nails an' a note sending Tony's kind regards to Frenchy stuck in his mouth, it looks as if Frenchy is beat to the game.

There's a meeting an' a sorta truce is arranged. Things are quiet for a bit an' even the fact that Frenchy is now only running one dump—the Honeysuckle an' Jasmine Inn—which is a roadhouse where anything you like can happen an' did—don't satisfy Tony. He has to have that. An' it looks like he figures to take the place over on the night I'm telling you about.

I was just interested. I thought maybe when these guys was finished bumping each other off, somethin' might come my way, and I'm a patient sorta cuss. I got medals for waiting for all sorta things—dough, dames, district attorneys and what have you—and I was interested in something else. I knew darned well that Lacassar wasn't really the big shot. I always had a hunch that there was some guy behind Lacassar, who was just a big mouth stuck up to hide the real feller. I also had an idea that this real guy is a feller called Siegella, who is really a big guy, an' is just poison. The things that this feller Siegella had done was just nobody's business.

I was telling you, it was about one o'clock in the mornin', an' I'm leaning up against a pillar watching Miranda doing her stuff with Yonnie Malas, who is Lacassar's star machine gun man. This guy Malas is good-looking and he can certainly dance. So can Miranda. I tell you that pair was good, but it sorta got me somewhere under the belt to see a nice piece of goods like Miranda, who was anyway American, dancing with a cheap yegg like Yonnie.

It was a hot night—one of them nights when every time you try to breathe you wonder where you're gonna get the air from. My collar was beginning to wilt. I had the sorta feelin' that I wished it would rain or somethin' just to clean things up a bit. The dance room was big, but it was hot. Dance rooms always are hot. The whole place was full of toughs, city fakers, play boys, "come-on" girls, an' all the rest of the hoodlums that you get round a place like that. I reckon about thirty per cent of the guys in that place had got a shooting iron stuck on their body somewhere or other an' knew how to use it.

After a bit I walked over to the bar at the end of the room an' ordered myself a high-ball.

"Nice place you've got here!" I says to the bar-tender.

"Oh, yeah!" he says, "ain't you original? So what?"

"Say, listen," I says to him, "there ain't no need to get that way. I was just passing the time of day, you know."

"That's O.K. by me," he says. "Passing the time of day don't hurt nobody, but that high-ball costs a dollar."

I told him that I reckoned a dollar was a lot of money to pay for a highball, to which he cracks back to me that a dollar is a lot of money to some guys anyhow. By this time I have come to the conclusion that this bar-tender is just about as much good to me for purposes of information as a couple of sick headaches. So I walk through the dance room again, out on to the veranda and round the back.

The garage which is at the back of the Inn is a long low shed running parallel with a road which curves round behind the main road in front of the Inn. Standing at the end of the garage shed, leaning up against a post an' looking down the road is some guy. He is wearing a tuxedo an' a white fedora. He is smoking a cigarette an' just thinking about nothing at all.

I have seen guys looking that way before, an' they are usually lookout men waiting for something to break. He sees me an' he takes a look at me, an' he puts his hand into his right coat pocket, which if you have been in America as long as I have is a thing you take notice of.

I throw my cigarette stub away an' I walk over to this guy. "Howdy, pal?" I say, "can you give me a light?" I take two cigarettes out of my pocket an' I give him one. He looks at me and by the look of his eyes this guy is a dope.

There he stands smiling and showing a whole lot of fancy teeth. He brings out a lighter and he gives me a light. Then he looks down the road again.

"Don't you like it inside?" he says.

I mop the back of my neck.

"It ain't so good in there. It's too darned hot. It's bad enough out here. Why the hell a guy hangs around this sorta place, I don't know," I go on. "When you come to consider all the things a guy can do an' he has to hang around a dump like this drinking lousy liquor an' getting hot!"

He looks at me. "Don't you like it, kid?" he says. "Well, why don't you scram out of it?"

"Well, where do I scram to?" I says. "It looks to me as if you don't like it either. What about coming an' having a little drink with me?"

He puts his hand back in his pocket. "Listen, kid," he says. "If I want a drink I can go buy myself one. Supposing you scram. I'm busy!"

I knock the ash off my cigarette. "Sorry, pal," I said, "I wouldn't know that. Expecting somebody?"

He looks at me like a snake. "Listen, baby," he says. "Didn't I tell you to scram out of here. You know you're one of those curious guys who is always liable to get himself into trouble."

I threw my cigarette stub away. "Well, there ain't no need to get that way about it," I says. "I never meant a thing. Good-night!"

I take a quiet look round an' there's nobody around this place. Then I make a movement as if I'm going to turn away, but just as I do this I spin round and I smack this guy right between the eyes. He just goes out like he was poleaxed. I take him by the collar an' I drag him to the far corner of the garage which is dark, an' I prop him up behind a car. I then proceed to frisk him.

This guy has got a Smith & Wesso

n Special in a shoulder holster under his left arm, an' a .38 Colt automatic in his right hand tuxedo pocket. Stuck in his pants' waistband he is packing a seven-inch Swedish sailor's knife. In his left hand pants' pocket he has got a small egg bomb. I'm tellin' you the New York armoury has got nothin' on this guy.

I prop him up against the wall an' I start pinchin' his nostrils which is a good way of makin' a guy come back to earth, an' after a bit he starts to shake his head. Then he opens his eyes.

"O.K. wise-guy," he mutters. "Just you wait a bit, will you? I'm goin' to do something to you for this, sucker. When I'm done with you I guess your own mother would change you for an old pair o' pants. You wait till Lacassar gets his hooks on you."

"Skip it, baby," I says smackin' him one across the puss. "Listen to me—I'm talkin' right now. I don't want to hurt your feelin's or anything, but I just want to know who you're waitin' for an' it's no good tryin' any cracks because I've got your cannons in my pockets. Now, sweetheart," I says, "do we play ball or do I bust in your face with a spanner?"

"Say, listen," he says, "I don't know nothin'. I was just takin' the air. Can't a guy take the air?"

"Hooey," I says. "I'm wise to you, pal, you're one of Lacassar's mob, ain't you? Say, do you think I'm so dumb that I ain't realised that about half the staff around this joint are his people. There's waiters in there that never waited on anything or anybody before—except maybe the cops—waitin' for something to break. The maître d'hô-tel has got a bulge under his left arm where he's packin' a shoulder holster that makes him look like he was deformed, an' if the bar-ten-der ain't carryin' a Smith an' Wesson in each of his hip pockets then I'm an Indian princess with the ague. In fact," says I, "there's a sorta atmosphere around this dump tonight that smells as if there might be a gun battle at any moment. So all you got to do is to talk an' talk quick, kid, before I start my big act with this spanner."

"What the hell," says he. "I don't mind telling you what I know. Maybe there will be a bit of trouble around here tonight."

"O.K.," I says, "that's fine!"

He grins. "That's all right by me, pal," he says, "now perhaps you'll give me my shooting irons back."

I tell him not to be silly an' I hit him some more. He goes down like a log an' I truss him up with some electric wirin' I find in the corner. I then stick a handkerchief in his mouth and push him inside a saloon car with one wheel off that is nearby. I reckon nobody is going to use this car for some time.

After that I take a walk round the road an' light myself a ciga-rette. After a bit I go back to the garage an' look at the cars. Presently I find a big roadster with "M. van Z." on the door, an' I start her up an' drive her down the road, away from the Inn. I put this car in a little spot behind three trees, an' I leave it with the engine runnin'.

Then I walk back. About a hundred yards down the road there is a rise an' from the top of this rise I can look over the country straight down a steep road. Right away in the distance I see the lights of some autos and I reckon these will be Frenchy's cars. I also reckon that they will pull up by the side of this road, off the main road, about fifty yards away where there is a copse.

I'm right about this, because fifteen minutes later they pull up there an' I can see that the fat guy in the first car is Frenchy Squills. I reckon it's now time for me to get back to the Inn, so I slide round the back way, get in over the veranda and walk back to the dance hall. I go up to the bar, buy myself another highball an' walk over to a corner.

After a minute I signal to some cigarette girl an' she comes over. "Listen, sister," I say to her. "How'd you like to make five bucks?"

She grins up at me. She is a pretty kid.

"What can I lose," she says.

I slip her five. "You see that dame over there," I says to her, "the one dancing with a slim feller. I want you to go over to her an' tell her that she is wanted urgent on the telephone. See? An' I reckon I'd do it right now. Tell her the call's in the booth down the passage way."

"O.K.," she says, "that looks easy."

She walks straight across the dance floor and she goes up to where Miranda and Malas is dancing, an' I see Miranda stop an' say something to Malas an' walk across the floor.

Well, I reckon I've got this in time pretty good, because just as Miranda gets off the dance floor the band stops. It stops for a very good reason. It stops because some guy has shot the saxophonist clean through the guts, and this feller is yelling like hell on the band platform. Right then the glass windows on the veranda side of the dance room is bust open and without so much as by your leave some guy starts across the floor with a tommy gun right into the thick of five Lacassar mobsters who are drinking scotch at a table in the other corner. At the same time three of the waiters who are Lacassar boys unload an' proceed to open fire on the windows. In about five minutes' time the place is like a butcher's shop on Friday night.

There is some fat palooka who ought to have been home with his wife and kids and who couldn't get off the dance floor in time, trying to drag himself off it with one leg broke by a bullet from the tommy gun. But he don't make it before he gets hit again. He has one in this time through the head so he decides to remain dead.

The cigarette girl, who has still got the five bucks I give her clasped in her fingers, is hit just as she is gettin' off on the other side of the floor. She flops down with a funny surprised look on her face, holdin' one hand, with the five dollar bill in it, to her side which is dyed red ... poor kid.

I just stand nice and quiet up against the wall. I've got a wooden pillar to one side of me, an' I reckon I've got as good a chance as anybody else. Out of the corner of my eye I can see Miranda, who has by this time discovered that the telephone call is phoney, an' has also heard the battle in progress, standing at the top of the passage-way leading away from the telephone booth, with her head round the corner watching the war.

Believe me that girl is a marvel, her cheeks are flushed and her eyes are bright. She has a little blonde curl which keeps swingin' over her left eye and she keeps pushing it back so as she can see better. Anybody would think that this dame had paid ten dollars an' was looking at a slug contest or a baseball game.

Presently things eases off a bit. Some of the Lacassar guys outside the Inn have opened fire on Frenchy's boys from the rear, an' the fight is proceeding to tail off down the back road towards the place where Squills has parked his cars. It looks to me as if he is getting the worst of it, and I am thinkin' he is a punk to try an' pull something on Lacassar who anyway is organised.

I think this is a good opportunity to make a move, so I start to edge over towards the passage-way where Miranda is. When I get near I call across quietly:

"Say, Miss Van Zelden," I say, "why don't you scram out of here. This ain't no place for you, sister. An' when these boys have fixed things up between themselves they're not going to get funny about bumpin' you!"

"Well, what do I do about it," she says smiling. "My car's in the garage. How do I make it. They're shooting out there now."

"Don't you believe it, Miss Van Zelden," I says. "Your car is just up the road away from the garage on the other side of the Inn. You'll find it parked just off the road behind three trees. I put it there myself. Now take a tip from me and scram out of it."

"O.K.," she says all brightly. "Say, that's nice of you, stranger, I like you for that."

"Don't worry about that," I says. "You'll be seeing some more of me sometime. So long, sister!"

She turns round and goes down the passage. I follow her and three or four minutes later from the front entrance of the Inn where I'm standing in the shade, I see the tail lights of her car going off in the dark.

This ain't so bad anyway. She was out of it. Now don't you get me wrong. Don't you think that I'm a little hero looking after forlorn women, because I ain't. No, sir! But I reckon it didn't suit me to have Miranda Van Zelden get into any spot of bother round that Inn. I had got my own ideas in pickle for that dame.

I stand there watching the tail lights of her car as they get fainter and fainter. Suddenly I get an idea that there's somebody around. I turn my head and standing just behind me looking at the tail lights too is Siegella.

In case you don't know Siegella is a tall guy nearly as big as I am. He is thin an' he has a thin white face and a thin hook nose. He has got eyes like a pair of gimlets and everything that is lousy in the world looks at you out of 'em.

He looks at me and he smiles. Then he looks at the Van Zelden rear lights again. Then he looks at me again. Then he says very quietly:

"A nice snatch, eh, kid?"

I put on a surprised look. "I don't know what you mean, pal," I says, but I'm not feeling so hot.

The fact that Siegella is around this dump at this time shows to me that my idea about his backing Lacassar is right, and any minute I expect to feel a lump of hot iron tearing into me from some place. But nothing happens.

Siegella takes a cigarette case out of his pocket and hands it to me. I take a cigarette an' he takes one. Then he brings out a lighter and lights my cigarette.

By the flame of the lighter I can see him grinning. He snaps out the lighter and puts it back in his pocket.

"Well, I'll be seeing you," he says. He nods an' walks down the passage towards the dance floor, where everything is quiet now.

I scram. I walk over to the cloakroom, take my hat. Then I slip out of the side door up the road, keeping in the shadows to where I've got my car parked in some bushes. I get in the car an' I step on it, because as I've told you before I'm not a guy who takes unnecessary chances, but I'm worried.

Whilst I am hitting up the road I'm thinking of that crack of Siegella's. . . . "A nice snatch, eh, kid?" I'm wondering whether Siegella is on to my game. . . .

It's funny how quick you can think; all this has gone through my head, as I am walking down Haymarket, London. By this time I am just about opposite the Theatre Royal. The show is just over there and the folks are coming out. I stand there for a minute because getting into a car on the other side of the road I see a very swell dame, an' I'm telling you that if I say that a dame is very swell then that is what that dame is. She also has a swell car. An' as she gets into it, I sorta get the idea that she has looked at me and given me one of them "come-on" looks.

Anyhow, whilst I am ruminating on whether this is an accident or whether this dame is giving me the once-over, the car drives off. It crosses the road and it crawls down by the pavement just a few yards in front of me. Through the back window of the car I can see this dame looking at me an' she definitely smiles. Then the car stops.

I'll try anything once, and what would you have done? I walk to the car an' I take off my hat. She looks at me out of the window, and I'm telling you that this dame is as pretty as paint. She has got this an' that an' she certainly knows how to wear clothes. I've seen a lot of dames, but I've got to admit that this one has got what it takes.

"Well, Lemmy," she says, "and so you were going to pass me up!"

I grinned. "Say, listen, lady," I say. "I think you're marvellous and I reckon you'll think I'm just no good at all when I tell you that I can't even remember you and how could I forget a dame like you anyway?"

She smiles and she has little even teeth like pearls.

"Listen, Lemmy," she says. "Don't you remember that night in New York when you drank some bad hooch and somebody took you home. You know that night Scholler threw that party at the Ritz?"

I whistle. "So it was you. . . ." I said. "Well, ain't life funny?"

I remember this dame. I got in some party an' I had some bad liquor an' bad liquor is poison, I'm telling you. This was the dame who took me home, at least that's what she said, an' it must have been her otherwise how would she know.

"Well, what do we do about it?" I say.

"Get in, Lemmy," she says, "I want to talk to you."

I tell you I'll try anything once, so I get in the car. It drives off and we turn down Pall Mall. There's no doubt that this dame knows me all right, because she is talking about people I know and places I've been. She also tells me that another dame I know called Lillah Schultz is over in England with her, and that we should drink a high-ball to celebrate. By this time we are in Knightsbridge. Way down in Knightsbridge we turn off some street, then we turn down another street, and then we stop in front of some swell block.

We get out and we go up in the lift; when we come to the door of the apartment she turns round and looks at me.

"You know, Lemmy," she says, "this is swell seeing you like this. It's marvellous meeting an old pal in this burg."

A lot of things is going through my head. I'm thinking that it's all wrong for me to get short-circuited with dames when I'm over here on this Miranda business. At the same time I'm also telling myself that a man must live, that this dame is a very swell dame an' I'm wondering just what she is thinking about me.

Whilst this is going on she opens the door an' we step into a hall-way. She snaps on a light. "Take your things off, Lemmy," she says, "and come in."

She goes through a door on the left of the hallway. From the room inside I can hear the clink of ice in glasses which is a very nice sound to me. I hang up my hat and I follow her through the doorway, and on the other side of the doorway I stop dead, because sitting on the settee on the other side of the room with an automatic which is pointing straight at my guts is Siegella.

"Well, sucker," he says, "come in."

Chapter Two
MONEY FROM HOME

Was I surprised? I'm telling you that for about ten seconds I am having a meeting with myself and the agenda is whether I am standing on my right ear or my elbow. Because, this is London, England, and here right in front of me is the whole Siegella set-up. Siegella is parked on the settee, looking like the model of the well-dressed gent from Squire's window on Toledo Boulevard. Around the room grinning at me and drinkin' highballs are Yonnie Malas, Lefty ("Twicer") Scutterby, the English dude who bust out of Auburn prison with a dummy pistol made outa cardboard, German Schultz, Willie Carnazzi and his brother Ginto—the finest bunch of hot killers that ever worked a tommy gun.

Behind Siegella is Toni Rio, Frank Caparazzi, Jimmy Rikzin the Swede, and some more thugs I don't know.

In fact if I hadn't known I was in London I mighta thought myself back in the Paris Club in Toledo or in any other mobster hang-out.

I looked at the woman. She had sat herself down on a sofa and was waitin' while Malas fixed her a highball. She was smilin' at me sorta old-fashioned.

I grinned back at her.

"Have a good laugh, sister," I says. "That was nice work I'm telling you. It was just too easy wasn't it? Just fancy framin' me like the young man who just come down from the butter an' egg farm! O.K. You're the berries an' you have your laugh whilst the goin's good because one of these bright nights I'm goin' to smack that grin off you with a wet bath towel."

They all start to laugh at me bein' so burned-up at this dame, which is just exactly what I require, because at this moment I need to do a spot of hot thinkin'. I do not like the look of this layout not one little bit.

Siegella nods to Malas and Malas walks over to me an' starts to frisk me. Now I do not mind bein' frisked by a copper, but I certainly am not goin' to have a gun I am *not* carryin' taken off me by Malas. So in spite of the fact that Siegella is still holdin' the gun I give Yonnie a smart Japanese clip on the neck gland an' he goes down like a skittle.

Siegella snarls but I chip in first.

"Say, listen, Siegella," I say, "I don't know what this lay-out is an' I don't care, but if you think that any of your thugs is goin' to go over me you're wrong. Try something funny like that again an' I'll make such a noise that some guy will ring a fire-alarm. If you want to talk turkey, I'm listening, but I don't want any fresh stuff from cheap mobsters. Get me?"

Siegella nods.

"I get you, Lemmy," he says. He looks at Malas who is gettin' up on his feet rubbin' his neck an' looking like a mug at bein' clipped like he was. "But ain't you gettin' a bit fresh?" he goes on.

"Look here, Siegella," I says. "Just pull yourself together will you? This ain't Toledo or Chicago or even New York. This is London, and if you think that you can get away with this sorta stuff around this burg, well, you ain't so hot as I thought you was."

Siegella looks at Malas again.

"Has he got a gun?" he asks.

Malas shakes his head.

Siegella grins.

"O.K., Lemmy," he says to me," now I'm goin' to tell you something. You're goin' to work for me. See? An' you're goin' to like it, an' the first thing you gotta learn is that if I tell Yonnie to frisk you then you're goin' to be frisked. Just so you won't forget I'm goin' to get the boys to give you a good beatin' up here an' now, an' we can talk afterwards— when you come to!"

Siegella nods to Scutterby and Schultz an' they are just movin' over to me when I shoot out my arm, and catch Yonnie Malas in a neck crook. I hold him in front of me so that if Siegella—who I can see has got a silencer on his gun—starts shootin', he has got to shoot Malas first, which is a fact that Malas is appreciatin' by the amount of wrigglin' he is puttin' up.

"Listen, Siegella," I says. "Just call your cheap bums off, will you, before I break this punk's neck? An' if I get another crack outa anybody here I'll break it just as sure as you're second class!"

Siegella is as white as death, but he sees that I have got the goods on him this time. He makes a motion with his hands and the boys sit down again. I think it is time that I made what the politicians call a gesture, so I make one. I throw Yonnie Malas against the wall hard an' he sorta crumples up an' flops on the floor—out for ten.

Now I reckon that this is one of them moments when anything you like is liable to happen. German Schultz is already slippin' his hand around to his hip pocket, an' Willie and Ginto Carnazzi are just gettin' outa their seats previous to doin' a big rush act, when the dame starts to talk.

Mind you there is something very come-on about this dame. She ain't exactly like the usual sorta mobster's pet, not by a long chalk when you come to think of it. She has got some sorta class, an' she is tall an' graceful and her voice is sorta low an' husky. I know a whole lot of guys would have gone for that dame in a big way.

"Listen, boys," she says. "What is this—a slug festival on Saturday night at the Bowery Club? Don't you think that the whole lot of you ought to be qualifying for some Home for Mental Rest. I go out of my way and I get Lemmy along here to talk turkey and before anybody can roll their own somebody has started something that looks like ending in the local morgue.

"Listen, Ferdie," she says to Siegella, "why don't you put that cannon away and be your age. You ought to know that Lemmy isn't the sort of guy to get frightened just because somebody starts doing an act with a gun. Yonnie got what was coming to him. He got fresh, and guys who get fresh always get smacked down some time. Now cut out all this palooka and let's have a drink and talk this thing out like regular fellers."

This sounds good to me, but I don't let on. I just look sorta casual, an' I walk over to where Yonnie Malas is picking himself up, an' I get hold of him by the collar an' I yank him up to his feet with a grin.

"Say, Yonnie," I say, "I'm kinda sorry I had to smack you down, pal, but you know how it is when a guy gets annoyed."

He manages to smile. He looks as kind as a couple of moccasin snakes with the earache.

"That's all right, kid," he says eventually. "Skip it, it's O.K. with me."

Siegella puts his gun away.

"Well," he says, "I reckon Connie is right. We won't do any good by startin' something here. One of you guys give Lemmy a drink an' let's talk."

I sit myself down in a big chair an' Connie mixes me a highball. When she brings it over I give her a quick once-over an' I see that she is lookin' at me very old-fashioned like. An idea runs through my head that it would be durn funny if Siegella's girl was to fall for me in a big way, an' that if she did I might manage to make things very uncomfortable for that guy. As she hands me the glass she looks right into my eyes an' believe me or believe me not I got a kick out of it . . . it was a swell look!

I grin over at Siegella where he is sittin' lookin' at me an' I take a drink.

"Well," I says, "let's talk."

He holds his glass up to the light an' looks at it. I am watchin' his eyes an' he looks more like a snake than ever. I'm tellin' you that this feller Siegella is pure poison.

"Well, Lemmy," he says, "here's the way it is. I reckon we need you, an' I reckon that you gotta string along with us because if you don't it's goin' to be curtains for you. You know me, I ain't the sorta guy to let anything stand in my way that I want out of it.

"I know what you're over here for. I reckon you're over here on the same racket as we are, an' I reckon I know when the idea first came into that head of yours.

"You're here after Miranda van Zelden. Well, am I right?"

I grin.

"Maybe you are, an' maybe you ain't," I says.

"O.K.," says he. "Now I've been aimin' to snatch Miranda for a long time, but I got too much sense to pull a snatch like that in U.S.A. The place wouldn't be big enough for any guy who snatched old man van Zelden's daughter.

"So we've been keepin' an eye on this dame for months. We knew sooner or later she'd come to Europe, an' I had everything set to come after her. Every guy in this mob was fixed up with a good an' proper passport an' we're all over here officially on some business or other. We're all business men.

"You gotta admit that the idea is pretty good. We snatch Miranda in England, an' we get the money out of the old boy over the long distance telephone. He don't even know which country his daughter is in. Maybe we tell him we got her hidden away in France or Germany or Italy.

"In other words he is goin' to get so scared at the idea of not knowing where his little girl is that he will pay plenty just for the chance of gettin' her back.

"We make him pay through the Dutch Bank in Rotterdam. He's got to put a credit there for us for three million dollars an' when we have drawn the dough well then maybe we'll let the girl go an' maybe we won't."

I nodded my head.

"Maybe it would be pretty dangerous to let that girl go after you got the money, Siegella," I says. "She's goin' to talk ain't she, an' we want to go back to the U.S. some time or other."

He grins.

"I don't think that we'll let her go home," he says with a leer. "Maybe I can find some other use for Miranda, an' when I've done with her, well . . . I reckon there's got to be some sort of accident . . . eh, boys?"

He takes a look around him at the mob. They are all grinnin'. You never saw such a bunch.

"O.K." he continues. "Now I had my eye on you up in Toledo, Lemmy," he says. "I guessed that you weren't hangin' around Miranda van Zelden just for the pleasure of lookin' at her, an' when she come over here an' you trailed along after, I took a couple of guesses an' I come to the conclusion that you have got some game on with Miranda yourself. Right?"

"O.K.," I says. "I might as well tell you that I had a scheme. You see, I got an idea that this dame Miranda might fall for me. I've spoken to her once or twice, an' I heard that she was a spot interested in yours truly. So I reckoned that I might come over here after her, an' rush her into a marriage. Then I calculated that when old van Zelden heard that his daughter was married to a mobster that he would pay me plenty to get her divorced quick."

Siegella nodded.

"It ain't a bad idea," he said. "but it's a piker idea compared with my set-up. Maybe van Zelden would have dropped a few grand for a divorce, but he wouldn't have paid what he's goin' to pay us for Miranda. I want three million an' I'm goin' to have it!"

Siegella gets up and walks over to me. He takes my empty glass outa my hand and mixes me another drink. Then he brings it back.

"Now, listen, Lemmy," he says, "I got you taped. I know all about you. You're the fellow who shot two coppers in Oklahoma City four years ago. You got a fifty years' sentence and you bust outa the big house sixteen months afterwards. That was a nice break, Lemmy. Sometime I'd like to know how you did it.

"You used to call yourself Price Fremer in those days, didn't you. Then you got mixed up with some mob in Kansas and you had to make a quick break outa there, because if I ain't mistaken you shot another guy round there, an' from then onwards you've been musclin' in on any job where you could muscle an' that looked good.

"You're the guy for me, Lemmy, because your record's too bad for you to rat on us and because you know me well enough to know that I don't stand any nonsense from any guy. Play ball with me and you're O.K., but get this—from the moment you leave this dump tonight somebody is looking after you, an' if you as much as move half an inch either way from the schedule I'm going to give you, then it's curtains for you, because I'll have you bumped whether you're in England, Germany, France or Iceland as sure as my name's Siegella."

He meant it all right. I grinned.

"Never mind the tough stuff, Siegella," I says. "I'm playing ball if I get my deal, an' I don't want any dealing from the bottom of the pack. How do I cut in on this job?"

He brings a piece of paper out of his breast pocket.

"There's twenty-five of us in on this," he says, looking round, "and everybody's got their share fixed. Do what you're told, Lemmy, and pull this job off, and you're on 250 grand."

I whistled to myself. 250,000 dollars is a lot of money. I must say it looked as if this guy looked at things in a big way.

"That suits me," I said. "250 grand is nice dough. After that I'll retire an' start chicken farming or somethin'. But you ain't told me what I'm doing."

Siegella laughs.

"That's easy," he says. "You just go ahead with what you was going to do. Contact Miranda. That shouldn't be difficult. Play around with her, take her places, be nice to her. You know you can make her fall for you if you want to, Lemmy. Why," he looks round at the boys with a grin, "I reckon there's more women looking for you in the United States than any other guy. You certainly have got a way with dames.

"All right, we all know what Miranda's like really, she's a nice kid, but she likes to pretend she ain't. She's one of them girls who's had too much money an' too much of her own way. I reckon she'll fall for you like a sack of coke.

"Now you've got to work fast. I reckon you've got two or three weeks to make Miranda fall for you. By that time I'm going to arrange a little house party way down in the country. I've got a house fixed, a nice quiet old manor house with lots of atmosphere. It looks like a film director's dream. I'm going to throw a party down there, an' you're goin' to bring Miranda.

"You've got to tell her that this party is something very special, that she's going to meet a whole lot of funny fellows down there, that she's going to get a thrill out of it, an' you've got to fix it that she comes down by herself. We don't want any maids or secretaries trailing around."

I nodded.

"Ain't she got anybody keeping an eye on her?" I asked.

Siegella grins.

"You bet," he says. "You don't think old man van Zelden is such a fool as to let his daughter go running round Europe without a watch dog. She don't know, but he's got a private tec, a big guy called Gallat, trailing round after the dame. Wherever she goes, Gallat goes too. He parks himself in a nearby hotel and he tails her."

"What do we do about him?" I asked.

Siegella grins and looks at Yonnie, and Yonnie grins back.

"Listen, Lemmy," he says, "don't you worry about Gallat. We're going to take care of him, and we're going to take care of him quick. It'll be done so nice that he won't ever know what's happened to him.

"Now that's all you've got to do. You get Miranda down to this house, an' then you're very nearly finished. After that you've got to keep out of the way, because people over here will have seen you getting round with her. Once she's down in that house you don't have to worry about her, we look after Miranda.

"An' what you do is this. You go back to London, and you put a long distance telephone call through to a guy in New York. I'll give you his name and address. This guy will go to van Zelden and tell him that his daughter's been snatched and he'll fix that van Zelden comes through on the long distance telephone to you the next day for more information.

"Now all you've got to do is to tell the old man that his daughter's been snatched, that you yourself don't know where she is, but you've got an idea I'm moving her over to Germany or somewhere.

"I've got a yacht over here and after we get her down to the house, we'll take her out of England in no time.

"Then you tell van Zelden that we want three million dollars placed to my credit in the Dutch Bank at Rotterdam. He can do it all right, he's worth about twenty millions, an' you can also tell him that if the money ain't there in ten days, including the day that you speak to him, I'll send him his daughter's ears in a registered envelope. You can tell him that if the money ain't there within fifteen days, he won't ever see his daughter again. She'll be dead! An' you can tell him that it won't do him no good goin' to the coppers because there ain't a police force in Europe will know where Miranda is."

I give myself another drink.

"It looks good to me, Siegella," I says. "He'll just *have* to put that money there."

"Right," says Siegella, "an' I shall go and get it myself.

"Now when you've done that, you lie low. Hang around London for a week or two, and then take a boat back to New York. But before you go you'll get an address near 42nd Street. Go round there and you'll find 250 grand waiting for you. Is it a deal?"

"It's a deal, Siegella," I says. "It looks easy to me. Why, I ain't doing a thing for the money."

"Well," he says, "you ain't doing as much as some of the other boys, but maybe your work is more important. We can't snatch that girl in London, we've got to get her down to that house, an' another thing," says Siegella, "nobody must know she's going down there. You've got to fix it so that you get her down sudden like. She mustn't even tell a maid or anybody where she's going. That's what you're getting your money for, and," he finishes with a little smile, "I wouldn't slip up anywhere if I was you, Lemmy, because if you do we're going to look after you, an' it won't be so nice for you."

"You needn't worry about that," I says. "This looks easy to me."

"O.K.," says Siegella.

He holds out his hand and we shake on it.

"Now get busy," he says. "I know where you're staying. You've got an apartment down on Jermyn Street. We've had a tail on you there for days, ever since you got to this country. You've got to start work tomorrow morning."

I got up.

"That's O.K. by me," I says. "I'll be getting along."

"Right, Lemmy," says Siegella, "I'll be in touch with you maybe sometime soon. Goodnight!"

I says goodnight, and I nods to the boys. I take my hat from the hall an' I walk down the stairs out into the street. I'm feeling pretty good because I reckon that muscling in on this racket of Siegella's is going to be a good thing for me, and maybe if I use my brains an' keep my eyes skinned, I can still find some means of double-crossing this guy.

By this time it's after one o'clock in the morning.

When I get into Knightsbridge, they are washing down the streets. It's a nice night and I went swinging along, feeling fine. The idea of me having 250,000 dollars made me laugh. Just think what a guy could do with that money.

An' if I could get hold of this money an' somehow upset Siegella's apple cart I reckoned it'd be all the sweeter.

By this time I'd got to the Green Park Station an' I asked some copper where there's a telephone box. He tells me that there's one in the station, and I go in. I have MacFee's number written in pencil on the tailor's tag inside my breast pocket. I get him right away.

"Well, Mac, how're you making out," I says.

"O.K., buddy," he says. "How's things with you?"

"Not too bad," I says. "Say, listen here. I just been having a meeting."

"You don't say," says Mac.

"I'm telling you," I says. "I just left Siegella. He's planning to snatch Miranda, and I'm in on the racket, an' it looks like big money, baby."

I heard him whistle.

"Pretty good, Lemmy," he says. "Are you going to use me?"

"Not for a minute, big boy," I says. "I've got to go easy on this thing because you know Siegella. He ain't a nice guy to cross. Just stick around, Mac, will you. I'll phone you in a day or two."

"O.K., buddy," he says.

I lit myself a cigarette and walked up the stairs out of the station. Just outside parked against the curb is a smart roadster. I take a look at it, and I see Connie, Siegella's girl, the dame who picked me up, sittin' at the wheel. She looks at me an' she grins.

"Did you have a nice phone call, Lemmy?" she says.

"Listen, Connie," I says, "ain't you the curious dame? I've been phoning because like a big mug I left the outside key to my rooms inside. I was ringing the porter downstairs to see if he was up, otherwise I wouldn't be able to get in."

She smiles.

"I'll drive you home, Lemmy," she says. "Get in, I want to talk to you."

I get into the car an' she drives me back to my rooms, where I have to go through a big business of knocking up the porter to let me in when I've got the key in my pocket all the time. When he opens the door, she's still standing there.

"Ask me up for a drink, Lemmy," she says. "I want to talk to you."

"Anything to please a lady," I said. "Come on, Connie."

I took her upstairs, opened up the flat, took her wrap and gave her a highball. As she stands there in the middle of the room, it strikes me that this Connie is a very swell dame. I wonder just how much I can trust her supposing I get the idea to pull a fast one on Siegella. But she soon puts me right on that point. She walks over to my big arm-chair, an' she sits down.

"Now, listen, Lemmy," she said. "I like you. You're a nice guy, and there's something about you that maybe I could fall for. Anyhow, I didn't come along here tonight to tell you that.

"Siegella sent me along to give you this. He didn't want you to have it in front of the boys."

She threw an envelope on the table.

"Inside that envelope," she says, "is 10,000 dollars. That's for expenses in toting Miranda around. Siegella wants you to do this thing in a big way, expense don't matter. Now, Lemmy," she goes on, "you listen to me. I know your sort. You're a born racketeer, you're a good crook and a nice worker. We know all about you, you've always worked solo, an' maybe you don't like the idea of having to string along with Siegella an' the boys.

"Now I'm giving you the tip off. You do what you're told, and like it, because Ferdie Siegella is wise to the fact that you might try to pull a fast one on him.

"Remember, he ain't quite certain of you, so he'll be watching you like a cat, an' if you side-slip he'll get you if he has to do it with his own hands."

She gives herself a cigarette outa the box beside her an' then goes on.

"You see, this Miranda snatch means a lot to him. The Feds are after him in America, he's got a record out there that's so black that it would make the devil's schedule look like a prayer book. He's got to have a lot of money and he's got to have it quick in order to straighten things out. He's made up his mind to pull this Miranda snatch, an' he's got the job so well planned that I know he's going to get away with it."

She walks over to where I'm standing in front of the fireplace, an' she stands right in front of me an' she looks right into my eyes. This dame Connie has got very deep brown eyes. I told you before that she was a swell dame.

"Now, Lemmy," she says, "string along, be a good guy, get your job done and take your money."

She walks over to the chair and picks up her wrap.

"When it's all straightened out," she says, "maybe you and I can have a little talk. Maybe I could fall for a guy like you, Lemmy," she says sorta sad.

I grin.

"So what, Connie?" I says, "an' you Siegella's girl?"

She smiles.

"That's the way it is, Lemmy," she says. "You don't have to tell the world but I don't like Ferdie Siegella, but what can I do? I've got to string along too, and I'm clever enough to like it. Still, there's lots of time."

I laugh.

"That's O.K. by me, sister," I says. "I'm a pretty good guy at waitin' around if it's worth it; but comin' back to the main job for just one little minute, there's one thing I don't like so much an' that is this guy Gallat."

She laughs.

"Be your age, Lemmy," she says. "This guy is a punk. He's a big broad-shouldered kid just out of college an' old man van Zelden pays him good to string along an' keep an eye on Miranda. Don't you worry about him, because Siegella will take care of him."

"That's as maybe," I says, "but it ain't so good my startin' operations on Miranda with this feller gum-shoein' around is it? Supposin' he gets wise to my game."

"Come an' help me put this wrap on, Lemmy," she says. An' when I hold it up for her she looks at me over her shoulder.

"Listen, kid," she says soft like. "Don't you worry about Gallat. Right now he's livin' round at the Strand Chambers, next to the van Zelden dame's hotel. Well, tomorrow night he's going to get a telephone call, see . . . a sorta urgent call, an' he's goin' to go out an' keep an appointment. I reckon he won't worry you any more after that. . . ."

I grin. "Siegella's going to take him for a ride, eh?" I say.

"Don't be so curious an' give me a kiss, Lemmy," she says.

That dame certainly can kiss. After a minute she goes over to the door.

"I'll be seeing you, Lemmy," she says.

I take her down to the street, put her in her car an' watch her as she drives off. It's funny that this dame should decide that she might like to fall for me some time.

Then I go upstairs and I lock the door. Then I open the envelope on the table. Sure enough there is ten grand inside it, twenty 500 dollar bills. I stand there looking at these bills for a few minutes an' suddenly I get an idea.

I go into my bedroom, an' I unlock my trunk. Down in the bottom drawer I got a book. This book is a pasting up book and in it I've got pages cut from the U.S. Federal Police news, because I've found that this is a very clever thing to do. It lets me know what the mobs are doing, and who the Feds are after.

Pretty soon I find what I'm looking for. Its a police report on the hold up of the Third National Farmers' Bank in Arkansas. Now everybody knows that this job was pulled by the Lacassar mob which means Siegella was behind it. On the next page is the page from the Police News giving the numbers of the stolen bank notes—the big denomination bills.

I take the book back to my sitting room an' I check up with the numbers of the notes that Connie has just given to me. I'm dead right. It was Siegella who pulled the Arkansas stick-up an' the ten grand he has given me is the ten grand that he pinched from that bank. This proves to me that Siegella has been planning this Miranda business for a long time.

I start to put the notes back in the envelope. Changing these notes over here in London will be easy. The stick-up was done in Arkansas six months ago, an' there won't be any check up in this country I figure.

I take the envelope an' I put it in a drawer in my bedroom. Right then I start thinkin' about this guy Gallat who is Miranda's protection man that she don't know about. I can imagine this guy—one of them big college kids with no brains an' full of la di da. I reckon this guy is not goin' to feel so good when Siegella gets his hooks on him.

But I think that it will be a good idea if some guy I know is keepin' an eye on this Gallat proposition, so I walk back into the sitting room and I telephone MacFee. I give him the layout an' I tell him that this guy Gallat is on the spot an' that Siegella will probably bump him some time tomorrow night an' that it might be better if MacFee hung around an' saw what was breakin'—just so I knew that everything was cleaned up properly.

I then go to bed because I am very tired havin' had a very busy day. As I go off to sleep I can see Connie's brown eyes—that dame has got nice eyes— lookin' at me.

I have got ideas about that dame.

CHAPTER THREE
GOYAZ CUTS IN

NEXT morning when I wake up the sun is shining, and I am feeling pretty good. I have a very good breakfast with six cups of coffee, and whilst I am drinking same I proceed to do a little quiet thinkin' about this Siegella set-up.

Its all the tea in China to an egg-flip that this Siegella has got a very swell organisation functionin' in this country; it is also a stone ginger that I have not seen the half of it. The bunch of tough eggs that I contacted round at the Knightsbridge flat are all guys—with the exception of about six—that I have seen around in the United States some place.

I reckon that there must be a lot more people in this thing. If Siegella has got somebody tailing me it must be somebody I don't know—otherwise I'm goin' to spot 'em right away, an' Siegella is too clever by a mile for that.

By the time I have finished with the coffee and started on a bottle of bourbon I am gettin' worried as to how I can figure out some way to get wise to the whole Siegella outfit here. I am a guy who likes to know what he is doin' an' what is goin' on around an' I do not fancy takin' some chances against something I don't know.

In the middle of this Siegella comes through on the telephone.

Say, Lemmy," he says, how're you feelin' this mornin'?"

I say I am feelin' O.K. an' he then asks me if I have got the jack which he told Constance to hand over to me—ten thousand dollars.

I say I have got it all right. I also say that I know where *he* got it from, an' I can hear him laughin'.

There ain't any flies on you, Lemmy," he says, an' suddenly his voice goes serious. This Siegella is a funny guy, when he means business his voice droops sort of—it gets thin, an' low an' menacin'.

Listen, kid," he says. Here's where you start work. We gotta get a move on an' I want you to get busy right away. Your little lady friend is stayin' down at the Carlton. What about gettin' along there an' makin' that contact. I want to get this job movin' as soon as I can."

"That suits me," I says. "Directly I've finished this bourbon I'll be gettin' right along."

"O.K., Lemmy," he says. "I'll be seein' you."

"Right, sweetheart," I says "an' don't do anything that you wouldn't like photographed."

I hang up on this crack an' proceed to do a little more thinkin'.

At twelve o'clock I get dressed. I have got some very good English clothes an' some swell silk shirts that I bought the day before, an' by the time that I am ready to go along and see Miranda I am lookin' like all the flowers in May.

I finish the bourbon, an' walk down the Hay-market and turn into the Carlton. I go up to the reception and I ask for Miss Van Zelden.

They tell me that Miss van Zelden is not there. Also they do not know when Miss van Zelden will be there. They think she has gone away for a few days.

This is not so good, I think. I then ask if Miss van Zelden has got a secretary or a maid, as I have some very urgent business, an' after a lot of palooka I go up in the elevator an' I am shown into a drawin' room. I give my name to the bell-hop and I sit down an' wait.

Presently in comes a jane that I take to be the maid. I am right in one guess. This dame is a neat baby an' she looks good an' knows it.

She hands me some stuff about Miss van Zelden bein' out of town for some days.

When she has finished I get up.

"Listen kid," I says. "I have got some very important business with Miss van Zelden, an' I am a guy that she will see almost any time. Now I want to get in touch with her an' it ain't no use your tellin' me she's away an' you don't know where she is. Now where is she baby? I guess you gotta know *something*?"

Whilst I am talking I have pulled a fifty dollar bill out of my pocket an' am foldin' it nice an' straight. I see her eyes fasten on the bill.

"Honest I don't know, Mr. Caution," she says. "But maybe this will help you."

She goes off an' in a minute she comes back with a bit of note-paper which she hands over to me.

"I found this waitin' for me when I went in with her early mornin' tea," she says.

I look at the note. It says:

"I shall be away for two or three days. M. van Z."

I give the maid fifty bucks.

"An' you haven't an idea where she is?" I says.

She shakes her head.

"Honest—I don't know a thing," she says.

I pass her a couple of wisecracks an' I then scram. Outside I start walkin' towards Strand Chambers which is where Gallat—Miranda's bull-dog—lives according to Connie, an' whilst I am walkin' I am still doin' some heavy thinkin'.

First of all it is a bit screwy Miranda bein' away at a time when Siegella. gives me the tip-off to contact her. I know Siegella ain't the sort of guy *not* to know what she was goin' to do. I do not like this one little bit.

Pretty soon I arrive at Strand Chambers which is a block near Trafalgar Square. I go into the entrance an' walk along a little passage until I come to a side window that looks out front. I have a careful look through this an' I see some guy standin' over the other side of the road pretendin' to read a newspaper. I guess this guy is keepin' an eye on the Gallat proposition. He is a fat, dark guy an' looks like a mobster, but I don't know him to look at. He might be one of Siegella's mob an' then again he might not.

I walk back to the elevator man, and ask if Mr. Gallat is around, an' he says yes, an' we go up. On the third floor this guy gets out an' shows me along the passage to a room. He knocks on the door an' I go in.

Inside, readin' a newspaper an' eatin' breakfast is a big, young-lookin' feller. He is a blond guy an' he has one of them faces that make you think of when you was young.

"What can I do for you?" he says. An' by the way he says it, I sorta get the idea that this guy is expectin' something to happen an' he don't quite know what, an' that is why he has given orders that anybody who comes along an' asks for him should be shown right up.

"Right now you can give me a drink, Gallat," I say, "an' then you an' me can talk a little bit. By the way," I says casual like, "I suppose you wasn't expectin' anybody about now?"

He goes over to a sideboard an' gets a bottle of whisky an' a glass an' he pours out a stiff one which he hands to me.

Whilst I am drinkin' this whisky he looks at me. I put the glass down an' I light a cigarette.

"You wouldn't know where Miss Miranda van Zelden was, would you?" he says.

I blew a puff of smoke an' grinned at him.

"Say buddy, I thought that was your job knowin' where that dame was an' what she was doin'," I says.

"And how would you know that?" he says.

I grin some more.

"There's an old proverb that says that two watchdogs are better than one."

He thinks this over for a bit.

"When did you find out she was gone?" he says after a while.

"Just now when I went round to ask for her," I say. "You see I've got some business with her. I've known her for some time."

He nodded.

"I reckon she knows too many bad eggs like you," he says.

I get up.

"Thanks for the whisky, buddy," I says. "An so long. If you don't know where she is, I guess you're no good to me. Remember me to your mammy when you write."

He gets up too.

"Say listen," he says. "Just who are you?"

I do some quick thinkin'.

"I'm John Mulligan, representin' the Illinois Trust Insurance," I say. "Miss van Zelden is carryin' a very big jewellery insurance with us, an' the firm ain't particularly sure that it's worth their while. You know how she gets about an' loses jewellery or just leaves it about where somebody'll pinch it."

He nods, an' I guess he is fallin' for this line of punk I am handin' him.

"Well, to cut a long story short I'm supposed to check up on Miss van Zelden an' see what the risk looks like, an' if my report is bad then the firm won't renew, that's all. I went round this mornin' to see her an' the maid told me that she had scrammed, leavin' a note sayin' that she'd be back in a few days. It looked a bit screwy to me.

"I knew about you because my firm was advised that old man van Zelden employed you to keep an eye on the girl, an' I thought you might know something about where she was, that's all."

He picked up my glass an' took it to the sideboard and filled it again.

"Sorry I was rude, Mulligan," he says. "But I'm a bit burned up about that girl. I wish I knew where she was. I've a scout in the hotel, but he couldn't tell me a thing."

I sat down again and lit another cigarette. The whisky wasn't too bad, but it was not as good as my bourbon.

"Listen, Gallat," I says. "Maybe I've been knockin' around a bit longer than you have an' I've seen one or two things. Now when I come in here just now I see some guy over the road who is keepin' tabs on this place.

"Now it stand to reason that either Miranda van Zelden has just slipped off for a day or so on some scheme of her own or there is something screwy goin' on. If there's something screwy afoot then whoever is behind it is goin' to keep an eye on you just to see what your reaction is goin' to be, an' it looks to me as if that is just what is goin' on."

I take him over to the window an' I show him this guy on the other side of the road, still readin' the newspaper.

In a minute he comes back to the table.

"It don't look so good to me," he says.

"Well, what are you goin' to do?" I says. "You can't do a thing. If you dash around callin' coppers into this an' Miranda is merely on some joy stunt she'll murder you an' she won't be so pleased with her old man for havin' her tailed, so you can't do that."

"Well, what can I do?" he says.

"I'll tell you what to do," I says. "Just you stick around here until this evenin' at about eight o'clock. Keep an eye on the other side of the road an' just watch what that guy does and who relieves him. Then at eight o'clock pick up a bag—just as if you were goin' some place—and go downstairs an' order a cab. Drive to No. 4 Priory Grove out at Hampstead. If what I think is right that guy or whoever takes his place is goin' to follow you.

"When you get to Priory Grove you get out of the cab an' you walk straight through the passage an' out the back way. This guy will come after you won't he? Well, I'll be waiting in Priory Grove an' I'll grab him. Maybe I can make him talk.

"Then you come straight back here pronto, an' wait until you hear something from me," I says.

He looks relieved.

"It's an idea," he says. "It's swell of you to take all this trouble."

I grin.

"Not a bit," I says. "I've got my job to do, an' I can't make my report until I've seen an' talked to Miss van Zelden an' made a lot more enquiries as to what she's getting up to over here. I tell you my firm ain't pleased with this jewellery risk. Maybe you'd like to have a look at this?"

I pull out a leather case and show it to him. It is an official card of the Investigation Department of the Illinois Trust Insurance—I pinched it off some guy four years ago, an' it's been very useful to me.

That clinched it.

"That's good enough for me," he says. "I'll do what you say."

"O.K. brother," I says. "Now get this straight. You leave here at eight o'clock tonight an' you take a cab to No. 4 Priory Grove, Hampstead, an' you walk straight through the passage an' you come straight back here. Have you got that?"

He said he had. So then I went straight back to my rooms on Jermyn an' telephoned MacFee.

I waited ten minutes. Then I went out. I had some lunch in a dump near Piccadilly Circus. I come out at two o'clock an' I got a cab. I drove to Green Park Station and took the subway to Knightsbridge, then I got out and took another cab and drove to the top of Park Lane. I changed cabs again here and drove to 4 Priory Grove, which is where MacFee hangs out. I reckon that if any guy was tailing me I have shaken him off by now.

MacFee is sitting playing solitaire at a table, drinking whisky. In case you don't know MacFee is a feller of about middle height, thin faced with a perpetual sorta grin that nothing could ever knock off.

He passes the bottle over to me.

"Well, what do you know, Lemmy?" he says.

"Listen, MacFee," I says, "something is breaking round here. This morning Siegella telephones me to contact with Miranda. She's staying at the Carlton Hotel. I go down there and she had blown out of it leaving a note for her maid that she will be away for two or three days.

"Now it doesn't look so hot to me because you can betcha sweet and holy life that if she was going away, Siegella would have known it. So I do something I don't want to do. I go down and see this guy Gallat, because I figure this way: Supposing somebody *has* got Miranda out of London, I reckon it ain't Siegella, an' I reckon I want to know who it is.

"Outside this guy Gallat's rooms is some feller keeping an eye on the job, an' it looks to me like this guy is a mobster. I see this feller Gallat an' he is sure worried. He knows Miranda is gone an' he don't know where she's gone. This guy looks like a kid that is chasing its own tail.

"I pull a lotta punk on him, an' I tell him that I'm John Mulligan, representing the Illinois Trust Insurance firm that is carrying a lot of jewellery insurance for Miranda, an" that I've been instructed to check up on the risk. He falls for this.

"I also tell him to stick around till eight o'clock tonight, an' that then he should come out of the place with a grip as if he were going somewhere, an' that the guy who is watching the place will follow him.

"I tell this guy Gallat to come along here to Priory Grove an' I reckon he is going to check in here at about 8.30. Now listen, Mac, at 8.20 you have the elevator on the ground floor. This guy Gallat will walk straight through the passage and out back way, after which he will go home. I reckon if this feller who is keeping tabs on Gallat is in earnest he will go through the passage after him. When he does you stop him—I will be right behind.

"We get this guy and we talk turkey to him, see? We find out where Miranda is, that is if he knows. Does that make sense to you?"

MacFee nods.

"I get it," he says. "You're going to give him the rough stuff."

"You've got a brain, baby," I says. "That's the way it is, because it looks to me as if some other guy is trying to muscle in on this job, an' I think we oughta know who it is."

"O.K." says MacFee.

I have a drink with him, an' I go back to my apartments on Jermyn. I go to bed because I have an idea that I'm going to be rather late. I sleep until five o'clock, when I have a cup of tea—English fashion—a bath, an' I stick around until half past seven. At half past seven I take a cab an' I drive round by Long Acre around to the Strand. At Trafalgar Square I pay off the cab an' I meander over to Strand Chambers.

After fifty yards off I stop, an' have a look round. Sure as a gun there's some guy leaning up against the wall just doing nothin'. I hang around in a doorway. At 8 o'clock Gallat comes out of Strand Chambers, an' he is playing his part very well. He has got on a big travelling ulster and has a suitcase. He stands on the pavement an' after a few minutes he signals a cab. He gets in an' he drives off.

The guy on the other side of the road orders another cab and goes after him, an' I jump a third one and trail on behind. Gallat is pretty good. He drives all round London before he makes for Hampstead with this guy sticking close on his heels.

Eventually at a quarter to nine Gallat pulls up in front of 4 Priory Grove. The other cab is about a hundred yards behind him, an' I am the same distance behind that. Gallat gets out, pays off his cab, an' the second cab stops.

I stop too. I give my cab driver a pound note, an' I walk over to the other side of the road, an' I watch. The guy in the second cab hangs around and watches Gallat go into Priory Court, and then very quietly he walks along after him.

I shoot over the road an' I go into Priory Court close on this guy's heels.

We can see Gallat walking down the passage an' going out the back entrance. The guy who is tailing him gets half-way along just to where the lift is when MacFee steps out.

"Just a minute, buddy," he says to this guy, "I want to talk to you."

This Priory Court is a deserted sorta place. There ain't nobody around. As MacFee speaks the guy slips his hand round to his hip pocket, but before he can do anything I'm there first. I take his gun off him an' as he turns round I just smack him right across the nose.

"Listen, baby," I says, sticking his own gun into his stomach, "I got an itchin' trigger finger, so just step into the lift and like it, will you?"

He gets into the lift—MacFee an' I get in after him. MacFee works the buttons and we go up.

We take this guy along to MacFee's rooms. He is a smartly dressed feller, young, an' he looks like any cheap mobster that you'll find around any city. I tell him to sit down.

"Listen, kid," I say, "we ain't got a lot of time to waste. You've been keeping tabs on Gallat at Strand Chambers. How come? Who're you working for, and where's Miranda van Zelden?"

He grins.

"Now wouldn't you like to know, big boy?" he says.

MacFee looks at me.

"Listen, kid," I says to this feller, "we don't want to get tough with you, but you're going to talk, see? Now are you going to cash in or do we give it to you?"

He takes a toothpick out of his pocket, and he starts picking his teeth.

"You make me laugh," he says.

I walk over to him an' I smack him right between the eyes. He goes over the back of the chair. He gets up an' he walks round to the other side of the table. MacFee gives him another one. This guy gets up and spits out a coupla teeth. I walk round to him an' I sit him down on the chair again. I pick the chair and him up, an' I throw the whole outfit against the wall. The chair busts an' this guy falls down on the floor. He is covered with blood an, he is not looking so hot.

As he gets up MacFee gives him another haymaker right on the point of the jaw. He goes down some more. I stand over him.

"Are you talking, buddy," I says "or do we really start work on you?"

He leans up against the wall, his nose is bust in an' one eye is closed. He is feeling around to see if the rest of his teeth are there.

"O.K." he says "I get it. I'm talking."

"Right, baby," I says, "suppose you have a little drink."

We fix him with a chair and we give him a drink. We sit down.

"Now spill it," I says.

He takes a gulp.

"I don't know anything much," he says. "I was told off to look after Gallat. You see, The Boss wasn't sure how much he knew. I'm workin' for Goyaz."

I looked at MacFee and he looks back.

"So Goyaz is in on this," I says. "Where's Miranda van Zelden?"

This guy is having a bit of trouble with his nose, so I lend him a handkerchief.

"I don't know," he says "but it's this way. Goyaz is working in with Kastlin. It looks like he figures that Miranda van Zelden will go for gambling. He contacts her some place and she falls for the idea that she can get a kick out of playing."

"And where's the play going on?" I ask.

"I don't know," he says.

MacFee walks over to him and he puts his hands up.

"Don't give it to me again," he whines. "I tell you I don't know."

I signal to MacFee to lay off.

"O.K. baby," I says. "Now you tell me where Goyaz is operatin' from, where d'you meet him? Where d'you go for your instructions?"

He gives me an address back of Baker Street.

We tie this guy up and we chuck him in MacFee's coal cellar. I'm hoping that MacFee or I will be around the place within the next two or three days to let him out, otherwise it don't look so good for this guy.

After this we have a drink.

"Where do we go from here, buddy?" says MacFee.

"Listen, baby," I says. "I got to find out where Miranda is. I think I'm going along to this Baker Street dump. Maybe I'll be trying a little strong arm stuff. Stick around here for an hour, an' if you don't hear anything from me, go down an' contact Gallat at Strand Chambers. Tell him you're working in with me—John Mulligan of the Illinois Trust Insurance an' stick around until you hear something from me. I reckon I'll phone you sometime before midnight."

"What about the punk in there?" he says indicatin' the coal cellar.

"You should worry," I tell him. "Just leave him there. If you get back within a day or so maybe he'll be alright. If you don't we'll have to think up something else, an' don't forget, when you meet Gallat, you're my assistant an' I'm Mulligan of the Illinois Trust Insurance."

"O.K. brother," he says . . . "but I don't like this Goyaz stuff one little bit."

I grin.

"I don't like it neither," I says. "It's tough enough trying to string along with Siegella—but with Goyaz too, it's like takin' tea with rattlesnakes."

"You said it," says MacFee. "Say, Lemmy, do you remember the time when we said we'd lay off all this stuff an' take that chicken farm down in Missouri—you know, that time that Krimp slugged you in the leg."

"Aw shut up," I says. "Chicken farmin'—you make me puke!"

But as I am goin' down in the elevator I think that maybe MacFee is right an' that it would be a durn sight more healthy for me to be kickin' around some chicken farm in Missouri than playin' ball with the mobs.

Outside I get a cab an' tell him to drop me off at Baker Street.

Chapter Four
ONE FOR SIEGELLA

SITTIN' back in the cab I am thinkin' about Goyaz, tryin' to make sense outa this thing.

Goyaz is sure one tough egg. He was runnin' a mob in Kansas in the old days when men was men an' hijackin' was a swell profession. He was mixed up in every big killin' that happened around there, an' Pretty Boy Floyd, who helped along in the Kansas City Massacre when they shot four coppers on the depot just to rescue some punk who didn't want to be rescued, coulda taken lessons from him.

Goyaz had contacts with Siegella in the old days. His racket was mainly gambling joints, an' he had a boat the Princess Christabel that used to lay off the coast towns and run games so big that a millionaire could lose his suspenders without feelin' excited about it. The games was crooked as hell an' anybody who won anything never got home with the dough. They either took it off 'em on the boat, or they chucked 'em overboard from the motor launch that used to take 'em back to the wharf an' talked big business with 'em before they pulled 'em aboard again.

One time, I know, Siegella contacted with Goyaz over some snatch he was plannin' an' he figured to use Goyaz' boat to make the getaway in.

But one thing was stickin' out a foot an' that is that this punk that we just beat up was no Siegella mobster—he talked too easy, one of Siegella's boys woulda put up a better show; an' the second thing that proves to me that there ain't any connection between Siegella and Goyaz on this particular business is that the punk told us that Goyaz was workin' in with Kastlin. Kastlin is a cheap mobster who works for anybody. He strings along mostly with Goyaz because he knows about runnin' boats, an' I know that Siegella wouldn't touch Kastlin at any price. He don't like him an' he don't trust him further than he can throw a coupla baby elephants.

Well, what's the answer? The answer is that Goyaz has some-how got wise to Siegella's game an' has muscled in an' made a try to hi-jack Miranda, an' it looks as if the job has come off.

Is this one for Siegella or is it? I can just imagine what Siegella is goin' to do to the Goyaz-Kastlin outfit when he gets wise to what has been goin' on.

It also looks as if this Goyaz has been puttin' in some very neat work on his own account. He must have been tailin' Miranda around an' contacted her at some party or racket or something—you must get it that this Goyaz is a nice, well-spoken sort of specialism in charm an' all that sorta stuff—after which he has told her the tale about his gambling ship an' Miranda has fallen for it like a dog for a hamburger.

She would. It's just the sorta thing that that dame would go for. The idea of losin' a lot of money aboard some boat would strike her as bein' excitin'. She wouldn't wait a minute to consider if the game was goin' to be on the level or just a common or garden 'take'. She'd just go for it. I gotta admit that this Miranda has got a good nerve.

By this time we have made Baker Street. I pay off the cab an' I walk down the street to the place that the Goyaz bird told me about. I turn down a side street an' there, at the bottom is a mews. I go along this mews keepin' close to the wall, an' way down at the end I see the flat, over some old stables. There is a light showin' between the curtains.

In my vest pocket I have got a little ·20 automatic. One of them nice things for killin' flies with. I am carryin' this in addition to the ·38 automatic I have got in my hip pocket. I take this little gun outa my pocket an' I fix it inside a clip I have fixed in the inside of the top of my soft felt hat—this is an old racket of mine an' has been very useful once or twice. This way the gun is restin' on the top of my head supported by the crown of my fedora.

I light a cigarette an' I walk up to the flat door by the side of the stables an' I knock two or three times.

After a minute the door opens a bit and a Japanese looks out at me. This gives me a bit of a kick because I know that Goyaz always used Jap servants.

"Is Mr. Goyaz in?" I ask, "because I want to see him pronto."

He opens the door.

"You wait here," he says, "I go an' look."

As he turns round I smack him just behind the ear—just where the bottom of the skull joins the neck—with a very pretty short arm jab, an' I catch him as he falls. I then prop this guy up against the wall an' shut the door an' I go upstairs.

At the top of the stairs is a door. I open this an' there is a passage in front of me with two or three rooms leadin' out of it on each side. At the end on the left there is a door half open with a chunk of light comin' through an' I can hear voices and glasses chinkin'.

I gum-shoe down the passage an' I stick my head through the door an' then I open it an' go in.

There is four fellers sittin' round a table playin' poker. In the corner of the room restin' her feet on a chair an' readin' a newspaper is Lottie Frisch, who is Kastlin's girl. It looks as if I have found the joint alright!

"Well, guys," I say. "How're you goin'?"

I have got my gun outa my hip pocket an' I let 'em see it. They don't move, they just put their hands on the table in front of 'em in the good old-fashioned way.

"Good evenin' Lottie," I say. "How's Kastlin? Now listen, people, don't let's get all burned up over this thing, just let's play along together. I don't want to waste your time an' you don't want to waste mine. Just give me a little information an' you can get on with the good work. Where's Goyaz?"

The guy opposite me—a big guy with dank hair, grins.

"Why, if it ain't Lemmy Caution," he laughs. "Just fancy seein' you around here—an' with a gun too! Ain't that too sweet? Say, piker, you don't think you can shoot that off here, do you?"

I grin.

"Listen, babies," I says. "You've known me to shoot it before. Cut out the punk. Where's Goyaz?"

"You search me," he says, "we don't know, do we, boys, an' if we did we'd forget about it. Say, Lemmy, I thought you was out in Missouri runnin' a liquor repeal racket?"

"Shut up," I says "an get on with it. If you don't tell me where Goyaz is I'm goin' to shoot your nose off."

The dame speaks up.

"Oh shucks," she says, "what's all the mystery about? If he wants to know where Goyaz is tell the sucker. I reckon Goyaz can deal with him direct in his own way. What're you tryin' to do Lemmy, muscle in on something? You won't do any good around here I'm tellin' you."

"Cut it out, Lottie," I say. "I'm dead serious. Where's Goyaz?"

She gets up.

"I got his address here," she says, shrugging her shoulders. "He's down some place in the country."

She picks up a little black silk handbag off the table and she opens it. It looks to me just as if she is taking a piece of paper out of her handbag, and then I learns somethin'. I learn that I can still be caught short on a bad market, because this jane has got a vest-pocket automatic in her handbag and she shoots through the bottom of it.

She gets me. I feel as if somebody has stuck a red hot poker through my right arm. My wrist drops, an' before you could say sap the four guys at the table are on top of me. They give me the works. By the time this bunch have done with me I'm feeling like a communist demonstration in New York when the coppers are bad-tempered. What those guys do to me is nobody's business.

Eventually they tie me up with some rope that the Japanese servant brings, an' they chuck me up against the wall.

The guy with the dank hair goes over me, an' I'm feeling very pleased with the fact that I'm not carrying the 10,000 dollars. I have just got a thousand dollars of my own money an' they help themselves to the wad. This feller then steps back and has a look at me.

"Well, sucker," he grins. "How do you like that?" Just fancy now, Lemmy Caution, the big mobster, being trussed up like a ten-cent chicken. Why don't you keep that big nose of yours out of things that don't concern you?"

Lottie walks round. She has a look at me an' she laughs.

"Ain't you the big mug?" she says. "Didn't they tell you that dames sometimes has a gun in their handbag? Have a piece of shoe, honey!"

She steps back and she kicks me in the face. I don't know whether you've ever been kicked in the face by a dame, but high heels can hurt considerable. I don't say anything much. I seem to be bleeding from everywhere an' my right arm is giving me hell.

"O.K. playboys," I say. "Just you wait a minute. Say, listen, do you think that a four-flushing twicer like Goyaz could ever pull anything on a feller like Siegella? What do you think is going to happen to you when he gets to hear about this?"

Lottie laughs again.

"Don't be a mug," she says. "After tonight Siegella nor anybody else won't be seeing us around here."

I fade out. I wriggle myself back against the wall, trying to make myself as comfortable as I can. They have tied my hands behind me, an' the pain in my right arm is not very pleasing. I reckon that Lottie's bullet has gone through a few inches above the wrist, but the bleeding is easing off and it looks to me as if she has missed the bone and the artery which is somethin' to be thankful for. She goes back to her chair an' goes on reading the paper. I can see she is readin' an article called "You must use Charm," and believe me if she was to use charm half as well as she kicked me in the face that dame would get some place. The other four guys go on playin' poker an' drinkin' highballs.

Somewhere in the neighbourhood I hear some church clock strike ten. I am feeling lousy, an' I think that I am a bit of a mug to have come along to this dump on my own. I'm still a bigger mug to be caught out by a jane like Lottie.

After an hour the guy with the dank hair, who seems to be winning all the money, rolls his wad up, and puts his coat on.

"Come on, fellers," he yelps, "we'd better be breaking outa here. Say, Lottie, what are we going to do with this punk?"

He looks at me where I am leaning up against the wall. I've got my eyes closed an' I am pretending to be almost out.

"Don't worry about him," she says, "you boys get along. Hirka and me'll take him along with us. Goyaz will fix him later."

She goes off into another room.

These four fellers put on their things and scram out of it, and the Japanese guy Hirka comes into the room an' starts cleaning up. Somewhere in the flat I can hear Lottie singing. Right under the table is my hat. It was a lucky break that when these guys rushed me my hat fell off and it fell down the right way. Inside the crown of that hat is my little gun, an' if I can get my hands free maybe I can still pull something.

I open my eyes.

"Say you," I say to the Jap, "why don't you listen to me. You don't think this sorta stuff is going to do you any good, do you? One of these days I'm going to get my hooks on you an' what I'll do to you, you yellow slug, won't be on any menu."

He grins.

"You make me laugh," he says.

Just then Lottie comes in.

"Say, listen, girlie," I bleat. "Why don't you have a heart? You know durned well you've plugged me through my right arm. It's bleeding like the garden spray. What about tying something round it or do you want me to die on you?"

"I'd like to put a hot poker on it, baby," she says, "but maybe you're right."

She goes to her handbag and she gets her gun out.

"Listen, Hirka," she says. "Untie his hands—he can't move, an' tie a towel or something round that arm of his, it's spoiling the carpet. An' listen, Lemmy," she says, "just you make one move an' I'm going to give it to you right through the pump, an' you know I can shoot."

"That's O.K. by me, sister," I say, "I wouldn't try an' do a thing."

The Japanese goes out an' comes back with a towel, some peroxide and a bandage. He cuts my arms loose, an' I move my right arm round and look at it. As I thought, Lottie has put one clean through my forearm, and the bullet has gone out the other side. The Jap cuts up my coat sleeve, washes the wound, plugs each end with a bit of cotton wool, an' ties the bandage round it. My arm is feeling numb and stiff, and the Japanese, remembering the smack on the nut I gave him, is not being too gentle.

I lean back against the wall an' I closes my eyes and groan. Lottie is standing over on the other side of the table, the gun in her hand, looking at me. The Jap has just straightened up an' is standing on my right.

"Don't you like it, sucker?" says Lottie, "I thought you could take it."

I let go a groan.

"Gee, I'm feeling bad," I moan.

As I speak I shoot my head forward. I pick up my legs which are tied together an' I kick out at the Jap. I get him just under the knees an' he falls forward across me just as Lottie fires.

The Jap gets it. I hear him howl. I push him off me with my left hand, and dive forward under the table just as she starts some more artillery practice. Right under my left hand is my hat an' about two feet away I can see Lottie's ankles. I skip the hat business for the moment. I take another dive. I get her ankle in my left hand an' I pull it. Over she goes like a ninepin. As she falls I get her right arm which has the gun in it, an' twist it. She drops the gun.

I take a quick look over my shoulder at the Jap. He is not so good. He is lying on one side coughing. I reckon that Lottie has got him through the lung. I pull her under the table an' I put my legs, which are still tied, across her so as she can't move. Then with my left hand I get the gun out of my hat.

"Now listen, sweetheart," I say, "just untie my legs, pronto."

She gets busy. In two minutes I'm standing on my feet, mixing myself a highball. The Jap is still doing a big coughing act on the floor, and Lottie is sitting in a chair on the other side of the room smoking a cigarette. She is not feeling so pleased.

"Well, baby," I say, "how do you like it now?"

She tells me all about it. She tells me all about me, an' my father an' my mother, an' what she hopes will happen to any descendants of mine. I've heard some tough dames in my life, but that dame could compete with the marines any time an' leave 'em cold. I finish this act by slinging a cushion at her which knocks her off the chair. She gets up.

"Well, where do we go from here?" she says.

"Don't worry your head, sister," I say. "You an' I are going places together, but first of all turn that guy over and let's have a look at him."

She turns the Jap over. As I thought, she's shot him through the back of the shoulder an' it looks to me as if she's got the top of the lung. I make her tie him up an' prop him up against the wall.

"Where's the car, Lottie?" I say.

"In the garage next door," she spits at me.

"O.K.," I say. "We'll just tie that guy up so as he can't move, an' then you an' I are going to get the car, an' if I were you I wouldn't try any funny business on the way."

After the Jap is tied up we go downstairs. Next door is a garage and in this garage is a big tourer. I make her drive it round to the front of the flat an' then we go upstairs again.

"Now, sister," I say, "you've got to understand this. I ain't letting this Goyaz guy an' your little playmate Kastlin get away with this Miranda stuff. Now you've got to talk an' you've got to talk quick. Where is Goyaz, Kastlin and Miranda?"

She looks at me an' she laughs.

"Go on, big boy," she pouts. "You try anything you like, I'm not talking."

I grin.

"O.K., sister," I say. "I've heard dames talk like that before. Go an' put your little hat on, honey, we're going riding."

I take her in next door an' I wait while she puts her hat on and powders her nose. Then we go downstairs. I shut the front door of the flat, put her in the driving seat an' I sit behind.

"Drive to Knightsbridge," I say, "an' step on it."

"O.K., Lemmy," she says, "but you get a load on this. One of these days my sugar Kastlin is going to get his hooks on you an' I'll just promise you one little thing. We're going to give you a paraffin bath an' I'll just love to light it myself."

About twenty-five minutes later we pull up outside the flat at Knightsbridge, the place that Connie took me to. I'm hoping to blazes that Connie hangs out in this place because if not I'm in a spot. When we get there I slip my gun in my right hand pocket an' I tell Lottie to get out.

"Walk in front of me, sweetheart," I say, "an' don't make any mistakes, because if you do there's going to be a nasty accident."

We go up in the lift an' we stop at the flat. I play a tattoo on the door and does my heart give a jump when Connie opens it. She is wearing a negligée that would make the Queen of Sheba look like the hired help.

"Well of all the—" she says. "Say, what is this?"

"Listen, Constance," I say, "this is just going to be a nice clean little party. Just keep your eye on this little dame, will you? She's working in with Kastlin and Goyaz, an' they've snatched Miranda."

"Well, may I be burned alive?" says Connie. "Come in, baby," she says.

She gets hold of Lottie by the nose and she pulls her into the flat, an' then she gives her a kick that sends her flying across the room. Lottie bounces off the wall and finishes up on the floor. An' is she peevish?

"Now, Connie," I say, "what is this Goyaz stuff?"

"Listen, Lemmy," she says. "It's easy. Here's the story. Goyaz was in with us on this snatch originally. We were going to use his boat. Then he got funny over money and Siegella gave him the air. He's pulled a fast one, that's all."

"You're telling me," I say. "He certainly has pulled a fast one. The set-up's easy. Goyaz has contacted Miranda, promised her a swell time on that gambling boat of his somewhere, got her aboard and unless we do some quick moving we ain't ever going to see that dame again."

Constance nods.

"You're right," she says, "where is this boat an' where is Goyaz?"

"You ask her," I say. "But she says she ain't talking."

I indicate Lottie who is sitting in a chair rubbing herself an' lookin' like Satan's ma-in-law.

"Oh, she ain't, ain't she?" says Connie. "Well, just fancy that now." She walks over to Lottie.

"Listen, pretty," she says. "You're going to talk an' you're going to talk quick. Just come in here with me, will you?"

She gets hold of Lottie by the back of the neck an' she pulls her to her feet. Lottie shoots out a foot and kicks Constance on the shin bone. Then Connie gets to work. She's a fine big girl an' what she don't do to Lottie is just nobody's business. Eventually, she drags her into the room next door.

I help myself to a cigarette from a box on the table an' light up. My right arm is as stiff as hell and the stiffness is going up higher and higher every minute. It don't feel so good to me.

Suddenly from the next room I hear a muffled yelp by which I gather that Connie is giving Lottie the works properly, an' has got a pillow over her mouth to stop the neighbourhood getting excited.

I'm right about this. Two minutes later Connie comes to the door. She is grinning like the cat that swallowed the canary. Inside the room I can hear Lottie sobbing.

"It's all right, Lemmy," says Connie. "She's talked. Goyaz has got his boat moored outside the three mile limit off the Isle of Mersea, which apparently is some dump near Colchester. But we're O.K. because the boat ain't pulling out till six o'clock tomorrow morning. We've got a lot of time."

"We've got a lot of nothing," I say.

Connie takes a look over her shoulder at Lottie, then she comes into the room, shutting the door behind her.

"Don't worry about her," she says, "she ain't got enough guts to do anything to anybody now I've finished with her. Now, where do we go from here? I'd better contact Siegella."

Now that don't suit me at all.

"Contact nothing, Connie," I say. "What we're going to do is this. I know this Goyaz and Kastlin mob. They ain't gangsters, they just think they are. I'm going to pull a big rescue act on my own. Don't you see how it would go over with Miranda if I get her out of this. Then I'm the little blue-eyed boy, an' I can do anything I like with her."

Connie nods.

"You're right, Lemmy," she says.

She looks at me old-fashioned.

"Say, listen," she says, "you ain't stuck on this dame Miranda, or anything, are you? You know she's a nice looking piece."

"Oh, shucks, Connie," says I, "I don't go for women, you know that. Miranda ain't so bad looking, but she ain't in the same street as you, is she, baby?"

I give her a hug.

"O.K., Lemmy," she says. "Skip that, we've got business to do."

"You're telling me," I say, "the first business you've got to do is to fix my arm. It feels like a bunch of red-hot pokers."

She gets busy. She leaps back into the bedroom, an' she takes a look at Lottie. Just to make certain of this dame she ties her to the bedposts with towels. I don't think I've ever seen a funnier sight in my life than Lottie Frisch. She looked like a Turkish bath attendant's dream.

"That's that," says Connie. "Now, listen. I'm going to scram out of here an' get some stuff to fix you up with. I'll be back in a minute."

"O.K., honey," I say, "and bring the car back with you because we're going to make this Isle of Mersea place right away."

Connie goes out. I wait till I hear the lift go down an' then I grab the telephone book. I get the number of the Strand Chambers an' I ring Gallat. Inside of me I'm praying that Siegella is not going to try to bump Gallat tonight, because if he does, there's liable to be a whole lot of trouble with MacFee kicking around.

Gallat answers the telephone an' I get him to bring MacFee to the wire.

"Now, listen, Mac," I say, "there's a whole lot of bezuzus flying about here. What's been going on ain't nobody's business. The inside stuff is this. Goyaz and Kastlin have snatched Miranda and have got her down on some boat, which will probably be the Princess Cristabel calling itself something else, moored outside the three mile limit off the Isle of Mersea. You get down there with that guy Gallat, but don't pull anything until I get there.

"Connie, Siegella's girl, is driving me down, an' I got to arrange to dump that dame somewhere before I meet you guys. When you get to this dump find the wharf, the place that a motor-boat from the Princess Cristabel would tie up, an' stick around there until I show up."

"O.K.," says MacFee. "When will you be there?"

I look at the watch inside my left wrist. It was a quarter to twelve.

"Listen, Mac," I say, "it's a quarter to twelve. This place is about sixty miles, an' as we're going to step on it I reckon we'll be there just after one o'clock. I'll be seeing you."

"O.K., buddy," he says. "So long!"

I hang up and I light another cigarette. Five minutes afterwards Connie comes back. She has rounded up bandages, iodine an' all sorts of stuff, an' she gets to work on my arm.

This Connie is a swell looker, I told you before. She has got nice curves and long tapering fingers, an' while she is doing my arm the perfume she is wearing smells good to me. She fixes up my arm good and bandages it.

"You can take it, Lemmy," she says, "you're a tough guy, ain't you?"

"What's the good," I say. "Nobody appreciates it."

She smiles.

"Don't you think so, Lemmy?" she says.

She gives me a kiss, and for just one minute I forget everything. For some reason which I don't know I start thinking about chicken farming in Missouri. Then I come to.

"Come on, Connie," I say, "we've got to scram out of here. I'm sorry to have to take you but you've got to drive."

"You bet you're taking me," she says. "We've got to get Miranda. Now, will Siegella be burned up when he hears about this? What he won't do to that Goyaz mob is nobody's business."

She gets me a hat an' we take a final look at Lottie. This dame is so done up that she ain't got a squeal left in her.

"I'll come back for you, baby," says Connie, "and when I come back I'll tell you what I'm going to do to you. Think it over, honey, it'll pass the time away."

We went down in the lift. Outside the roadster is parked. We get in an' Connie proceeds to step on it.

As we move off she takes a big Luger automatic from the door pocket.

"Have a piece of this, Lemmy," she says. "I gotta idea you'll want it tonight."

Was she right or was she right!

CHAPTER FIVE
MERSEA ISLAND BLUES

CONSTANCE is swell with a car. The only time we ain't doing round about sixty is when we are near some copper. We get across London, and pretty soon we are going through Stratford—and by this time it is about half-past twelve—and I am having a meeting with myself as to how I am going to ditch this baby, because one thing is certain an' that is that it's going to do no good at all for her to meet MacFee and Gallat who will be hanging around down at this Isle of Mersea dump.

It ain't so easy to pull anything on Connie because as you will have guessed by now she is a very clever dame, in fact I would go out of my way to say there are no flies worth swatting on this young woman at all.

I savvy that I have got to get away from her somehow before we get to Mersea. Stuck in front of me in the pocket of the car I see an Automobile Association book and a flash lamp. I take this book out an' I turn on the flash lamp an' I make a big play that I'm looking up the distances to the Isle of Mersea, but what I am really doing is seeing where the nearest garage is. Eventually, I get the set-up. Ten miles from the place we are going through is a garage.

I keep my eye on the speedometer and I wait until we have done over five miles. Then I proceed to do my stuff.

"Say, Connie," I say, "just pull up for a minute, will you? There's a nasty rattle somewhere round the back nearside wheel, an' I don't like it. We don't want any accidents, so hold everything while I go an' have a look."

I've got a very old-fashioned idea. I always carry a safety razor blade in a little holder in my vest pocket. I use it for clipping cigar ends and things. I get out of the car and I walk round the back an' I stick this blade right through the rear near side cover. I leave the blade there because I reckon when the wheel has revolved a half a dozen times this blade is going to work out an' there's going to be a blow out. After a minute I get back into the car an' I say everything is O.K. an' we go on.

It works. We do about another two and a half miles, an' Connie is getting the speed up to a clear fifty, when the tyre goes pop. We skid across the road an' it's only due to some nice handling by my girl friend that we keep outa the ditch. I get out and I look at the tyre.

"Now what do you know about that?" I say. "Ain't it like women not to have a spare wheel?"

She looks glum.

"This would happen," she says. "I punctured the spare and it's being fixed at the garage."

"Well, that ain't goin' to help us," I say, "you can't drive that car like that. Stick around here. I'm going to see if I can find a garage."

I pull the A.A. book out once again an' I tell her that there's a garage two miles away. I tell her I'm goin' to scram down there, pick up a car an' come back for her. She says O.K. I break into a quiet trot an' I make this garage, which is not so far away, very soon. My arm is givin' me hell!

They have got a Chevrolet for hire.

I rent this car, an' then I write a little note to Connie. I tell her that I reckon it's so late that I'd better get straight along to Mersea Island, that I'm sending the garage man back to fix her flat, an' that she had better come along afterwards. That when she gets there she had better hang around at the nearest railway station an' pick me up, this being the only place I can think of to meet at.

I give this note with a pound bill to the garage man, an' he says he'll go an' locate Connie. I step on it. I bet nobody in this country has ever seen a car driven the way I drove that car, an' it is about a quarter to two when I get to this Mersea Island. That place ain't really an island, there's sea all round it except the back where there's a little stream that is crossed over by a bridge. It's a funny sorta place, murky dark an' damp.

I drive along until I pass some guy an' I ask him if they have got a pier or a landing wharf round here, an' he tells me where it is. I go down till I get to this place, an' leave the car by the hedge at the side of the road, an' I walk down to the wharf.

This wharf is a deserted flat platform supported by piles. There's nobody on it. I look around but I cannot see any sign of MacFee or Gallat, an' I begin to wonder whether they have been held up too, or whether MacFee, thinking that somethin' else has happened to me, has taken a chance an' gone out to the Princess Cristabel.

I meander around this place but I cannot see any guy at all. Way out I can see some ship lights twinkling, an' I reckon this is Goyaz' boat all right. I walk back off the wharf an' I turn off a side road leading off the main road through which I have come.

Way down on the left I can see a light twinkling in a window along there. It's a sorta fisherman's shack and standing in this doorway is a feller with a blue jersey smoking a pipe.

"Howdy, pal," I say, "it's a nasty night, ain't it? You don't happen to have seen a coupla mugs round here, have you? They was due to meet me down at the wharf."

He smokes for about twenty seconds before he says anything. This, guy must be one of them saps you read about in the papers who always think what they're saying in case they talk too quick. After a while he starts to talk:

"Oh, yes," he says, "there was two men down here. I reckon they was looking for you. Then they thought that maybe you wasn't going to turn up, thought perhaps you'd had some trouble gettin' down here."

"Fine," I say. I slip him a ten shilling note. "Where'd they go to, pal?" I ask him.

"They've gone out to that there ship," he says. "They hired Jim Cardew's launch."

I nod.

"When was this?" I ask.

"Maybe twenty minutes ago," he says, "maybe half an hour. I don't know."

"Have you got another boat round here," I ask, "something that will take me out there?"

He shakes his head.

"Cardew was the only feller round here with a motor launch," he says, "an' he's a bit fed up because they wouldn't let him go with them. They hired the boat and went off on their own. He charged them plenty though. There ain't nobody will row you out this time of night. The tide's too strong, you wouldn't make it."

"Thanks, buddy," I say, "you're a great help."

I say goodnight an' I walk down the road back to the wharf.

I am in a jam, an' I don't see what I can do, but it seems that it ain't any good sticking around on this wharf, an' when I am thinking I like to walk about. So I turn off the wharf, an' I walk up the road past the car, wondering what the hell I am goin' to do. I reckon I must have walked a hundred yards down the road, when I hear something coming along.

It's pretty heavy and sounds like a lorry. Suddenly an idea strikes me. Supposing for the sake of argument that the four mobsters who were around at Baker Street with Lottie Frisch had left early because they had to pick up provisions or stores of some sort for the Princess Cristabel, this might be them!

I stand in the shade of the hedge at the side of the road, an' in a minute the lorry comes along. I give myself a pat on the back because I am dead right. It's a big ten ton truck and it's loaded up with all sorts of cases an' stuff. Right on the top where the tarpaulin cover has blown away I can see a case of whisky. Sittin' in the driver's seat is the big guy with the dank hair. Two other fellers are sitting alongside of him, an' I reckon the fourth man is somewhere on the back.

The lorry goes straight past me, but instead of drivin' down to the wharf it turns right and goes towards the shack where I spoke to the fisherman. Presently it stops. I skeedaddle across the corner over the grass towards it, an' I hear a lot of palooka goin' on, an' it's obvious to me that the driver has taken the wrong road an' is preparing to back the lorry on to the right one, so as to get her down to the wharf. The road being very narrow he has some trouble about this, an' while he is about it I scram back, get into my car, an' drive it straight across an' park it right in the middle of the side road.

I then get out an' stand round behind the car. In a coupla minutes the lorry backs towards the car and stops about ten feet off it. The driver pops his head round an' yells to me to take that so-and-so car out of the way an' can't I see he is trying to make the wharf.

I don't say a word. I just crouch behind the car. After a coupla minutes I hear 'em getting down. As they walk past my headlights

I can see it is the whole four of 'em in a bunch. When they have got round the car I am waiting for 'em with the Luger in my mitt.

"Reach for the sky, suckers," I say. "Well, how're you feeling? You didn't expect to see me, did you?"

The guy with the dank hair don't look so pleased.

"You dirty so-and-so," he says, "so you made a getaway, did you?"

"You bet I did," I say, "and will you tell me why I shouldn't slip you a coupla slugs a piece an' chuck you in the lake? Just come an' line up here facing the car with your backs to me, will you?"

They line up with their hands up in the air, an' I am feeling very glad that this Isle of Mersea is a deserted place and there ain't nobody kicking around, otherwise they might think this was Barnum Circus, maybe.

I frisk these guys. Each one of 'em is packing a rod an' I drop 'em in a little heap behind me. I also help myself to the 1,000 dollars which the big dank guy took off of me round on the Baker Street Mews, an' I help myself to another 400 which he has won off these other guys playing poker. I don't see why I should not make a profit out of this deal. Naturally this guy does not like this and becomes very abusive about me personally.

Then I get rough. I smack the first three guys over the head with the butt of my gun. They just flop on to the ground. Then I talk to the last feller, the little one.

"Listen, buddy," I say, "I am a tough feller, an' I wouldn't like you to die before your time. Now I tell you what you're goin' to do. You're goin' to load these three guys back on that lorry an' you are goin' to drive it back to London an' you are goin' to keep goin', because if I see you anywhere round here I'm goin' to blast daylight into you. Now you get outa here an' don't stop till you see Charing Cross."

He looks pretty scared. I guess he ain't feeling so good. After a lot of trouble he gets these three saps loaded back to the lorry. I move the car an' he backs it down on the road.

"Listen, kid," I say, "just a minute before you go. In about five minutes' time you are going to be off this island. You see that telephone box over there." I point to the booth at one end of the wharf. "When you've been gone five minutes I reckon I'm going to put a phone call through to the Essex Constabulary. I am going to tell 'em that I am a resident round here an' that I have seen a lorry driven by a suspicious looking guy with three unconscious fellers on it heading for London.

"Now I reckon if you was to get pinched by these English coppers they'd want a whole lot of explanation from you, wouldn't they? It wouldn't be so good for you. It wouldn't be so good for Goyaz or Kastlin. Now you get out a here and keep running. Got me, sweetheart?"

"O.K.," he says, "but you bet your sweet an' holy life somebody is goin' to get you some time for this, an' when they do they'll get you good!"

"Don't make me cry, sweetheart," I say. "Get a move on before I give you the heat."

He drives off an' I see his tail-lights disappear in the distance. I reckon I won't have no more trouble with this guy. Needless to say I don't telephone no police, because at this moment I wouldn't like to have any truck with any coppers from anywhere.

I then chuck the guns into the water, after which I go into a huddle with myself and do a little more heavy thinkin'.

Two things is stickin' out a foot. The first one is that it is a certainty that some boat is comin' in to the wharf from the Princess Cristabel to meet the lorry an' take the stores aboard, an' the second thing is that it looks as if I have got to do something about Constance who will be hangin' around the railway depot—wherever that may be— and will start something if I do not head her off. This Constance will certainly get some sort of action because she is not the sorta dame who will stick around doin' nothin' at a time like this.

So I reckon that my first play must be Constance. So I start up the car an' I drive off. I reckon that the railway depot will be somewhere along the main road along which I have come, an' a spot of investigatin' soon tells me that I am right first time.

This railway depot is a little dump off the main road on the left. It is quiet an' deserted because this Mersea place is the sorta place that only has trains on Christmas Day an' Leap Year.

Outside the palings I can see Connie's car. This dame is very pleased to see me. She is sittin' behind the wheel smoking a cigarette.

"Howdy, Lemmy," she says. "I'm glad to see you all in one piece. Say, why did you make that breakaway like you did? What did you have to ditch me for?"

"It's durn lucky I did," I say.

I tell her what has happened an' that if I hadn't been around these four thugs would have made the Princess Cristabel an' I wouldn't have stood a dog's chance of gettin' aboard.

She looks glum.

"Look, Lemmy," she says. "Just what is goin' to happen when you do get aboard? What do you think Goyaz is goin' to do to you. Do you think he's goin' to be pleased with you. This guy is goin' to bump you an' throw you in the ditch afterwards just as sure as my name's Constance."

"Grow up, baby," I say. "Get a load of this. Goyaz don't know anything about me in this set-up, does he? Alright, when I blow aboard I tell him some fairy story about how I was kickin' around with some boys I met in town an' how they told me that he has muscled in on Siegella's racket. I then tell him that Siegella has got wise to the game an' has hi-jacked the lorry that was comin' down here an' beaten up the boys.

"Well, Goyaz is goin' to listen, ain't he? I then proceed to wait my chance to pull a fast one, an' you can bet your life I'm goin' to find some way to do it."

"O.K.," she says. "It's your funeral, Lemmy."

"Maybe," I crack back, "but you shut your head an' grab your earphone. I reckon that some boat is comin' off the Princess Cristabel to pick up the stuff off that lorry. You an' me has got to get down to that wharf. When the boat comes in we gotta see how many guys there is aboard, an' you gotta fix it so's you get 'em ashore somehow."

I then get her to park her car alongside the palings an' I load her into mine an' we drive down to the wharf. I pull up in the shadow where the car can't be seen an' we wait.

It is about three o'clock when we hear the chug-chug of a motor-boat, an' presently we see a twenty-foot launch slipping up to the wharf. There is two guys in this launch. They pull alongside an' one of 'em ties the boat up whilst the other feller gets out an' looks around.

Connie, as we have fixed, is standing at the end of the wharf in the shadow. She walks across and she goes up to this guy.

"Say, listen," she says, "I'm Connie, Lottie Frisch's pal. Things ain't so good. The lorry had a smash up gettin' down here. She's about two miles away with one wheel off. Lottie says that you guys had better get down the road an' give a hand."

"Oh yeah!" says this guy. "Where is she?"

"She's down the road," says Connie.

He goes back and he has a few words with the feller in the boat. Then he comes back to Connie.

"O.K.," he says, "I'll come along with you, but this guy has got to stay with the boat."

He an' Connie walk down the road. I wait ten minutes an' I slip over the grass on to the main road an' start walking down towards the wharf as large as life. The guy in the boat is sitting in the stern smoking.

"Hey, you," I say, "we need you, come down an' give us a hand. It's all we can manage."

"Yeah," he says, "well, I ain't comin'. I ain't leaving this boat; it looks to me as if there's something screwy going on around here."

I am sorry I have to get tough with this guy, but I have no option.

"Get out of that boat, kid," I say, "an' look slippy, otherwise this cannon might go off."

He don't say anything but just gets out an' steps on the wharf. As he straightens up I let him have it with a left hook that jolts this feller considerable. He crumples up an' I drag him round an' stick him in the car. I go over him but he hasn't got a gun.

I am very sorry to leave Connie to carry the baby but I have no option. I ran back to the wharf, jump in the boat, untie her an' start her off. I turn her nose out to sea. Away in the distance I can see the lights of the Princess Cristabel.

It is a nice night although it is dark. There is a big tide running an' I am very glad that I didn't try to get out to the Princess Cristabel in some row boat. I light a cigarette an' I begin to think of all the stuff that has come my way since two nights ago when I was walking down the Haymarket just before Connie picked me up. It is funny what a lot of things can happen so durn sudden.

But I am feeling a bit worried. What is going to happen when I get on this boat, I don't know. I don't know what MacFee an' Gallat have pulled, whether they are on top of the situation or whether they have got in bad. I am also wondering just what Connie is going to do with this guy that she took down the road when he finds out that there ain't no lorry an' I wonder what the guy I have left in the car will do when he comes round.

Still I reckon that Connie has got enough brains to handle this stuff. I also make a mental note that when I go ashore again, that is if ever I do get ashore again, I must do something about this guy that we left in MacFee's coal cellar. I reckon this feller must be considerably bored by now, but maybe he likes the dark.

It seems a long time before I get anywhere near the Princess Cristabel. I steer the launch towards her stern, an' believe me there is plenty noise coming from that yacht.

The Princess Cristabel is a long smart rakish looking yacht that was built for some millionaire. How Goyaz got it I don't know, but he has made considerable money outa this boat.

Right now I can see the lights in the portholes an' somewhere aboard a band is playing. I reckon this Goyaz does things in style. By this time I have switched off the motor an' have floated up under the stern. Most of the noise on this dump is coming from the fore part an' the saloon amidships. I take a chance.

There is a coil of rope in the launch an' after throwing one end of it up at the stern rail a half a dozen times, I get it over the rail an' back to me. I tie up the launch to the two ends of this rope an' I shin up. In a few seconds I am aboard. The stern of the Princess Cristabel is deserted. There is a big deck house running three-quarters the length of the boat, an' there is plenty noise coming from this.

Way forward I can see couples in evening dress sittin' on deck chairs with coats on an' there are one or two tough looking guys in white jackets serving drinks. When the breeze comes my way I can hear somebody talking French, an' reckon that Goyaz has brought this boat over via one of the French ports. If I know anything of him he has probably got aboard the usual crowd of cheap playboys and their sugar babies.

You gotta hand it to this guy Goyaz that he has got plenty nerve to come bustin' around this part of the world workin' a racket boat just as if he was layin' off San Pedro or some place in U.S. where men is men an' women are durn glad of it. The idea of his doin' his stuff just outside the three mile limit off the English coast is good because no other guy has thought of it. Outside the limit you can do what you durn well please an' nobody can pinch you.

I reckon I have got the Goyaz set-up alright. It looks to me like Connie said that Goyaz was comin' in on the Miranda snatch with Siegella; that the first idea was that this guy should load up his boat with this mob, bring her over to England an' get Miranda aboard an' scram with her. But it would be like him to want all the dough an' I reckon that Siegella found out that Kastlin was workin' in with Goyaz an' turned 'em both in. Siegella wouldn't trust Kastlin, who is a guy who got a nasty smear on his record when he turned State's Evidence in Kansas on Freddy Frickle—the guy who got boozed an' shot two Protective Association men thinkin' they were cops—an' so saved himself from the chair. Freddy got fried an' Kastlin went free.

My arm is givin' me the jumps. It has got sorta stiff up to the elbow an' although I can use it don't feel so good. Still I reckon I was lucky to get properly tied up by Connie who is swell at that sorta stuff.

Sittin' there in the darkness I got to wonderin' where Siegella picked up Connie. That guy has certainly got brains an' he don't make a lot of mistakes where dames are concerned. Too many mugs who have been swell racket workers have slipped up over bein' too chancy in pickin' their janes, an' more mobsters have been dragged in by the cops just because some dame has got a fit of the jealous blues an' gone off shootin' her mouth to the cops outa spite, than I could count on both hands.

I reckon women is alright so long as you don't tell 'em anything an' so long as you got a whole lot of 'em at once. It's the single dame that gets you. Play 'em all an' it's swell. Stick around with one an' as sure as you're born one of these fine days she won't be feelin' so good about some little thing an' she'll go an' put her little blonde head on some guy's shoulder an' spill the works, an' in nine cases out of ten this sympathetic guy with the nice ways is a Federal Dick

or a copper of some sort, after which the fireworks begin an' she's
sorry for ever afterwards.

Which is a helluva lot of good to you when you are all set to take
a nice long rest-cure in the electric chair. You're tellin' me.

But this Constance was different somehow. It seemed a sorta pity
that she should be kickin' around with a man like Siegella, although he
certainly has brains an' he goes for the big stuff like this Miranda snatch.

All this is goin' through my head whilst I am sittin' in the shadow
of a capstan or whatever they call the durn thing, gettin' my wind
back an' tryin' to fix up some sorta plan in my head.

I am all burned up about MacFee, because I cannot understand
why this guy has not done his stuff like I told him an' stuck around
an' waited for me. The only thing I can think of is that this guy Gallat
was all excited about Miranda bein' aboard an' was hot to get on the
boat an' that MacFee couldn't stop him an' had to stick along.

When I was a kid I can remember some guy tellin' me some
proverb which says "When in doubt don't." I have always found
this a very good proverb, an' whenever I am uncertain about some
situation I just stick around an' don't do anything. I guess somethin'
always turns up.

It looks to me as if there must be a whole lot of mugs on this
boat. I can see 'em coming out of the deck house forward, an' there
is no doubt about it that most of them is just about as full of hooch
as they can be. Knowing the sorta cheap liquor that Goyaz usually
totes around on his boat I reckon that most of these guys aboard
will be so blind that I could get in amongst them an' nobody would
notice me, except maybe Goyaz or Kastlin an' any members of the
crew or the mob, who I reckon would jump right outa their skins if
they knew Lemmy Caution was aboard.

Just at this moment a door in the darkness at the end of the
deck house facing the stern opens and some dame comes out. She
is a heavy blonde, a swell looker, an' she is dressed in a white satin
evening gown covered with diamante or whatever they call it. She also
looks as if somebody has dragged her through a coupla hedges. Her
hair is all mussed up an' she is staggerin' about like as if she didn't
know where she was. I reckon that this dame has either been look-

ing on the wine when it was very red or else some guy has slugged her with a blackjack.

She comes staggerin' over towards where I am sittin', so I think I had better do somethin' about it, an' I get up.

"Well, honey," I say, "how is it goin'? You don't look so good to me."

She looks at me an' her eyes are glassy. She is not a bad looking dame. She has got a nice mouth, except she's using the wrong sorta lipstick, an' she's licking her lips which I reckon are pretty dry. She looks at me just as if she couldn't see anything.

"I feel lousy," she says. "Say, don't you think that Goyaz is a mug to start pulling this sorta stuff on this boat? Why can't he lay off rough stuff, there's plenty trouble in the world without making some more of it."

She looks almost as if she is going to take a fall, so I put my arm around her an' I walk her over to a seat by the stern rail an' sit her down.

"Say, I'd like a drink of water," she moans.

"Take it easy, sister," I say. "What's eatin' you? What's going on around here?"

"It's them guys," she whispers, "the stiffs! When we left the U.S. coast I told Goyaz I reckoned there'd be trouble on this trip. Why couldn't he stick around there, where he's always made good money. No, he has to take the boat over to France an' the mug gets stuck inside the three mile limit an' we get chased out of it. Now he's got some other scheme over here. He's got some dame aboard, an' he's taking her for plenty. I reckon that girl's lost twenty grand tonight."

I listened. This must be Miranda.

"Well, that's all right, sister," I say. "That's how it goes, you know. But nobody can't do nothing to Goyaz here, he's outside the three mile limit."

She looks at me again.

"Don't talk hooey," she says, "you can't get away with what he's been doin' tonight any place, three mile limit or not. Gee, would I like some water?"

She hangs over the rail an' it looks to me she is so keen on water that she's going to jump into it in a minute. It is stickin' out a mile that this dame is not feeling so good. I pat her on the shoulder.

"O.K., kid," I say, "take it easy, I'll get you a drink."

I get up an' I walk along the deck. Suddenly out of one of the doors on the port side this end of the deck house comes a guy in a white jacket. I take a chance.

"Hey, steward," I say, "I want you."

He looks at me, and he comes towards me.

CHAPTER SIX
CURTAINS FOR THREE

I'M A bit windy whilst this steward guy is walkin' towards me, but in a minute I see it is O.K. This feller has been samplin' the rye himself an' is not quite certain about anything very much. He asks me what I want.

"There's a lady here ain't feeling so well," I tell him. "Go get me a glass of water, will you, an' bring along a big shot of bourbon. I could use it."

He goes off an' I go back to the dame. Presently the guy in the white jacket comes back. He has got a bottle of bourbon, a carafe of water an' a coupla glasses. I take these off him an' he goes off.

I give the dame some water an' I help myself to a shot of bourbon, after which I feel a little bit better.

"Now, girlie," I say to this dame, "what are you gettin' so excited about? Life ain't so bad. Howdya get on this boat? You been with Goyaz long?"

She nods.

"I've been kicking along in his racket for years," she says. "I work ashore round the coast ports, an' get 'em to come an' play. It ain't bad in the States, but I don't like this business of going away from the U.S. coast. I sorta got suspicious tonight when he told me to keep away from the cabin—the one he uses as an office. You know how it is, big boy," she goes on, "if somebody tells you you shouldn't do somethin' you must go an' do it. When they started playin' I went along an' I poked my head round the corner of the door, an' it wasn't so hot."

I nodded.

"Was that when you come out just now. Out of that door over there?"

"That's right," she says, "I didn't want to go back the same way, otherwise he might have tumbled to what I'd been up to, so I came through the kitchens an' I got out this way."

"O.K.," I say. "Now listen, sister. You must be feeling pretty cold, eh, baby? Take a walk round the deck an' go in the saloon through the forward companion way. He won't know a thing, he'll think you've been on deck for some air."

She just nods an' she gets up and meanders off.

It's evident to me that this dame is not at all pleased with herself. Right now, at the back of my neck, I am beginning to feel a bit hot, because I have got one or two ideas in my head which are not very pleasin'.

Directly she has scrammed out of it, I get up an' I walk towards the back of the deck house, an' I slip through the door where she came out. Inside it is as dark as hell, but somewhere ahead at the end of a passage I can see a light an' hear a lot of dishes being rattled. I gum-shoe along this passage an' I look through the door at the end.

It seems to me as if I am lookin' into the kitchen because there are a couple of guys in dirty white coats washing up dishes an' pullin' corks. I wait there for a minute an' then I walk straight through putting on a bit of a roll as if I was tight. I reckon so many guys are tight on this boat that nobody ain't goin' to notice one more.

Anyhow, neither of these guys says nothin' an' I walk through the kitchen and out through the door the other end. I find myself in another little corridor. There is two doors on the right and three on the left. I open the two doors on the right of the passage but these are just sleeping berths—empty—so I try the left. The first two are open—they are berths too—but the third one is locked an' if this is the cabin that the dame I have just been talkin' to got into I reckon she must have had a key.

The fact that this door is locked gets me curious. The lock is just nothin' at all, an' it takes me about two minutes to fix it. I go inside and shut the door behind me. This cabin is as dark as Marpella Alley an' for some reason which I don't know I get a sorta feeling that I am goin' to get a coupla nasty surprises.

I strike a match an' take a look round, an' believe me I am right. On a desk in the middle of the cabin I can see an electric lamp an' I switch this on.

Lying against the wall opposite in a pool of blood are two stiffs. It don't take me long to see that they are Gallat and MacFee. It is also quite plain to me that they are both very dead. It looks to me as if Gallat has been shot two or three times through the stomach while MacFee has got it through the neck an' head. These two guys evidently have not been popular on this boat.

I reckon I have seen a lot of killing in my time, an' I don't get burned up every time some guy gets himself bumped off, but I feel very annoyed that these two guys have got theirs like this, especially MacFee who is an old buddy of mine, an' who has been stringing along with me for more years than I care to remember.

On the table are two guns. One of 'em I can see is MacFee's iron, an' the other one I suppose is Gallat's. I look at these guns an' I smell 'em. Neither of them has been used so it looks to me as if somebody has given these two the works without their having a dog's chance, an' I reckon that this must be Goyaz.

I stick MacFee's gun in the waistbelt of my trousers because I have, got a feeling that I would like to pack another rod just in case somebody is goin' to start some more skullduggery around here. It looks like this Princess Cristabel can be a not very healthy place sometimes.

I then switch off the light, open the cabin door, get out into the passage an' walk back to the stern through the kitchens. When I get on deck I walk up the starboard side of the boat past a dozen couples who are necking about the place or arguin' about cards or money or somethin', an' right forward leaning over the rail I find the dame I was talking to. I had an idea that this dame wouldn't go back to the saloon. She'd be frightened that Goyaz would call her up for what she'd done.

"Hulloa, sister," I say. "Take a little walk with me. I wanna talk to you."

I take her by the arm an' I walk her back to the stern. She comes like a. lamb—it looks to me as if this dame would do anything that any guy told her. I sit her down on the seat by the stern rail.

"Now listen, baby," I say. "It looks to me as if what you were saying about this outfit is correct. I don't think that Goyaz has got any sense either. You tell me somethin'," I say. "Do you know how them two stiffs in the office cabin got theirs?"

She looks at me an' her eyes are wider an' glassier than ever.

"So you've been there? Say, who are you?"

"If you don't ask no questions you won't get no lies," I say. "Maybe I am Santa Claus an' maybe I ain't. But if you're a wise little girl you're goin' to tell me what's been happening round this boat tonight. Did you see them guys come aboard?"

She starts to cry. Another rule of mine is that when a woman turns on the water I never stop her, they always feel better afterwards. She sits there sobbin' an' shakin' just as if she was real sorry about somethin' or other. Presently she quietens down a bit.

"Come on, baby," I say, "spill it. You've got to talk sometime, you know."

She gulps.

"I was with Goyaz in the saloon," she says, "when these two guys came aboard. They came in some motor-boat from the shore. Selitti, the chief steward—one of Goyaz's—comes in and tips off Goyaz. Goyaz don't say anything for a bit, but he's thinkin' and thinkin' hard. Presently he signals to me to go over. Then he tells me that there are two guys just come aboard who can make plenty trouble for everybody if they want to, an' just at this moment he don't feel like having that trouble.

"I ask him what, an' he says I am to go up on deck an' take these two guys along to his cabin, an' that I am to tell them that he will be along in a minute. He says that I am to get them talking in front of the desk an' that when I hear a gramophone start playing in the berth next door I am to move to the right of the desk.

"I get an idea that Goyaz is goin' to pull something screwy, an' I tell him that I don't want to be mixed up in any business that is really serious, but I reckon that he has got a lot on me an' he tells me that if I don't do what he says he will give me the works. Then he looks at me, an' he sees I am looking a bit shaky I suppose, so he tells me to lay off, an' he puts Freda—another dame who works for him—on the job.

"She don't mind, she's as tough as hell. She goes up on deck, but I am plenty curious to know what is goin' on in that cabin. After a bit I see Goyaz go, so I slip out the door on the other side up on the starboard side, an' I walk down round the stern, an' I look through the ventilator of this cabin because it is not quite closed. Inside I can see Freda talking to these two guys. Just then I hear somebody coming, so I scram out of it down in the shadow at the end of the deck house, an' at this minute I hear the gramophone start playin'.

"Just then Goyaz walks along the passage. He has got a gun in his hand with a silencer on it, an' he fires six shots through the ventilator. Then he scrams an' the gramophone stops."

She starts cryin' some more an' I light myself a cigarette an' watch her. After a bit she eases up.

"Well, honey, it ain't no good cryin' over spilt milk an' these dead guys are certainly spilt," I crack. "After all, they asked for it musclin' aboard without an invitation an' Goyaz has got to look after his business, ain't he. You gotta remember these guys might a been dicks."

"Supposin' they was," she says, "he mighta given 'em a chance—the dirty so-an'-so."

She gets a big idea all of a sudden an' gives me a smart look.

"Say," she says, "who the hell are you, anyhow? I ain't seen you on this boat before."

"Correct, sweetheart," I say, "an' if you don't stop askin' questions you won't see nobody any more, because if I have any smart cracks outa you I'll throw you in the lake as sure as my name's Lemmy Caution."

She sits up—her eyes poppin'.

"My, are you Lemmy Caution!" she says. "I guess I heard about you."

"Yeah," say I, "an' what did they tell you, baby?"

"That you was about the toughest mobster that ever bumped a copper," she says.

"All right, that's about how it is," I say, "an' if I was you, sister, I'd just keep my little trap shut about me bein' on this boat an' anything else about yours truly, otherwise I'm goin' to give you the works, just like they told you about me."

"I ain't sayin' a thing," she whimpers. "I don't wanna make any more trouble around here."

"That's fine," I say, "an' now that you an' I understand each other, honey, everything's okey doke. Now you scram outa here an' just go forward an' become part of the evening's festivities once more, but you don't have to say one little word about seein' me, otherwise I'm goin' to fix you."

"That's O.K. by me," she mutters. "Honest—I'm just dumb."

She went off forward, an' I lit myself another cigarette.

I am very sorry about this dame being in such a state because if she'd had any guts I reckon I could have used her. I'm telling you I was feeling pretty lonely aboard this boat because it was as plain as the nose on your face that Goyaz wasn't being particularly nice to anybody who came butting in on his racket but was doin' his talking with a gun. I reckon I had it in for this guy Goyaz. I owed him one for MacFee.

I sat there for a few minutes an' then I made up my mind that I would take a chance an' go forward an' see what was happening. As I got up off the seat I heard the chug chug of a motor boat somewhere near me, so I waited. Presently I can see a little motor launch coming towards the stern. By this time the moon has come up an' do I get one big surprise when I see that the guy driving the motor launch is none other than Yonnie Malas, Siegella's head man.

I reckon this is a bit of luck. I start giving him the Indian eye sign over the stern rail an' he sees me. He gets his boat under the stern an' ties her up to mine. As he looks up I can see he is grinning all over his face.

"What do you know, Lemmy?" he says. "Say is this a party or is it a party?"

"I don't know, kid," I say. "Are you asking me or tellin' me. Listen, you cut out all that big stuff an' shin up that rope an' get aboard. I want to talk turkey to you."

He comes up the rope hand over hand like a trapeze artist. I'm telling you this Malas is strong, maybe nearly as strong as I am. He gets over the rail an' he sits down beside me.

"Well, you son of a so-and-so. What are you doin' around here?"

"What do you think," he says. "When Connie went out to get that dressing for your arm at Knightsbridge, she phoned Siegella an' he told me I'd better scram down here just to see that nobody bumped you. He thought you might need me around, an' he told me I'm taking orders from you."

He grins.

"Connie sends her love," he says. "She's going to tell you all about it when she sees you."

"Say, is that dame burned up, Yonnie?" I say. "But what could I do? I just had to get aboard."

"That's O.K. by her," he says, "only it was lucky I arrived. When I got here I saw her car away down the road past the station an' she is in a tough argument with the two guys that you left ashore. They ain't so pleased neither. Well, I fixed 'em. We got them tied up on the wharf. They won't trouble nobody. Now what's the layout?"

I do a bit of thinking.

"Say, listen, Yonnie," I say, "I bet Siegella ain't so pleased, is he?"

He grinned.

"Is he burned up?" he said. "What he won't do to Goyaz when he gets his hooks on him ain't nobody's business. I reckon this guy Goyaz muscling in the way he has has upset Siegella considerable, an' it has upset me too because we are all set tonight to bump this guy Gallat."

"You don't say!" I say, "an' just how was you goin' to do that?"

"This guy's living in a place called Strand Chambers," says Yonnie, "an' I was putting a phoney call through to him to meet me some place. We reckoned we was goin' to push him in a car, give him the heat an' chuck him out some place in the country. But I found when I phoned that this guy ain't in. Just when I'm gettin' good and bored with this proposition one of the boys comes along from Siegella an' says that Connie's phoned that Goyaz has snatched Miranda an' you two are going after her. Siegella tells me to string around. He also phones for a boat to be waiting for me down here, and here I am. Where do we go from here?"

"Don't ask so many questions," I crack back at him, "an' listen, Yonnie, as for Gallat you don't have to worry about that guy because Goyaz has bumped him an' a pal of his."

He looks surprised.

"You don't say, Lemmy," he says.

"I'm telling you," I told him.

I then proceed to spill the beans about what has happened on this boat, except that I told him that this guy MacFee is a friend of Gallat's an' that I don't know him.

"Now listen, Yonnie," I go on. "Here's the set-up. The main job is to get Miranda off this boat, an' the sooner we do it the better. Now it looks to me as if most of these guys round here is blind, the question is whether we are going to be brainy or tough."

He grins.

"If they are boozed, Lemmy," he says, "let's be tough."

"O.K.," I say. "The gaming saloon's way forward. Here we go!"

I get out the Luger automatic in my right hand, an' MacFee's gun that I had got stuck in the waistband of my trousers in my left. Yonnie is packing two, one under each shoulder. We walk forward along the starboard side of the deck house. It's pretty cold by now, an' most of the people have gone inside. I am gettin' a kick out of this business, so much so that I am almost forgetting about my arm which is burning like hell.

When we get forward I signal Yonnie to stop an' we look through one of the ventilators into the saloon. This saloon is big and is about half the length of the boat. It is crowded with people an' you never saw such a bunch in your life.

There are guys an' their dames that I have seen playing around the U.S. Coast resorts for years. There is a very hot syndicate that used to work the race track game at Agua Caliente. There is Mardi Spirella, the star thug from Oklahoma, an' Persse Byron who shot Augie Siekin in Ma Licovat's because he didn't like the colour of his shirt; there is Big Boy Skeets from Missouri an' Rachel Manda his girl; there is Wellt from Los Angeles, an' Pernanza who used to run the liquor around San Pedro.

All these guys are there with dames, most of 'em a bit screwy, an' they are all on holiday, you bet. I never saw such a lotta jags in my life; also there is about sixty other people I never saw before. But none of these others are English guys by the looks of 'em, so it looks like Goyaz had laid off gettin' anybody from off the shore here. Evidently he is takin' no chances, an' I think he is right.

Right in the middle of this saloon is a roulette table an' everybody is crowding round this. Goyaz is runnin' the bank an' on one side of the table facing us, her lace flushed an' her blonde hair sparkling in the light of the electric lamps, wearing a swell gown an' looking like a million dollars, is Miranda. She looks swell. Say, has that dame curves or has she curves?

I look over my shoulder at Yonnie. He is just lighting himself a cigarette. A little bit further on there is a slidin' door half open leading into the saloon.

"Let's take 'em, Yonnie," I say, an' we step in.

Everybody is so struck with this game they don't see us, an' the first thing they know is when Yonnie bawls out:

"Reach for the sky, suckers, an' keep 'em there!"

You should have seen these people's faces when they turn round an' see us. About eighty pairs of hands went up at once. It was obvious to me that these guys had been stuck up before the way they put their hands up.

"Now ladies and gentlemen," I say, "if anybody wants to start anything they had better start it now, because we are very very busy, an' we are not nice guys."

I look at Goyaz. He is standing at the head of the table lookin' very sick, but he makes a good attempt at a grin.

"Say, what is this," he says, "a stick-up?"

"What do *you* think?" I tell him. "Does it look like Mother's day in Oshkosh?"

He grins some more.

"What do you want, boys?" he says.

"Nothin' much, Goyaz," I say. "We just want Miss van Zelden. I reckon her Pa'd be all burned up if he knew that you had a little idea to snatch this dame."

I put my guns away seein' that Yonnie has the situation in hand, an' I walk round the table. The crowd parts an' I go up to Miranda.

"How's it goin', Miss van Zelden?" I say.

She smiles. Has that girl got nice teeth or has she?

"Why, if it isn't Mr. Caution," she smiles. "Now what is all this about? it seems to me that every time I go some place I find you around there."

"Listen, lady," I say. "I'm little Lord Fauntleroy an' I'm your good fairy, but you don't know it. My middle name's Santa Claus an' I come down chimneys. Do you remember the Honeysuckle and Jasmine at Toledo?"

She laughs.

"I'll never forget it," she says. "I got a kick out of that."

"You're too fond of kicks an' thrills, Magnificent," I crack back. "One of these times you're goin' to get such a real kick that you'll think you was in the ice box you'll be so thrilled."

I point to Goyaz.

"I'll tell you a coupla things about that guy an' the rest of these hoodlums," I go on. "First of all this game is as screwy as hell, an' the only time Goyaz ever played a game straight the other fellow got paralysis through shock. Secondly all these thugs round here have committed so much crime that if they was added up they would make Hell look like a charity committee of the female Elks Society at Cold Springs, Pa. Point number three is that this sucker was goin' to snatch you this mornin' an' hold you for ransom, an' how d'ya like that?"

She clasps her hands.

"You don't say," she says, "how thrilling!"

But for the first time in my life I see her lookin' surprised.

"That's how it was, sister," I say. "Now what have you lost?"

She opens her evening bag an' looks inside.

"I had 10,000 when I came here this evening," she said, "an' it looks to me as if I have got about five hundred dollars left."

"O.K.," I say.

I turn to Goyaz.

"That's goin' to cost you plenty, Goyaz," I say. "I want the 9,500 Miss van Zelden's lost, an' I'll take 10,000 interest, an' you will like it."

"Say, listen," he starts—but just at this moment Yonnie sticks a gun in the middle of his back an' he shuts up.

"O.K.," he says, "but I'll remember it."

"You're telling me," I say. "So will I."

I help myself to 20,000 off the table an' I give 10,000 of it to Miranda.

"Now, baby," I say to her, "you're goin' home."

She don't say a word. On the back of a chair behind her is a wrap an' she puts this on. Then we make for the door with Yonnie backing behind us with his guns on the crowd. When we get to the door I talk to 'em.

"Listen, mugs," I say, "nobody's moving outa this saloon for ten minutes, an' if they do we are goin' to give it to 'em. Get it?"

They get it.

We get out on deck an' I shut the door. I lead them towards the stern.

"Now listen, Yonnie," I say, "I tell you what you're going to do. You get into your boat with Miss van Zelden, take her back to the wharf and hand her over to my sister Connie."

I give him one big wink, an' he gets it.

"What about you," he says, "you ain't staying on this health resort, are you?"

"You betcha life I'm not," I say. "But I have got some business to do right now. Get busy."

I watch the pair of 'em as they go towards the stern, then I see Yonnie help Miranda over the rail. As she goes down the rope I can see her laughing. I reckon she's gettin' a thrill outa this. Then Yonnie goes after her an' a coupla minutes later I hear the chug chug of the motor as the launch goes back to the wharf.

I walk back to the saloon an' open the door, the Luger in my hand. These mugs are still standin' there, an' we have got 'em so well trained that as I put my foot inside, their arms reach up for the ceilin'.

"Listen, Goyaz," I say, "I want to talk to you. Come here an' keep your hands up."

I step backwards through the door, an' I wait for him to come through.

"Now boys," I say to the crowd, "my pal has got you covered through the ventilator on the other side of the saloon, so don't move for another ten minutes."

I shut the door.

"Say, Lemmy," says Goyaz. "What is this, what are you doin' over here an' what are you trying to pull?"

"You come with me, Goyaz," I say, "an' I'll tell you."

I take him to the stern. When we get there I tell him to sit down. He sits down. He is lookin' puzzled because he cannot get this business.

"You know, Lemmy," he says, "I don't get this at all. What are you easing in on this job for, an' what have you held me up for 20,000 for.

You ain't got an interest in this dame, Miranda, have you? Besides, if you have, let's do a split. I'm always fair—"

"Shut up, Goyaz," I say. "Now listen, I don't like you an' I never have. You're a punk, you're not a mobster, you're yellow. Do you know what I am goin' to do to you?"

He looks up at me an' I can see some beads of sweat standin' out across his forehead.

"I'm goin' to give it to you like the lousy rat you are," I say.

He starts to whimper.

"Jeez, Lemmy," he says, "give me a break. I'll give you plenty dough. I ain't done nothing to hurt you, I ain't—"

"Skip it," I crack. "You gave them guys Gallat an' MacFee a hell of a break tonight, didn't you."

Then I grin.

"Well, maybe I was wrong, Goyaz," I say, "I got sorta angry with you, but perhaps I'll change my mind. Say, look at that!"

I look over his shoulder as if I was seein' something on the water. He gets up an' he turns round to look an' I let him have it. I shoot him five times through the heart an' the spine, just a couple for Gallat, two for MacFee and one for myself. He slumps over the rail. I put my foot under his legs an' I kick 'em up, an' he slides over with a plop into the water.

I look back at the saloon, everythin' is quiet there. Then I shin down the rope into my own boat, start her up an' head for the shore.

A mist is beginnin' to come up an' as the lights of the Princess Cristabel get dim I can hear the noise start. Over the water I hear the sound of a champagne cork poppin' an' somebody starts up some dance music on the radio.

Sittin' steerin' the boat an' smokin' I reckoned I was pleased with the evenin'.

Except for MacFee it was nice work.

CHAPTER SEVEN
SOME MORE LOTTIE

WHEN I floated up alongside the wharf I was wondering what the set-up was going to be. I reckoned that Yonnie and Constance had had lots of time to get rid of the Goyaz boys they'd got parked around there, an' I was right about this. There was nobody around the wharf except Constance, Yonnie Malas an' Miranda, an' I must say they put on a very nice act for Miranda's benefit.

We go along an' we get the cars. Constance goes back in her own car an' Yonnie is driving my hired car back to the garage. I go back with Miranda in her car which we get out of the local garage where she left it.

Going back Miranda is burbling good an' plenty about the evenin's work. Is she pleased with herself? Anybody would think that to get into a racket that she'd just got into an' then to get yanked out of it was funny. I reckon this dame has got a screwy idea about what is good, but that's how a lot of 'em are.

You will know by this time that I am not a guy for any sorta moralisin', but it looks to me as if a lot of these dames whose fathers have made plenty money are just plain nuts. In nine cases outa ten the old boy starts as a farm hand up in some hick town, works like crazy for about fifteen hours a day, goes into the big city and works some more an' eventually pulls a coupla lucky breaks and makes himself a few millions.

Just when he starts gettin' old, one of his kids will start sky-rocketing all round the place, gettin' into trouble looking for thrills just because they don't know any better, an' they think that's the works. I reckon that's how it was with Miranda.

Yet this dame has got a certain amount of brains.

While I am thinkin' all this she is telling me how she got into this Goyaz thing. It looks like that one night she goes out by herself an' has dinner at some swell joint. Then she goes to a theatre. Just as she is coming out some good-looking guy comes up an' tells her he met her some place in U.S. Miranda has met so many guys that she wouldn't know anyhow, so she falls for it.

This guy then proceeds to spill a lot of stuff about the Goyaz gaming boat an' of course Miranda falls for this an' chips in an' says she wants to go along. So she goes.

All this time I am waitin' for her to ask me how I knew she was down there an' all about that, an' I start thinkin' up a story for her. After a bit she notices that I am having some trouble with my arm, which by this time is feeling like an iron bar, an' she takes the wheel over.

She is driving so fast that she ain't got any time to talk, for which I am very grateful, an' I get my story all set.

I tell her that I see her coming out of the Carlton the other day, an' that I strung along to say a few kind words an' that the maid has told me she has gone off for two or three days, an' that as I was comin' out I meet one of Goyaz' boys an' we have a drink together an' this guy tells me he reckons that she was goin' down to play on the boat.

I tell her that I knew that Goyaz was running a crooked game an' that in any event he will probably try a snatch, so I come along there with my sister an' a friend of mine an' muscle in on the job.

She looks at me outa the corner of her eye, very old-fashioned like.

"Why didn't you go to the police, Lemmy?" she said with a little smile.

"Listen, Miranda," I say, "do you mind keeping your eye on the road otherwise we'll be in the ditch, an' as for that police stuff don't you know better than that. I don't like cops."

She laughed. I tell you this dame Miranda has got a swell laugh.

"I bet you don't, Lemmy," she says. "Say tell me, what do you do? You're a gangster, aren't you? What's your particular line of business?"

I grin. I feel that I had better make myself out to be a little hero whilst the goin' is good, so I lay it on a bit.

"Aw hell," I say, "I suppose I am maybe, but I'm being a good boy now. I ain't done a thing for a long time."

She smiles.

"Didn't you shoot a police officer in Oklahoma?" she says.

I tell her yes.

"I had to shoot this guy," I say, "if I hadn't shot him, he'd have shot me. It was just a matter of who squeezed the gun first."

I also proceed to tell her a lot more hooey about myself an' by the time I have finished with this dame she thinks I am a mixture of Paul Revere, Dick Turpin, Robin Hood an' what-have-you.

"I guess your arm's pretty bad, Lemmy," she says. "What's the matter with it?"

"Here's where you have a big laugh," I say, "but when I am gettin' over the rail of that boat tonight I have got a gun in my hand an' I slip an' it goes off, an' I give myself one through the arm. What do you know about that? I'll get it fixed up when we get back to London, it wants a new dressin', that's all."

She smiles.

"I'll do it, Lemmy," she says softly.

It is seven o'clock in the mornin' when we get back to the Carlton Hotel. We go upstairs to Miranda's suite an' she gets the maid up and sends for some stuff to do my arm with. I am pretty lucky about this arm, because it looks like the wound is clean an' there is no inflammation. I am a pretty cough guy an' I reckon in a coupla days it is goin' to be all right.

Whilst Miranda is tying up my arm I am havin' a look at the maid who is running about with the bowls and bandages. This maid is a pretty neat piece of goods an' also she looks as if she has got some brains sortie place. I think maybe I can use this jane.

When Miranda has tied up my arm we have some coffee an' I tell her I have got to get along. She says O.K. but that she wants to see some more of me an' that I should come back an' have dinner with her at nine o'clock that night. This suits me very well.

After a bit I go, Miranda is yawning her head off, an' I tell her that she needs a piece of bed. The maid shows me to the door, takes me along the corridor an' rings for the lift, I have a look at her.

"You know, honey," I say, "has anybody told you that you're: easy to look at?"

She smiles.

"I got an idea some guy told me that once," she said, "but it didn't get him any place."

"Too bad," I crack back. "We gotta do somethin' about that. What about taking a bowl of chop-suey with me one night, that is if they've got chop-suey in this country?"

She smiles again slowly. She is a cunning looking little piece.

"Well, what can I lose?" she says.

I grin.

"Well, it looks like a date, sister," I say. "Do you have any time off?"

"I shall tomorrow night," she says, "Miss van Zelden's taking dinner with some friends of hers."

"O.K.," I say.

I make a date to meet her at a restaurant I know in Greek Street, an' I go off.

I walk along Pall Mall an' up St. James's. When I get to the end of Jermyn Street I look down the street. Sure enough opposite my apartment is some guy smoking a cigarette an' lookin' tired. I reckon this is one of Siegella's boys who is keepin' an eye on my apartment just in case I get lost or somethin' an' it looks like Siegella ain't trusting me any yet.

When I get into my apartment, I give myself a shot of bourbon an' I sit down and think things out. I reckon everything is going along very nice but it looks to me that the guy that things are goin' nice for is Siegella. I also reckon that MacFee being bumped off like that has made things very difficult for me, an' I do not like that one little bit.

But I reckon it is no good trying to think anything out very much just now, I am good an' tired an' my arm is aching, so I go to bed. I reckon that bed is a great place. If more guys was to stay in bed for longer instead of gettin' around so much, there would be a lot less trouble in the world.

Now it is six o'clock that evening when the valet at the apartment comes in an' tells me that there is a gentleman of the name of Siegella would like to have a few words with me. I say O.K. an' to show him in an' also to bring some whisky an' some coffee.

In a minute he comes back an' Siegella is with him. The man is lookin' very good. He has got evening clothes on with a white tie, an' I reckon the pearls in his shirt front cost a whole lotta money.

I sit up in bed an' I yawn.

"Well, how does it go, Siegella?" I say.

He sits down and gives himself a cigarette out of a platinum case. He has got a thin mouth an' it is smiling. I reckon Siegella is one of them guys who always smiles with his mouth an' never with his eyes.

They are always just cold an' hard, just like bits of blue ice. Most big mobsters have got eyes like that. He lights his cigarette an' he takes a few puffs, then he looks at me.

"You know, Lemmy," he says, "I got to hand it to you, the way you handled this situation aboard the Princess Crisabel last night. You can be good when you want to."

"Aw, hell," I say, "you're telling me. That was easy stuff an' anyway who the hell is Goyaz?"

He grins and blows a ring of smoke across the room.

"Well, I reckon Goyaz ain't goin' to worry anybody no more," he says.

He looks at me straight in the eye.

"What do you mean, Siegella?" I say.

"I mean it was nice work, Lemmy," he says. "That guy is better outa the way than stickin' around. I'm very glad you gave him the heat."

"You don't say," I crack back, "an' how d'you know I gave him the heat?"

He grins. He has got very nice teeth.

"What do you think I was doing last night, Lemmy?" he says. "When Constance came through on the telephone an' told me that Goyaz had got Miranda on that boat, it didn't look so good to me, specially when I heard that Lottie and that mob had held you up on Baker Street. So I got around. You didn't know it," says he, "but myself an' six of the boys was hangin' around on the sea side of the Princess Cristabel for three hours last night just in case you slipped up.

"After we saw you introduce Goyaz to the high diving act over the stern rail I reckoned we could call it a day, so we went home."

"Oh, well," I say, "These things happen along, an' I reckon Goyaz was gettin' too fresh."

He nods.

"You didn't do so badly last night, did you, Lemmy?" he says. "Did you give that 10,000 back to Miss van Zelden, the ten grand she lost?"

"What do you think?" I say. "Of course I did." which was quite true. "An'," I go on, "I made another ten grand on the deal that I took outa Goyaz that I didn't give her. She didn't have to make a profit anyway."

"That's O.K." says he. "Well, you ain't doin' so bad, are you, Lemmy? You get ten grand from me for expenses, you get ten grand out of Goyaz an' the pleasure of bumping him. Are you satisfied?"

"You bet I'm satisfied, Siegella," I tell him. "I got medals for looking after myself too."

He grins again and pours himself out a little shot of bourbon.

"That's the way I want it to be, Lemmy," he says. "I like everybody to be happy. I think you are a good guy, an' I think you're doin' your stuff nice an' pretty. So just so you'll feel good an' comfortable here's another five grand."

He puts five monkeys down on the table an' stands there smilin'.

"That's to pay for the arm," he says. "You know, Lemmy," he goes on, "I got a lot of ideas about you an' me. I reckon that when we have pulled this Miranda snatch after things have blown over, we'll go back to the U.S. an' we'll run every mob in the country."

I laugh.

"Listen, Siegella," I say, "when I get my cut outa this I don't have to be a mobster no more. 250 grand is good enough for me."

He laughs.

"What are you goin' to do, Lemmy?" he says.

"I wouldn't know," I say, "but I've got a whole lot of ideas about chicken farmin'."

He brings me over a shot of bourbon, which I drink. As he hands me the glass I look at his long white fingers. I reckon if hands can be cruel this guy has got the cruellest pair in the world.

"I can imagine you on a chicken farm, Lemmy," he says. "I reckon you'd be screwing their necks every day just to keep your hand in. But now let's get down to cases."

He draws up a chair by the bedside an' he lights another cigarette. I have one myself an' I look at him through the smoke.

"I reckon we get a move on this weekend," he says. "Today is Wednesday. On Friday I'm taking the boys down to the house I am taking. It is a place called Branders End near Thame. Now this is a fine old place an' I reckon I shall have about thirty couples down there. They are all very nice an' they all know me very well. Now have you got the set-up for gettin' Miranda down there?"

"That's easy," I tell him. "Miranda is strong for me, especially after this Princess Cristabel business. I'm dinin' with her tonight. But I'm not goin' to say anything about the weekend. Between now an' then I will pull some story on her about being in a little bit of trouble myself, somethin' that necessitates her coming down to this Branders End dump with me, somethin' that is so personal and confidential that she don't even tell nobody that she's going. Well, I reckon I got her out of a coupla jams an' I reckon she's just got to say yes."

Siegella grins, then he passes his tongue over his lips, a habit he's got.

"That's the lay, Lemmy," he says. "You get her down there on Saturday night, an' then you're very nearly through."

"An' after that?" I ask.

"That's easy," he says. "Your job's very nearly done. You come back here on Sunday an' you put the call through to a man in New York whose address I'm goin' to give you when you get down there. This guy will arrange that on Monday morning van Zelden himself will ring you an' you'll spill the beans to him.

"You'll tell him that his daughter's been snatched an' that she'll be moved outa England within two or three days. You'll tell him that we're goin' to give him one week to get that three million credit in the Dutch Bank, Rotterdam. If he don't," says Siegella—and here he starts to grin some more—" you can tell him that we've got a very swell idea. Ask him if he knows what his daughter's teeth look like, because every day after the week that the credit is late we're goin' to send him one of her teeth by registered post, an' you point out that we ain't goin' to give her gas either when we take 'em out."

He gets up.

"I'll be gettin' along, Lemmy," he says. "There's just one little point I'd like to mention before I go. You've got a lotta brains, an' you're tough. Maybe you think you've got as much brains as I have. Well, that's all right, but don't try anything—remember you can't do a thing or go any place unless I know it. It ain't because I don't trust you particularly, Lemmy," he says, "it's just because I'm a guy that don't take any chances, an' I tell you that if you try to cross me, I'll know about it before you've done it, and I'll get you."

He stands there looking at me like a whole bunch of snakes.

I grin.

"Listen, Siegella," I say. "What do I do, get frightened and take a run-out powder? Be your age. I reckon it's payin' me to string along with you an' I'm stringin'. I want that 250 grand."

"O.K. Lemmy," he says. "Do your stuff an' you'll get it. So long!" He goes out.

After the guy had gone I lay flat in bed smoking an' looking at the ceiling. You gotta understand that I am pretty burned up about this big punk Siegella. He is just one piece too durn sure of himself for one thing, an' secondly I reckon he is right when he says that he has got a whole lotta brains an' wisecracks me about thinkin' I have got as much as he has. Well, maybe I have an' maybe I haven't, but I reckoned that before I was through I was goin' to pull a fast one on that thin-faced grinnin' baby that he wouldn't forget in a helluva hurry.

But I gotta watch my step. When he said that if I crossed him he'd get me he was about right. An' when I remembered all the stunts that Siegella had pulled in the States I calculated that I had got to be pretty good to pull one on him. Feds, State coppers, an' every other sorta copper had been tryin' to get their hooks on him for years an' they never had a dog's chance because that baby never come out in the open but always has somebody frontin' for him whilst he financed the jobs and thought out the: set-ups.

Siegella had the low-down on most of the cheap mobsters, because he had education in a sorta way an' because nobody ever knew who was working for him an' who wasn't.

But the idea of me goin' in with him in a big way after we had pulled this Miranda snatch, made me laugh in about sixteen places at once. I reckoned I would as soon string along with Siegella as go to bed with a coupla boa-constrictors—in fact I would rather kick around with the snakes.

An' it sure looked as if he had got me well tied up over the Miranda snatch. I had been relyin' on MacFee to give me a hand when we come down to the brass end of things an' that silly palooka has to go an' get himself shot up just at the time that I needed him.

I was worryin' around tryin' to think up something that I could pull good and fast before the weekend. It was stickin' out like the Manilla Bay pier that if once he got Miranda down to the Branders

End place he would get me back to London so as to put through the long-distance call for the ransom an' then I could scram out of it an' get back to U.S. an' collect my dough an' go to sleep.

I am sure in one big spot because now that MacFee is dead there ain't anybody I could trust so's you would notice it. I can't wiseup Miranda as to what is goin' to happen because she would simply scram outa the country an' Siegella would get her some other place as certain as sure, an' it looks to me as if the only other way I could spoil his racket is by goin' an' blowin' the gaff to the coppers here. An' that just now would be bughouse anyway because Siegella hadn't got any record in any country—the coppers had never had their hooks into him any place at all, an' he would simply laugh the whole durn thing off an' wait until he could get Miranda over in France or Spain or some other place, an' snatch her there.

Suddenly I get an idea into my nut that Siegella has gotta whole lot of ideas about Miranda besides gettin' ransom money outa the old man. He was very keen for women an' he had a nice taste in 'em— Connie for instance, an' she was good to look at, I'm tellin' you—an' it looks as if he might collect over Miranda an' then try some funny stuff with her. Afterwards you can make about six guesses as to what would happen to that dame when Siegella was through with her.

I reckoned he'd get the ransom money all right. He'd get it because he was talkin' straight when he said he's send one of her teeth to old man van Zelden each day. He'd do it all right an' he'd probably get a helluva kick outa watchin' some guy pull 'em out; he was like that, because I remember MacFee tellin' me that when the Lacassar mob pulled a fast snatch out in Kansas City—a job that was laid out by Siegella—an' the husband whose wife was snatched wouldn't ante up, the mob used to send him a handful of her hair that they'd pulled out every day, an' when after a bit he got the ransom money together why the jane was very nearly bald as a coot. I reckon this was Siegella's idea of humour by which any guy could see that he had a durn funny brain about that sorta stuff.

It was pretty fly of him to know that I had bumped Goyaz too, that was one little thing that I thought nobody wouldn't know, an' it was clever of the guy to stick around off the Princess Cristabel, lyin' out there somewhere in the darkness, an' watch what my game was after I had sent Yonnie Malas an' Miranda off. It just showed me that this guy Siegella wouldn't trust nobody an inch; that he was a hot guy when it come down to business.

Anyway I reckoned that the only thing I could do would be to play along an' after a bit I got up an' looked at the five grand that he had left on the table. I got out my pasting-up book an' checked up on the notes an' I see that this lot also is some of the take from the Third National Bank pinch in Arkansas. I put these notes with the other lot because I am goin' to save as much money outa this business as I can, an' one way an' another I am not doin' so bad what with the money I had got outa Goyaz an' the fifteen grand that Siegella has cashed in with. I must say when it comes to money he certainly is no mean piker.

By this time it is nearly eight o'clock so I get up and take a shower and begin to get into a tuxedo. I take my time over this dressin' business, an' I walk around and do a little quiet thinkin', because I am already playing with the idea that it might be possible for me to cross the guy up somehow although it is plain to me that if I am goin' to do this I must somehow fix to pull it down at this Branders End place.

I have already wised you up that I have got an idea at the back of my head, but this idea is not one that I would like to pull unless I have to because it looks a bit chancey to me. But I reckon to figure it out some more before I keep the date that I have got on Thursday night with Miranda's maid.

I reckon that by now I am darned tired of thinkin' round about this business so I light myself a cigarette an' go out. It is a very nice night too, an' the idea of eatin' dinner with Miranda is certainly a swell one.

She was waitin' for me in the hall down at the Carlton an' I must say that this girl was an eyeful. She was wearing some shimmery sorta gown made of some stuff that just clung around as if it liked her plenty.

When she saw me she comes forward holdin' her hand out and smilin' like some turtle dove.

"Well, Lemmy," she says, "it's good to see you. How's the arm?"

I tell her that it is goin' on fine an' we go outside an' get into her roadster. We have an argument about what place to eat at an' eventually we decide that we'll go to some place called the Cafe de Paris out on the Maidenhead Road.

Drivin' along with Miranda I felt swell. She don't say nothin' much but she just puts her hand on my arm sorta friendly an' it makes me feel good. I wonder just what this dame would say if she knew that I was up to my neck in a deal to snatch her within the next two or three days, but sentimentality ain't a long suit of mine an' so I put this sorta punk outa my head.

When we get on the Kingston Road, I put my foot down, an' we made some nice speed. Then, as I look into the drivin' mirror I get an idea that there is a big black roadster coming right behind me an' sorta stayin' about fifty feet in my rear. Every time I put on more speed this car does likewise. It is a big horse-powered Stutz an' it can pass us easily if it wants to.

For a minute I begin to wonder if Siegella has got somebody tailin' me, but it is as plain as the nose on your face that if he was—an' he ain't likely to be keepin' tabs on me while I'm with Miranda—he wouldn't be doin' it so that the whole world would know. In fact it looks like this car behind is makin' it obvious that it is tailin' me an' that it wants me to know it.

I don't say nothin' to Miranda, an' when we get to this Cafe de Paris, an' she goes off to powder her nose I watch this car, which has passed us an' gone on, come back again.

It swings around and pulls in the courtyard in front, an' then it stops. I am totin' the Luger in a shoulder holster under my left arm an' I sorta slip my hand on the butt just in case of accidents when the car door opens an' out gets Lottie Frisch.

She has a look round and then she comes in my direction. I sorta walk off to a corner where I can't be seen from outside an' she comes after me.

She steps up an' she says:

"Listen, Lemmy, we don't want no post mortems on last night. I reckon you was too good that's all, but I'm here to tell you from Kastlin an' the rest of our boys that if you wanna talk turkey we're willin'."

I have one eye on the door of the ladies' room just in case Miranda comes out in the middle of this business, but everything is O.K.

"What's the set-up, Lottie?" I ask. "I hope you don't think you can get away with any fast stuff."

"Be your age, Lemmy," she says. "I know who I'm talking to. There ain't nothin' funny or screwy about this. Here's the lay-out: The Princess Cristabel sailed early this morning, but Kastlin stopped off here. He ain't goin' with her. Some punk—one of Siegella's men I reckon—has shot Goyaz, so Kastlin has handed the boat over an' stayed ashore.

"Now here it is. It looks like you was workin' on your own the other night except that you got Yonnie Malas along they tell me, an' Yonnie is stringing along with Siegella—he's his head man. Now Kastlin an' me reckon that if you was to string along with us we could make Siegella look sicker than an old cow. We could cross him up to hell, an' we could get away with a packet of jack. Well . . . . are you listenin'?"

"I might," I say, an' I think that maybe I can use these guys. Anyhow I ask her where we can talk.

"Kastlin an' me are stayin' at the Parkside Hotel," she says. "Come around at two or three tonight. We're registered as Mr. an' Mrs. Schultz of New York."

"O.K. baby," I say. "I'll be there, but I wouldn't try any funny business if I was you. By the way, how's that Japanese sap that you put a bullet into?"

I grin at her an' she grins back.

"You certainly slipped it across us, Lemmy," she says. "I gotta hand it to you. Well, that guy is gettin' on pretty well, except that every time he coughs it sounds like the tide coming in. So you'll come around, Lemmy?"

I nod.

"I'll be seein' you between two an' three o'clock," I say, "an' tell Kastlin not to get any ideas about who's goin' to do the talkin', otherwise I'm goin' to get tough. Now scram outa here."

She goes out an' in a minute she gets into the car an' it goes off. As it turns around I reckon that I get a glimpse of Kastlin sittin' in the back, an' I reckon it's like that dirty little dog to get a woman to do his talkin' for him.

Just then Miranda comes out, an' we go an' eat.

We talk about all sorts of things an' we have a swell meal. I sorta get the idea that this Miranda is pretty well interested in me an' I am doin' my stuff plenty.

Then we go off an' dance an' we drive about the road till midnight. This England is a good place for drivin' around after dark.

It is one o'clock when I pull the car up outside the Carlton. Miranda gets out an' stands there lookin' at me.

"Aren't you comin' up for a whisky an' soda, Lemmy?" she says, lookin' at me old-fashioned.

I say no, because I am hot to get on to this Kastlin proposition, an' this gives her the needle.

"Maybe there'll be a time when you'd like me to give you a whisky an' soda," she says, "an' maybe then I won't feel like it."

I think now is the time, an' I do my stuff.

"Listen, Miranda," I say, "I got some place to go now an' I gotta make it, but if you want to do somethin' for me I guess you can, an' I don't know anybody else in this burg who could do it."

She comes close to the car an' looks at me.

"Why, what's the matter, Lemmy?" she says.

I tell her, an' do I do it good? I tell her that I am being black-mailed by some woman who has got a lotta papers that could get me well balled up an' that this dame was goin' to be at some house party over the weekend at some place down the river an' that I was goin' down to meet her. Then I ask Miranda if she will come along an' see if she can help me to pull a fast one over on this dame and get back the papers.

She falls. She falls for it like a bird for a worm, an' she promises me that she won't say a word about it to anybody an' that nobody will know where she's gone to, so that everything will be O.K. for me.

I tell her that I will pick her up at four o'clock on Saturday after-noon an' that we will drive down, an' then I say goodnight.

She shakes hands with me an' she is lookin' at me with her eyes shinin' like stars.

"Goodnight, Lemmy," she says. "You know I think I'd do anything for you."

I said somethin' . . . . one of them things you say at that sorta time, but I wasn't thinkin' of what I was sayin'; I was wonderin' what the

Kastlin set-up was goin' to be and whether I could use those guys to double cross Siegella.

CHAPTER EIGHT
SADIE GREENE

IT IS half past two when I get to the Parkside Hotel, an' I reckon that when I get there I have shaken off any of Siegella's boys who are tailing me. After I left Miranda I hired a car from a garage. I drove out to Wandsworth after this, just to make certain nobody was coming after me, left the car there, took a cab back via Hammersmith, an' I went into the Parkside Hotel through the back door.

The night porter was expecting me an' I went up in the lift. On the third floor in a drawing room I found Lottie Frisch, Kastlin, the four guys who gave me the works in the Mews flat on Baker Street an' about three other fellers. I reckon these guys are the remnants of the Goyaz mob who have been operatin' over here with him.

On the table is cigars and a lot of liquor. Kastlin is a fat guy. He is seated in a corner an' looking very depressed. I told you I ain't got any use for Kastlin. He was a cheap yellow dog but I reckon he was desperate an' when a guy gets desperate maybe he'll have some guts because he's got to have 'em. Anyhow, I reckon I got to use these boys an' you can't pick and choose when you're in a spot.

Kastlin is half German an' he speaks slowly and distinctly just as if it was a trouble talking.

"Listen, Caution," he says, "I reckon this is a showdown. I got Lottie to tail after you an' try an' get you to come up here an' see us because we're in a spot. She can talk better than I can so she'll do the talking."

Lottie who is wearing a pink silk wrap an' fluffy slippers, gets up an' pours me a shot of whisky. She pushes the cigarettes over the table.

"See here, Lemmy," she says, sittin' down again an' lighting herself a cigarette. "I reckon we know you're on top of the job, you've got the lowdown on us, but maybe you'll be interested in doin' a spot of business."

"I'm listening, Lottie," I say, "I'll always do business any time. I'm a business man."

She nods.

"Here's the way it is, Lemmy," she says. "I don't know whether you know what Siegella's game is; I don't know whether you was in it in the first place—although I don't think you was—an' I don't know whether you just happened to be around in this country an' muscled in last night. Because I reckon it wouldn't be the first time you muscled in on somethin'; but Siegella, who is a dirty double-crosser, has given us the air, an' given it to us good, an' we don't feel so hot about it."

I nod.

"Wasn't you in with him on this thing originally?" I ask.

"You betcha," says Lottie, stubbin' her cigarette out. "I'm telling you we found the money for this job."

I get interested.

"So what?" I say.

"Here's the way it is," she goes on. "Last year a guy who is fronting for Siegella comes to Goyaz an' Kastlin, an' tells us that there is a hell of an idea goin', nothing more or less than snatching Miranda van Zelden. But he says that this thing has got to be done in a big way. He reckons that the girl will be goin' to Europe within the next eight or nine months, an' the idea is to snatch her some place out of the States. Now it is stickin' out a foot that two things is required for this job. One is plenty dough and the other is a boat. That's where Goyaz an' Kastlin here come in on the job, because Goyaz is the only guy in the States who has got a seagoin' boat with a proper captain and crew who know how to work an' who can mind their own business and not shoot off their mouths about what's goin' on aboard.

"Well, it looks as if Siegella is pretty clever this time because he has one hell of an idea for raisin' the dough. Just before this meetin' Siegella has muscled in on the Lacassar mob's racket, but Jake Lacassar ain't feelin' so good about the deal he is getting, an' Siegella reckons to kill two birds with one stone, to get the money out of Lacassar an' to get rid of Lacassar at the same time.

"Well, it's easy. An idea is put up to Jake that it will be a good thing to stick up the National Farmers Bank in Arkansas. This job is easy an' Jake says O.K., but Siegella has got a double-cross waiting for him because the idea is that after the stick-up Jake Lacassar an' the three boys who are pullin' the job with him are going to change cars at the cross roads near Little Rock.

"Siegella's guy suggests that the Goyaz boys shall be waitin' there with a new car, but that instead of changing cars and letting Lacassar make a getaway, they bump him an' the three boys and take the dough. This kills two birds with one stone. It finances the Miranda snatch an' it gets rid of Jake.

"Well, it works. Three of the Goyaz boys wait around for these mugs on the cross road on Little Rock an' when Jake Lacassar's car comes they let him an' his mob have it. They hi-jack the dough and it is handed over to Siegella.

"Now everythin' is hunky dory. We have the jack. We have got the boat. A set-up is all laid out. Now you can betcha life that it cost Goyaz an' Fritz here plenty money to get that boat over from the States; plenty money to get that crowd aboard so as to make it look like a party, but when we get over here an' contact with Siegella he gives us the air. He pulls some phoney story about not likin' Fritz here, an' he tells Goyaz that if he don't like it he can go an' give himself a coupla hot baths.

"It looks like he has bought himself a steam yacht with some of the dough that we hi-jacked outa Lacassar, so he's sittin' pretty.

"Well, what can we do? Siegella has got a bunch of gorillas over here that would just burn babies for the fun of doin' it, so Goyaz has to say yes, but he don't like it, neither does Fritz, an' neither do I."

If you could have seen this jane sittin' there with her eyes glitterin' like a rattlesnake, you bet she could have done something' pretty to Siegella if she had him tied up. She gives herself another cigarette.

"Well, can you blame us if we tried to slip one across him, Lemmy?" she asks. "We made a big play that we was fadin' out of the job, but Goyaz has an idea that it's goin' to be easy to get this van Zelden dame to go aboard any boat where there's a game goin' on.

"An' he's right. Some of our boys have already got fed-up with the whole works an' gone back to the States, but there's still a bunch of us stickin' together round here, an' we are reckoning that we can pull this Miranda snatch ourselves.

"An' I reckon it would have come off except for two things, one is a smart private dick called Gallat who is keepin' tabs on Miranda an' he somehow gets a line that she is comin' down on the boat. This guy Gallat an' some other mug that we don't know come aboard an' instead of playin' them along nice and quiet Goyaz, who is feeling brave for once, has to put a lotta hot work in with a gun. By this time— nobody knows why—you're stringin' along in this thing, Lemmy, an' the upshot of this bezusus is that with Goyaz dead—an' we don't know who bumped him but we reckon it must have been Yonnie Malas— Frenchie, the skipper of the boat tells Kastlin he's pullin' out good an' quick. There is one hell of a row an' what with some of the guys we've got on that boat going funny an' one or two other little things that is happenin' around there, Fritz here began to get a bit jagged about the nerves, so he comes ashore an' let's the boat go.

"Now here's the thing. You ain't done so bad outa this, Lemmy. You hi-jacked Goyaz for twenty grand, ten grand he took outa the van Zelden piece, an' an extra ten you took for luck. Well, that ain't so bad to start with, is it?"

I grin.

"It's all right," I say, "but what's twenty grand to me? I've had jack before, you know. Twenty grand won't get me no place."

"You betcha," she says, "but I reckon we can still make some real money outa this Miranda business, Lemmy."

I give myself another drink.

"Well, spill it, Lottie," I say, "I'm burnin' to hear the answer."

"It's easy," she says. "You can take it from me that Siegella is goin' to pull this snatch, an' he's goin' to do it quick. Now we ain't quite dead from the neck up, an' it looks to us as if you're workin' in with him.

"Now with Goyaz runnin' the mob, we wasn't so good, but I reckon if you was runnin' it, Lemmy, we could get some place, an' I reckon we could pull a fast one, because you're tough, you've got brains an' you've been runnin' around in the States for years doin' what you like an' nobody's got their hooks into you.

"Siegella reckoned to get three million outa this snatch, an' here's our proposition. Come over to us, take over the mob here—we've got nine good boys—muscle in on the Siegella business an' snatch this dame ourselves. Well, how do you like it?"

"It looks all right to me," I say, "how do I break?"

"We've talked that over," she says, "we reckon that you take two million an' we'll split the third. That's pretty good terms, ain't it, Lemmy?"

"It suits me," I say. "But how do we get this dame out of England, because you know these English cops are pretty hot an' although they ain't got any idea what's goin' on over here, if they start smellin' around they can be very funny, an' another thing is they tell me you can't graft 'em either."

"That's right enough," she says, "but don't it stand to reason that Siegella has got his boat stuck around somewhere. Why shouldn't we play along an' let him snatch this girl? If we can get our hooks on that boat we've got him taped."

"It's an idea, Lottie," I say, "but it wants a whole lotta thinkin' out."

I think for a minute an' I make my mind up quick.

"Now listen, you boys," I say, "I'm goin' to tell you somethin'. Siegella is goin' to snatch this dame on Saturday. I happen to know because I'm the guy who is gettin' her down to the place where she's goin' to get it. Now I am coming in with you, I am running this mob, an' I am taking two-thirds of the dough. Another thing, you're goin' to do what I tell you an' like it from now on. Believe me," I say, "I would also like to slip one into Siegella, an' I reckon we can do it.

"I don't know where they're goin' to take her, where they've got the boat or anythin' else, an' Siegella ain't likely to tell me, because he don't trust me further than he Could throw a coupla baby elephants.

"Now here's the thing. We gotta fix it so that on Saturday or Sunday your mob is way down in the country near this dump of Siegella's, stickin' under cover. We have got to wait until Siegella has let the van Zelden dame know what the works is. Instead of me coming back to town an' puttin' any ransom call through, I reckon I gotta stick around. We have got to pick our time an' hi-jack Miranda. In other words we've got to do another big rescue act.

"An' we've got to try an' do this nice an' quiet. Maybe there'll be shootin' an' maybe there won't. If there is any we have got to do it, but if we can do without it we've got to.

"Now get this. Once we have got Miranda back in London away from that mob, we got Siegella where we want him because we've got a criminal charge on him an' Miranda herself can prove it. You've got to realise," I tell 'em, "that nobody in this country has got a thing on Siegella, an' until he actually pulls that snatch everythin' is O.K. legally, but once he's done it an' we're sittin' pretty with Miranda, why it's just easy.

"It looks to me as if when Siegella has found out that he's beat there's only one thing he can do, he's got to take his boat an' scram back to the States just in case Miranda goes callin' coppers around here, and then we are well away.

"We are sittin' pretty with the dame, an' we go back to my original scheme. One that I came over for."

Lottie looks at me an' raises her eyebrows. She grins.

"An' what was that, Lemmy?" she says.

"Just this," I say. "I reckon I'm goin' to get Miranda to come over to France with me, an' I reckon I'm goin' to marry her, an' I reckon that when old man van Zelden hears I've done it, he's got to pay plenty money to get his one an' only daughter out of a marriage with a first-class mobster like I am, especially havin' regard to the fact that I have saved this jane from being kidnapped about three times.

"It's soft an' it's easy. The only tough part is hi-jacking this dame from Siegella."

Lottie gives herself another drink. Round the room I can see the boys grinnin'.

"Gee, Lemmy," says Lottie, "you've got one helluva brain."

I tell her to lay off of that sorta stuff, because compliments don't mean a thing to a guy like me, an' I then proceed to get the set-up for this job. I have to be pretty spry about what I am doin' because I am thinkin' from two ways at once. First I am thinkin' what is likely to happen to Miranda on Saturday night an' just how I can cross this guy an' get away with this dame myself, an' secondly I have to make the set-up look good an' legitimate from the Kastlin point of view.

Kastlin himself don't worry me any because he is a big sucker anyway, an' anybody could play him along for a mug, but Lottie Frisch is no gargoyle above the neck, that baby knows her stuff I'm tellin' you, an' she is one of them cantankerous sorta dames that when she's crossed-up she's just as likely to blow a hole in you as the next guy. She'd just have to turn the heat on somebody.

I smoke a coupla cigarettes an' Lottie gets some coffee an' we get down to hard cases. It looks like there is five of these guys who has the necessary nerve an' is tough enough to pull this job off. These are the four guys who bust into me at the Baker Street dump—Merris—the one with the dank hair—Durient, Coyle, a half-breed Canadian, an' a man called Spegla; there is also another guy who they tell me is a sorta half-brother of Lottie's.

It looks like that Lottie has got a Tommy gun that Kastlin—who came off the Princess Cristabel with this half-brother of Lottie's—has brought with him, an' I reckon that this will come in plenty useful.

After a bit I give them the say-so. This is how I have got it figured out: Merris, Durient an' Coyle will go down to this dump Thame on the train very early on Saturday mornin'. They will look around at this Branders End place an' case the job so that when we start something we know which way they are goin'. These three guys will fix themselves up at some little roadhouse, an' they will stay inside all day. They will not take any chances of any of Siegella's gorillas havin' a look at them.

Late on Saturday night Spegla an' Lottie's half-brother Willie Bosco will go down in the car with the Tommy gun, besides which everybody will be carryin' a rod, if not two.

Now I reckon that Miranda an' me will arrive at this Branders End place at about five o'clock on Saturday, an' I also reckon that Siegella is not goin' to pull anything at all that day. He'll have this party he's talking about an' when it's over, good an' early on Sunday mornin', I reckon he will wise up Miranda as to the real situation an'—carryin' out his usual layout—will get her to write a letter to old van Zelden askin' him to pay the dough good an' quick, so that this letter will reach Pa van Zelden about five or six days after he has got the say-so over the long-distance telephone, an' will gyp him up a bit over gettin' the money.

Well, I reckon that Miranda will put up one helluva show an' that she won't write the letter an' that Siegella will get burned up an' will start workin' on this dame good an' plenty. If it goes like this then he is goin' to get her aboard his boat—where-ever he has got it—on Sunday and scram out of it.

So it looks to me that everything that we are goin' to pull has gotta be pulled early on Sunday mornin'. I fix this time because I reckon everybody will be sorta thinkin' that the job is O.K. an' maybe most of the gorillas will be blind to the world.

Lottie says yes to all this. She reckons it's the works, so the set-up is that about midnight on Saturday night Merris an' the rest of the boys will meet at some place near Branders End. They will get up as close as they can an' that I will look out for them an' make a contact. Then as soon as I get a break I bust out of it with Miranda an' if any of Siegella's mob start to get funny then Merris an' the boys will turn on the heat an' cover up my getaway.

Once we get away we stand a chance because Siegella will be all set to leave anyhow an' he will have to get out of it somehow just in case Miranda takes it into her little head to go about shoutin' the story around town.

Well, we sit around and we talk this thing out until we have got all the details fixed and everybody knows just what they are doin' on the schedule.

An' it is fixed that Willie Bosco is to be my contact man, an' that on Saturday afternoon when I call down at the Carlton for Miranda he will fix to slip me a note givin' me a plan of what the neighbour-hood is like down there. I reckon this will be safe enough because by that time Siegella will have taken his tails off me.

Havin' fixed all this I say goodnight to this mob, an' I scram outa the hotel by the back door—like I come in. It is good an' late, but I walk around by Hyde Park for a bit turnin' things over in my mind, an' I come to the conclusion that I am takin' a big chance if I trust this Lottie Frisch an' the Kastlin crowd all the way.

After all it is as sure as anythin' that there ain't nothin' to stop this crowd pullin' a fast one on me after we have crossed up Siegella an' I know the mobs too well to take any chances.

But still I reckon that pullin' in with Lottie an' the remains of Goyaz' mob is goin' to help me some in fixin' Siegella an' you gotta take a chance sometimes.

I am pretty satisfied with things in my mind when I get back home. I open the front door an' start walkin' up the stairs which is a thing I do not like, but naturally the lift ain't workin' an' I am feelin' good an' tired.

Just when I am goin' up the last few stairs an' my eyes are on a level with the landin' above me I look along the passage an' I see a light under the door of my sittin' room.

I stop an' have a meetin' about this. What guy is in my sittin' room anyway? It might be Siegella an' it might be Constance, but I reckon that neither of these is goin' to hang around an' wait for me when they could phone.

I slip out my gun an' gum-shoe along. When I get to the door I throw it open an' step into the room.

Sittin' in an arm-chair in front of the electric fire is Miranda's maid—the jane I have got the date with. She looks good an' cold to me an' she has a coat wrapped round her.

I told you this dame is a neat piece. She has got a nice fresh skin, an' big blue eyes, an' her face is open an' frank like she was one of them dames—an' they are few an' far between they tell me—who just couldn't pull a fast one even if she was paid for it.

She gets up, as I throw my hat on a chair, an' put the shootin' iron back in its holster.

"Well, if it ain't Sadie," I say. "Well, baby, who's been run over or what; or is it my sex-appeal? How long you been here?"

She gulps.

"I been waitin' for hours I guess, Mr. Caution," she says, "because I'm worried sick an' I don't know what to do. So I thought I'd come around an' ask you an' I got round here just before midnight.

"I told the valet that it was important that I just gotta see you, an' he said that he didn't know when you'd be in an' I better wait."

I tell her to sit down an' I light myself a cigarette.

"Take it easy, kid," I say. "There ain't nothin' so bad that it couldn't be worse, an' anyway worry is bad for the eyes. What's on your mind?"

"I got this," she says.

She hands me an envelope an' inside is a letter. I pull this out an' I read it an' as I go along I begin to think that this guy Gallat was not such a mug as I thought he was.

The letter is addressed to Miss Sadie Greene, care of Miss Miranda van Zelden at the Carlton Hotel, an' it says like this:

"Dear Miss Greene—I am only writing you because it is necessary that I make a contact with someone close to Miss van Zelden.

I am a private inquiry agent employed by Mr. van Zelden for the purpose of keeping near Miss van Zelden and maintaining some sort of protective influence. You will know her aptitude for making strange friends and seeking thrills and excitement which are not always conducive to her safety.

I have contacted a servant at the Carlton and it seems that Miss van Zelden has disappeared. I have also contacted two other men, one of whom purports to be an investigator to an insurance society which carries Miss van Zelden's jewellery insurance.

At the instigation of these people I am going down to the Isle of Mersea as they tell me that Miss van Zelden is there.

But candidly, I am not quite satisfied in my mind. I feel that a closer check should in future be kept on Miss van Zelden's movements, and I propose when I return from this journey to contact you and, with your help, to maintain a closer watch on Miss van Zelden in the future. I am relying on your assistance and help because you know that this is what her father would desire you to do.

Naturally you will say nothing of this to Miss van Zelden who objects strongly to any sort of surveillance.

I shall therefore get into touch with you almost as soon as you receive this. If I do not contact you by midnight on the day of the receipt of this letter then you may take it that something serious has happened and I would like you to telephone at once to Scotland Yard the English Police headquarters and after showing them this letter request their assistance.

I am, Yours truly,

Robert Gallat."

I folded the letter up, wonderin' as I did so, just what this dame has done.

"I got that this mornin', Mr. Caution," she says, "an' I been waitin' all day to see if this Mr. Gallat turned up, but there's never even been

a smell of him. Tonight about eleven o'clock I thought I would ring
up the Police like he said, an' then I reckoned that if I done this an'
Miss van Zelden got to hear of it, she'd give me the air just as soon
as she could hand it out.

"Then I thought of you. I knew you'd been with her wherever she
was, because you brought her back, an' I sorta liked you. Say, Mr.
Caution, what am I to do?"

I grin over at her.

"You're a good kid," I say, "but you're worrying that little head
of yours over nothin'. This guy Gallat is a proper punk, I'm tellin'
you, an' the fact of the matter is he has been made a sucker out of.

"This is the way it was," I says, "this guy Gallat thinks he is one
helluva dick, an' so some of the boys—friends of Miss van Zelden's—
strung him along that she had gone over to France. So the big sap went
over there after her, an' I suppose he wrote that just before he went.

"Anyhow," I say, "you don't have to think about it. You can take
it from me that everything's O.K."

She looks relieved an' so am I because I have got the jitters about
this business. That letter of Gallat's might have caused plenty trouble
if she'd gone flashin' it around the place.

"Gee, I'm glad, Mr. Caution," she says. "I was gettin' myself
worried about all this business an' I just didn't know what to do.
You know it's not so easy bein' maid to Miss van Zelden. She's very
easy to upset an' I wouldn't do that for the world. Well, I'm glad I
came an' I reckon I'd better be goin' along now."

She gets up an' I go over an' give her a squeeze, an' she likes it.

While she has been talkin' I have been doin' some fast thinkin',
an' I have got a set-up in my mind that looks to me as if I can look
after myself down at this Branders End place supposin' I can get this
Sadie Greene to listen to reason an' do what I want her to.

"You don't want to go yet, baby," I tell her, "because I wanna talk
to you. I'm glad you come around here tonight because I got something on my mind about Miss van Zelden that I was goin' to tell you
when I saw you.

"It ain't anything to get worried about, it's just a little thing you
can do that would maybe save a whole lotta bother, an' you won't be
doin' yourself any harm neither because when I get back to the States

I reckon I'm goin' to tell old man van Zelden that you did your stuff an' I reckon he'll probably slip you a very nice present."

She looks pleased.

"I reckon I'll do anything I can for anybody," she says, "an' I would certainly like to please Mr. van Zelden."

I tell her to sit down, then I go off an' make some coffee an' I bring it back. I give her some an' a cigarette an' I proceed to tell her one helluva story, because I have got it figured out that she can't do any harm anyhow an' if she strings along then I reckon I can protect myself against anything that Lottie and the Goyaz boys might try to pull down at Thame.

She sits there holdin' her coffee cup an' lookin' at me with her big blue eyes.

"Listen, honey," I tell her. "Here's the way it is."

CHAPTER NINE
HOT MONEY

SHE sits there drinkin' coffee an' smoking a cigarette an' lookin' at me, an' I proceed to tell her the hell of a tale. I tell her how I am goin' down to some house party with Miss van Zelden on Saturday afternoon an' the guy who is giving this house party is very keen on the van Zelden dame. I tell her that I am goin' along because I have got an idea in my head that this feller may try to get funny, an' that she need not worry because if there is any nonsense I will knock seventeen different kinds of hell outa this guy.

She falls for this all right. She tells me she knows just how it is an' there is always a certain type of guy who does not know how to be fond of women without makin' himself objectionable. I say fine an' I see she has got the whole idea.

I then go on to tell her that it looks to me like this party might be a bit rough, an' that her coming round to see me tonight over this Gallat business has given me a swell idea. I say that I am goin' to suggest to her that without sayin' anything at all to Miss van Zelden she should put herself in the train on Saturday evening about six o'clock an' take herself down to some hotel in the neighbourhood and just stick around there just in case this party should get so rough that I might decide to take Miss van Zelden away.

"I get it, Mr. Caution," she says, "you mean if this party gets really sort of objectionable like, you bring Miss van Zelden back to me an' I can look after her at the hotel."

"You've got it, Sadie," I say, "an' there's another little thing you might do. Suppose everythin' goes O.K. an' the party is nice an' quiet, then I reckon you'll want to be back at the Carlton Hotel in case Miss van Zelden comes back some time Sunday."

She says yes, she reckons that's how it is. I then arrange with her that she should telephone from the hotel at which she is stayin' at Thame to the Branders End House. I tell her she can get the number from the inquiry directory. I also tell her I reckon she should stick around until about three o'clock on Sunday morning an' if by that time she ain't seen Miss van Zelden or me, she is to phone through to the Branders End House and ask to speak to me.

Now I reckon this is a wise move on my part because I calculate that by three o'clock on Sunday morning I shall know just how the works are down at Branders End, that Siegella will either have shown his hand an' we shall have crossed him up an' got Miranda out of it or else having done so Lottie Frisch an' her mob will have had time to try any funny business that they're goin' to try. If they do then havin' this girl around at the hotel in the neighbourhood is goin' to be pretty useful for me.

First of all I can park Miranda there if I am in a jam, an' secondly I have got somebody who can do some heavy phoning if I want 'em to.

While Sadie is gettin' herself another cup of coffee, I go an' get the ABC directory an' look round for an hotel. Then with the aid of an A.A. map that I get off the valet I find some place called the Holly-bush Hotel which is about fifteen miles from this Branders End place.

This looks like the only place that would be suitable for Sadie because I do not want her stuck around anywhere near Branders End where any of the mob could get wise as to what we was at. The only bad thing about this hotel is that it is off the main road, an' the road leadin' from Branders End to this place is a bad one, an' it is goin' to take a bit of time to drive over. Still I reckon if I ain't in a hurry the road won't matter, an' if I am I won't be able to let it matter, so that's that.

Maybe you might think I was a mug for pullin' Sadie Greene in on this racket, but what's a guy to do? I reckoned I was goin' to be stuck down there at this Branders End right in the middle of the finest bunch of thugs that ever went after some jack. I am also goin' to be totin' around a very temperamental dame—this Miranda woman—an' the idea of having somebody who looks as if they was at least straighter than a corkscrew somewhere around the neighbourhood looks good to me.

While Sadie is drinkin' her second cup of coffee, I do some more come-on stuff with her. I tell her that she has got the loviest eyes that I ever saw except maybe some film star that I once knew by accident up Hollywood way, an' by the time I have finished doin' my stuff with this dame she is ready to eat outa my hand.

When I have got her nice an' docile I tell her that when she rings me through at the Branders End dump she is to do it at three o'clock in the mornin' sharp, an' when she speaks to me if everything is O.K. then I will tip her off, in which case she can get up early on Sunday mornin' an' get back to the Carlton so that she's there if Miranda should decide to go back that day. If everythin' ain't all right I can tell her so an' tell her what I want to do.

I'm feelin' not so good about this telephone call because I have not got any idea what is goin' to be happenin' around this Branders End at three o'clock, but I have always found you have got to take a chance sometimes.

Sadie falls for all this. It looks like this dame is an adventurous sorta cuss, an' I think she is rather enjoying the idea of stringin' around on this thing. I give her a hundred dollars as a sweetener, an' when she's finished her coffee I go downstairs an' I look up an' down the street. There ain't nobody around. I go upstairs an' tip her off that she can go, an' she goes.

I now think that there is nothing else that I can do about this job. I have just got to sit down an' wait an' see what happens, but I reckon I can cross up Siegella with the Goyaz boys, an' that if they try anything funny afterwards I've got to rely on usin' this dame Sadie Greene to get me out of it. I then go to bed.

Next day is Friday, an' I stick around an' don't do anything very much. I called off the date I had to eat chop-suey with Sadie Greene because I reckon there is not very much sense my being seen around any more with this dame at this moment. I stick around most of the day an' smoke because I reckon that Siegella will maybe get in touch with me some time during the day, an' I am right about this because at seven o'clock Constance arrives.

She is lookin' pretty swell an' is wearing an outfit that would knock your eye out. Siegella is evidently very fond of this dame, because he buys her plenty clothes.

Constance gives me the tip off that everything is ready, that Siegella an' the boys have already gone down to Branders End, an' that they will be expecting me about five o'clock next day.

She tells me the idea is that I shall stick around there on Saturday night, when she says there is goin' to be a nice party, an' that I shall leave on Sunday morning, which makes my idea look right that Siegella will not try anything on Saturday night.

Connie says that when I come back on Sunday I am to stick around until she either sees me or telephones me either on Sunday night or Monday morning an' lets me know the name of the guy I am to telephone in New York, the feller who is going to make the contact with van Zelden an' get him to ring me.

I tell her this is all fine. Then I ask her just what the guy is goin' to do with Miranda on Sunday. She smiles.

"Listen, Lemmy," she says, "you oughta know better than that. Curiosity killed the cat, didn't it? I reckon that when you've got that jane down there an' come back here, your job's done. All you've got to do is to take your money an' sit pretty."

"That's O.K. by me," I say, "but you're forgettin' one little thing. I reckon one of the things that you was thinkin' of when you pulled me in on this job is that I've been pretty clever in my time at gettin' outa jams. Now it is all very well for you to say that when I get this dame down there I'm finished, an' that's O.K. so long as somebody don't start somethin' afterwards an' the cops don't get to hear about it. If they do I reckon I ain't finished. But what I want to know is that Siegella has got this job so laid out that there ain't goin' to be no comeback."

She laughs.

"Be your age, Lemmy," she says, "you oughta know better than that. Don't you know Ferdie well enough to know that he looks at everythin' about six hundred times before he moves an inch. That guy is the most cautious an' the most desperate feller that I ever struck. He cases a job until there ain't no possibility of a mistake, an' I reckon he's got this Miranda thing worked out fine.

"Anyway, nobody ain't goin' to talk to coppers, Lemmy," she says, "or anybody else, because you can take it from me that if Siegella just as much as smells somethin' that looks like a dick's grandfather, he'll put a coupla bullets into this dame an' scram. After which I reckon we can all look after ourselves. You're gettin' plenty money for this job, you know, Lemmy."

I say alright because it looks as if Connie is not very keen on tellin' me anything, an' I think it will not be a good play to try an' find anything out now.

"O.K., Connie," I say, "I guess I don't wanta hear anything that I shouldn't, only"—an' I look at her with a come-on look in my eye—"I guess I wanted to know when I was goin' to see you again."

She thinks this over for a bit an' then she says:

"You'll be seein' me alright, Lemmy, I guess I'll be knockin' around town some time on Monday mornin' an' I can contact you some place. Maybe I'll phone you."

Now this gets me thinkin' because if Connie is goin' to hang around town on Monday next it looks to me as if she ain't goin' along with Siegella after he has pulled the Miranda snatch. Maybe just he an' one or two other guys are aimin' to make a quick getaway with the Miranda dame an' don't want any other women stringin' along.

I give Constance a drink an' then she looks at her watch an' says that she guesses she'd better be getting along, as she is drivin' down to Branders End right away.

She stays on for a few minutes an' we wisecrack a bit, an' then she comes over an' gives me one of them kisses I told you about— you know the sort that makes you feel as if your hair's standin' on end—an' then she scrams out of it.

I see her to the door an" we shake hands.

"Well, you great big beautiful brute," says Constance, "I reckon I'll be seein' you, an' don't you go makin' a play for the Miranda bit on the way down. I know you an' your little ways with the dames."

"Hooey, Magnificent," I say, "since I seen you I ain't even looked at a woman—they just don't mean a thing to me, an' I wear your picture next my heart an' it's burnt a hole in my undervest."

Constance smiles at me as she steps into her roadster.

"You're the little smart guy, ain't you, Lemmy?" she says. "Well, baby, you wait till we got this Miranda business in the can, an' when we're all sittin' pretty then I guess I'll have a little time to devote to you. Goodnight, sweetheart, an' don't do anything I wouldn't do myself."

She slips in the gear an' she goes off, an' I stand there lookin' after the car. This Constance is a funny dame I'm tellin' you. She's that sorta woman that you never quite know how to take; you never know whether you'd do yourself more good with her by rushin' her or by standin' off an' usin' the old ice-box tactics. She's one of them janes that you never really get to know.

But she is also one of them janes that causes all the trouble. When I look back an' I remember all the stuff I've seen in my time, an' the tricks that the mobs have pulled, one thing is always stickin' out a mile an' that is the fact that there would be durn little crime if it wasn't for women like Connie. Fellers get into rackets because they want to buy some dame swell clothes, because they wanta make her, or because they wanta look like great big he-men, so they get around the place, shootin' and racketin', bumpin' off coppers an' each other, heistin' banks, snatchin' people and generally kicking hell out of everything.

I once read in some magazine that crime costs the American people four million dollars a year, an' I reckon if somebody had dipped Constance in a bucket of cold water five minutes after she was born that maybe the U.S. taxpayers would have saved one million, which shows you that I think this dame is pretty good.

But as far as I am concerned she makes me wonder whether she is a bit batty over me or whether she is just jollyin' me along and does the same to every other guy.

After a minute or two I go upstairs again, an' mix myself a highball. I'm just sinkin' this drink, when the telephone goes an' this time it is Willie Bosco. I gave him my number at the Parkside meetin', in case anything urgent should break that he wanted to contact me over.

"Listen, Lemmy," he says. "Everything is nice an' orderly. Siegella and his bunch left town about two hours ago. We watched 'em drive off an' I been stickin' around your place just to see if I could contact you an' talk about this Branders End place.

"I just seen that dame of Siegella's leave your apartment an' I reckoned that it would be O.K. to telephone you."

"O.K., Willie," I say, but I am doin' some hot thinkin' while I am sayin' it because it is a new one on me that Lottie an' Kastlin should know where Siegella was hangin' out in London—which was a thing that I didn't even know myself—so that they can watch him go off, an' I am wonderin' just how many more things they know that I don't.

He goes on:

"We got the ground cased out, Lemmy," he says. "Here's the way it goes. This place Branders End is a big swell sorta house standin' in its own grounds, about a quarter mile off the main road. There is a wall around the grounds but not enough to keep anybody out.

"There is a sorta lawn all round the house an' paths leadin' off this lawn to different gates in the wall. At the back of the house is a thick shrubbery place an' there is two paths leadin' through this. One of these paths leads to a gate in the wall directly facin' the centre of the back of the house, an' the other path which is just a little one, a sorta footpath, leads to some place where the wall has broken in an' you can get through. Now this path is the one for you because we reckon that Merris will stick around by the wall at the end of this path from late Saturday night until the time when you contact him an' give the word to blow the works. On the other side of the wall, near this path, is an old road runnin' through some trees that leads to the main London road. We reckon we can park two cars here an' make a swell getaway.

"Now we had a whole lotta luck. Coyle went down last night an' nosed around this place an' he found a furnished cottage not a quarter mile from this Branders End dump that was for rent. So we took this place for a month an' paid for it, an' the gang's there. They're stayin' under cover an' they got the car parked in some bushes at the back of the cottage. Nobody is goin' to put his foot outside the cottage until the balloon goes up so there ain't a chance of Siegella gettin' to know a thing.

"I'm goin' down late tonight with Lottie, who reckons that she might as well be in on this job. We are leavin' Kastlin behind because anyway he is a mug an' likely to ball things up at the last minute by gettin' het-up an' jittery.

"I am takin' the T. gun an' half a dozen pineapple bombs in the car with me an' we shall go straight to the cottage an' park the car in the bushes with the other one. Both cars will be loaded up with petrol an' ready for a quick scram tomorrow night. We have got all the roads cased out an' if you say yes we reckon to do this:

"When we've snatched this dame we run straight across country, back to London, through London to Camber. Lottie has it fixed that we got a thirty-foot motor-launch waitin' for us at a place near there where there's a sea-wall, near Dymchurch. We run both cars into the sea an' ditch 'em there, take this boat an' land on the French coast early Sunday mornin'. Kastlin is fixin' fake passports for the lot of us an' one for this Miranda jane, because Lottie reckons to slip her a coupla Spanish drops that will keep this dame quiet good an' plenty, an' we can say she is a sick jane. Directly we make Paris, we are O.K. because Lottie has plenty connections over there an' we can lay low an' let you handle the thing the way you want. How does that go?"

"It doesn't go at all," I say. "It's all O.K. except that French stuff. We ain't goin' any place except London when we have got that jane. There ain't no reason to scram over to France an' it's out an' that's all there is to it."

"That's O.K., Lemmy," he says. "If you say so, only Lottie is afraid that if Siegella gets burned up he is just as likely to start a gun battle in the middle of Hyde Park as not. You know that guy, he ain't got no sense of decency at all, an' he just don't give a hell for anything if somebody gets him good an' annoyed."

"I'm chancin' that, Willie," I say. "An' with the exception of the pleasure cruise the set-up's O.K.

"Now get this: I'm arrivin' down there with Miranda about some-where between five an' six tomorrow evenin'. There's goin' to be a party an' I reckon that everybody will have a first-class jag on by about eleven o'clock. You tell Merris that at twelve-thirty I'm goin' to get outa that house somehow an' get along that path through the shrubbery at the back—the one that leads to the hole in the wall. You tell him that he's gotta be stickin' around there at twelve-thirty, because by that time I shall know just what the works look like an' I shall have got some idea of what we are goin' to pull.

"All the boys will be standin' by from that time on, an' the cars ready with the engines runnin' but no lights on, at the back of this cottage.

"One of these cars will have to be ready to come down to this hole in the wall if I say so, an' you wanta see that the boys drivin' these buses know their business.

"Every guy has gotta have a silencer on his gun, an' if you gotta use that Tommy gun, which is a thing I don't want, then you'd better fire the thing through an old blanket or a cushion or somethin' just so that the inhabitants don't get the idea that somebody's declared war on England some more. Another thing is that if I find any guy has been drinkin' too much I guess I'm goin' to beat him up with a piece of lead pipe.

"The last thing is that when you an' Lottie get down there tonight you get into that cottage an' no guy is to stick his nose out of it except Merris, an' he stays there until it's time for him to contact me tomorrow night. Got it, Willie?"

"I got it, boss," he says. "Well, here we go an' good luck."

"O.K., Willie," I say, "an' the same to you an' here's mud in your eye and a million dollars."

I hang up.

I reckon that you guys have heard of somethin' called instinct, well that is a thing that I have got. After all it stands to reason that a feller cannot get around with the mobs the way I have for the last two-three years without gettin' an idea ahead of the starter that something hot is blowin', and I get just this idea after the talk I have just had with Willie Bosco—nothin' definite, mind you, just a sorta vague idea that there's something wrong somewhere.

All this stuff about thirty-foot launches an' takin' Miranda over to France all sounds screwy to me after I have taken the trouble I have to explain to these guys that I can handle this thing nice an' easy if I am left to myself an' allowed to hand Miranda the stuff I figured out.

Another thing that I do not like is that Willie Bosco should telephone me instead of slipping me the layout on my way down to pick
up Miranda as arranged. It is a fact that I have given this guy my
telephone number so that he can contact me in case of some urgent
slip-up, but I have not asked him to telephone the set-up through to
me, because I know by experience that telephone conversations can
be very hot things sometimes an' talking over a telephone can be as
bad as talkin' too much to a dame.

I am doin' a lot of considerin' as I get into a dressing gown an'
figure out just where I am breakin'.

First of all this guy Siegella is not to be priced cheap. He has got
a brain an' he is as reckless as a coupla rattlesnakes when it comes
to the push. If Siegella is crossed murder don't mean a thing to him
an' he would just as soon bump off any guy who crossed him up as
he would look at him twice, even if the bump meant that he had got
to fry in the chair for it.

An' I am not too certain that Siegella ain't got an idea that I am
trying something crooked. If I was him I would think so.

Another thing. Supposin', just for the sake of argument, the guy
should pull a very fast one on me. Supposin' that after I have got
Miranda down there he figures out that there is no further necessity
for my kickin' around. If he got an idea like this into his headpiece I
reckon it would take him about four minutes to give me the heat an'
chuck me in the sewer. After all he has bumped plenty fellers before
an' got away with it.

Also it is goin' to be very simple for him to get some other guy to
telephone the call through to the man in New York who is to contact
old man van Zelden about the ransom money—any guy could do that.

So this is where I have got to get some sorta scheme to look after
myself, just in case somethin' breaks while I am down at this Branders
End place, because although I am a guy who has taken a lotta chances in his lifetime, I have a very strong objection to becomin' very
dead like Gallat or MacFee for a few years, because there are quite
plenty things I want a do before I start gettin' measured up for some
angel's wings an' totin' a harp around instead of a Luger automatic.

But here is one place where Siegella has not been quite so wise.

I go into the other room, an' I open the drawer of my travellin' trunk, an' I take out the money that Siegella has given me. Altogether I have got fifteen grand here, all of which is part of the dough that came from the Third National Farmers Bank hold-up in Arkansas. I take this money back into my sitting-room, an' I get the typewriter which I have got, an' a sheet of plain paper, an' I sit down an' I type a letter to the Assistant Secretary of the American Embassy in London, an' this is what I say:

"Dear Sir—Maybe it would interest you to know that a guy called Lemmy Caution who is over here in this country on a dud passport, has this mornin' changed fifteen 1,000 dollar notes for English money at the London branch of the Third National Farmers Bank in Pall Mall.

This money is some of the dough that was pinched from the head office of this bank in Arkansas eighteen months ago. You will remember this holdup. It got plenty publicity.

This guy Lemmy Caution is living at the Carfax Apartments on Jermyn Street, and whilst I have not got any proof that he was in this Arkansas hold-up I reckon that the Feds in the States might like to ask him one or two questions about how he got it, because you will know that they are still looking for the guys who pulled that job.

This guy is going off for the weekend he tells me, but I reckon he is coming back to London some time Sunday night, and maybe you would like to slip the word to these English dicks over here so that if they want to ask him any questions about it they can.

I am giving this information because I reckon I aim to be a good citizen, and also because this guy Lemmy Caution once four-flushed me for a century in a poker game, and I reckon here is where I cause *him* a little inconvenience."

At the foot of this letter I type the signature "A friend of law and order"—which I think is a good one! An' I then seal this letter up an' stamp it because I reckon that next morning I am going down to change this fifteen thousand an' I am also goin' to post this letter so that they get it at the Embassy on Saturday night.

Now I reckon if it looks like Siegella is goin' to pull some funny stuff on me down at this Branders End then I can tell this guy that I have got very good reason to believe that the English dicks will be looking around for me just in order to ask me about this money, an' that England is not a very big place, an' that I have read in a book somewhere that these English coppers are very efficient guys an' have got an old-fashioned way of cleanin' up anything they go out for.

I reckon that this is goin' to make Siegella think a bit, because he will know that if I am alive I can get away with some explanation to these coppers, because I have done a lot of explaining to coppers in my time, but that if I am good an' dead then they are goin' to want to know why, an' they are goin' to keep a very close eye on ports an' railways so that it won't be so easy for him to make a getaway with Miranda.

In other words I reckon I have created a situation that will make it look to Siegella, if he is goin' to get hot with me, that he had better have me kickin' around alive than dead. After I have done this I give myself a shot of bourbon an' I light a cigarette. I reckon there ain't anything else that I can do, an' from now on this business is in the hand of fate as the guy said when he fell off the skyscraper.

I reckon this Siegella is clever, but when they was handin' brains out they also handed a few to this baby.

I look up an' I see myself in the mirror over the mantelpiece, standin' there with a glass of bourbon in my hand. I hold it up. "Here's to you, Lemmy," I say, "an' Miranda, here's mud in your eye, an' good luck all the way." I drink the bourbon, an' I go to bed, which as I have told you before is a good place, that is if you like beds.

CHAPTER TEN
THE SNATCH

THE sun is shining an' I am feeling like a coupla million dollars as I drive down to Thame with Miranda parked beside me. She has got on some flowered sorta dress with a cunnin' coat an' a little hat, an' she looks like the Queen of Sheba only better. As we are doin' a mean fifty on a nice piece of road I am thinkin' to myself that if there wasn't

such a lotta hot business breakin' round about now that maybe I'd
think I was sittin' pretty for once.

An' is this dame pleased with herself! I'm tellin' you that the
idea of thinkin' she's helpin' me out of a tough spot is going like
jake with Miranda.

When I met her at the Carlton I told her that the dame who is
pullin' this blackmail racket on me has got some letter which could
put me on a spot, an' that I, knowin' this dame like I do, reckon that
she will fall for Miranda an' that the idea is that Miranda should sorta
pal up with this dame—who will be at the party—an' that later when
my girl friend has had a coupla drinks, which I say she is certain to
do, that Miranda who has by this time found out which room this
wild cat is sleepin' in will scram upstairs an' try to lay her hands on
the letters. This is as good as anything else I can think of an' it keeps
Miranda quiet, so it's O.K.

On the way down she is workin' the pump handle like steam.
It is as plain as a breach of promise plaintiff that Miranda is very
interested in me, an' she is askin' me this an' that an' tryin' to find
out everything she can, which, havin' regard to my come-backs, is
just about enough to put in your eye an' lose it.

It is a quarter to six when we pull in at Branders End, an' I'm
tellin' you that when Willie Bosco has said that this is a swell place
he is just about right. I have seen millionaires' dumps on Long Island
which ain't got anything on this place.

It is a big house standin' right back off the main road, an' round
it there is a ten-foot wall. When we go in we go through some big
iron gates an' we drive along a wide carriage drive that winds in an'
out of the lawns an' trees until we see the house.

Behind the house, in a sorta half-circle, is a thickly wooded bit
of ground, and stretchin' away from the front an' sides of the lawn
around the house I can see the paths that Willie has told me about.

Siegella an' Constance is waitin' for us on the front steps an'
behind them is some other people. There is a butler—at least there
is some guy called Chicago Bull, who I knew in the States an' who
beat a rap for murder an' escape—pretendin' to be a butler—an' so
far as I can see the place is full of people an' servants an' what have

you. I gotta hand it to Siegella that when he fixes to do somethin' he certainly does it good.

Constance takes Miranda off to powder her nose, an' I am still sittin' in the drivin' seat when Siegella comes down the steps an' leans over.

He is grinnin' like the cat what swallowed the canary an' he is sure pleased with himself.

"Swell work, Lemmy," he says. "Now we're gettin' some place. I reckon it won't be long before you're nearly a millionaire an' able to buy yourself that chicken farm on Missouri that you wanted."

I grin back.

"Well so long as the chickens lay gold bricks, that suits me," I say, an' I start up the car an' drive round to the back which is where they tell me the garage is.

Whilst I am handin' the car over to the guy who looks after the garage I have a look round and get next to the look of the land around the back of the house.

Right behind is a lawn about thirty yards across, an' on the other side of this is a wood runnin' round the back of the house. Away on the left I can see a wide pathway runnin' through the trees, an' on the right, as I stand facin' the wood I can see the little footpath that Willie Bosco has told me about.

I reckon that is about all I want to get acquainted with, so I walk back round to the front of the house an' go in.

Just inside the double doors is a big hall all done in old oak panellin' an' lookin' very good to me if it is a bit dark. Away on the right hand side of this hall there is a bar an' there is another opposite on the left, an' there are plenty guys at these bars an' a lot of janes swillin' up liquor like they never had a drink before they got down here.

An' I see plenty folk I know, I'm tellin' you. All these people are all dressed up an' lookin' fit to go to the White House, but here an' there I pick out guys I have known in the States an' they are all bad men and proud of it. I reckon that two outa every three guys stickin' around them bars was a killer an' some of the women had squeezed a mean gun trigger finger before now, an' I don't mean maybe.

An' there is more than a sprinklin' of foreign guys around. French an' Germans mostly an' a coupla Italians that I don't know. It looks like Siegella is pullin' an extra meetin' of the League of Nations around here.

I go to some room off the hall, an' I wash up, an' then I go over to the bar and order myself a double shot of whisky. I get crackin' with some of these guys an' everybody is talkin' nice an' polite and being perfect little ladies an' gentlemen so that you would think that none of 'em had ever been inside in their lives, although lookin' around I reckoned if you added up the jail sentences that there was in that hall you would have enough to last you until the last instalment was paid on the grand pianner, an' that's sayin' something.

Siegella is just gettin' around sayin' a word here an' a word there an' bein' the perfect host. I reckon he musta been readin' it up somewhere because he was good that I will say.

Presently a bell starts ringin' an' everybody goes off to dress for dinner. I stay put because I am not dressin' anyway as I have not brought any dress clothes because I am not stayin', but I put in some very good work in the bar because the liquor is English liquor an' it is very good.

After a bit I begin to stroll around and sorta get acquainted with the layout. Right at the back of the hall are some more big doors an' on the other wise is the dinin' room. This is a helluva big room with big windows, but they have all got the curtains drawn although it is still daylight. Runnin' down the centre of the room is the dinin' table which is already laid an' I can see that there is seats for about sixty or seventy people.

After a bit I go back to the bar where folks have begun to drink some more, and pretty soon Miranda comes down. It looks like Miranda was rather pleased at bein' at this party, because she is smilin' an' lookin' about her an' she tells me that even if the company is a bit strange it's interesting.

I sit her down at a table in the room on the right of the hall, which is used as a sorta bar-lounge with fellers in white coats servin' drinks, and I get her a sidecar. She drinks this an' she asks me where is the dame who is workin' the black on me, the one who has got the letters, an' I say that she has ditched me by not comin' down here, an' that bein' so we had better forget her an' make the best evenin' we can.

"Alright, Lemmy," says Miranda. Suddenly her voice changes an' she becomes sorta confidential. She leans across the little table an' she says:

"You know, Lemmy, there's something about you that I like. I don't know what it is but it's there. What do you think it is?"

I grin a lot, because I am thinkin' that if this dame knew what was in the bag for her she wouldn't be so stuck on me but would pick up her skirts an' run like a couple of boa-constrictors had come up an' asked for her telephone number.

Pretty soon after this some guy comes in an' says that dinner is served an' we all go into the big dining room. Siegella comes up an' takes Miranda off an' I find a card with my name on it half way down the table. Siegella is sittin' at the top with Miranda on his right hand an' Connie on his left, an' I can see him doin' his stuff an' talkin' to Miranda who is smilin' back and wisecrackin'.

Dinner starts an' it was a good one. I don't know who organised this thing but it was good an' the service an' wine an' everything was perfect. It was a slow meal though an' took a whole lot of time, an' after about an hour I can see that a lot of these guys an' their dames are beginnin' to get a bit part worn. There is some guy near me who is already dead drunk, an' away down the table a coupla janes are tellin' each other all about it an' tryin' to get at each other. Two guys are holdin' them off an' laughin' their heads off.

Near the top of the table, drinkin' water an' keepin' an eye on everything I see Yonnie Malas. When his eye catches mine he slips me a wink an' I return it. Yonnie is lookin' pretty well pleased with himself an' I reckon that he thinks he is goin' to do himself some good outa this snatch.

Presently, after a helluva time, Constance gets up an' the women go out. A whole lot of them is not walkin' so well, an' one dame who has been mixin' Bacardi with champagne is singin' a song an' tryin' to accompany herself on a silver fruit plate which she thinks is a ukelele.

But all around the room, watchin' everythin' an' behavin' like a lot of statues, are the servants with the butler—Chicago Bull—supervisin' everything.

By the time I have got out into the hall it looks like Miranda has disappeared an' after a minute Constance comes up to me an' tells me that Siegella has taken her to see some interesting collection of photographs that he has got which is in the drawin' room upstairs.

I think it is about time that I start to do a little bit of plannin' for myself, so I take Constance along to the bar in the hall which has now opened up again, an' I begin to take a lot of liquor an' to put up a front that I am gettin' good an' tight. I can see the little curl on Constance's lip as I start hiccuppin' all over the place an' it looks like she is fallin' for the line I am puttin' up.

Pretty soon a whole lot of people go upstairs to the drawin' room where there is some sorta concert or something goin' on an' I take Constance up an' we sit down on some settee an' begin to talk. While Connie is sayin' her piece I look over at Miranda who is lookin' through the book of pictures with Siegella. She is wearin' some pretty flowered dress an' with her blonde hair all wavy she certainly looks a picture. Connie, sittin' beside me in her black frock with one big diamond brooch an' her dark eyes an' black hair is certainly a handsome piece, an' I think to myself that I could be pretty good an' comfortable with either of these dames, that is if I had a certificate that Connie wouldn't cut my throat some time when I was sleepin'.

All the while the waiters an' people are bringing cigars an' coffee an' more liquor, an' I go on drinkin' an' pretendin' to get more an' more boozed. After a bit I get up an' I go down to the hall an' I get the waiter down there to give me a large glass of Bacardi rum. I take the glass in my hand an' I go outside an' I gargle with the Bacardi an' then spit it out, after which I go back upstairs, staggerin' a bit an' flop down beside Connie. As she turns I breathe at her an' she pulls a face as the smell of the Bacardi hits her.

"Gee, Lemmy, are you a sap?" she says. "Just fancy drinkin' Bacardi after all that champagne an' stuff you been drinking. If you don't lay off you're goin' to feel good an' ill before the night's out."

I hiccup so it could be heard a mile away.

"You're tellin' me, Connie," I say. "Ain't that just like my dear lil sister to worry about her big bad brother. Say, Connie, I reckon that I don't feel so good, an' wanna go an' lie down."

She gets up.

"Come on, Lemmy," she says. "You give me a pain in the neck. I thought you was a guy who could carry his liquor."

I start mumblin' a lotta stuff about not feelin' very well all day, an' she takes me along a passage on the first floor an' shows me into some bedroom an' tells me to lie down for a bit an' then wash up in the bathroom that communicates outa the bedroom an' then come back to the drawin' room.

I say O.K. an' I lie down on the bed an' pretend that I have fallen asleep. I lay there breathin' like a coupla elephants an' she is standin' by the bedside watchin' me.

After a bit she switches off the light an' I can hear her singing hey-nonny-nonny as she goes. She is a cool cuss—this Connie.

After a minute I get up an' go over to the window. I look out and see that this room I am in is on the west side of the house lookin' towards the front an' that there is a drain pipe within arm's reach of the window an' that I can use this to shin down to the ground.

I take a look at my watch an' I get a surprise because it is twenty minutes to one o'clock, an' I have never realised how the time has been goin', an' I think that I had better get some action.

I open the window an' get my leg over an' make a jump for the drain pipe. I catch it an' it stands for my weight. It don't take me long to shin down this an' trot round the side of the house until I am at the corner an' I can see the little footpath leadin' through the wood to the place where Merris is supposed to be waitin' for me.

I reckon that if I can get the Goyaz boys through this wood an' sorta concentrated on the edge of it we can easy get into the house an' take the whole durn lot of them directly somebody starts something.

I pussyfoot round the edge of the lawn at the back until I reach the shadows where the trees are an' then I run for the footpath. Just before I turn into the little wood I take a look round at the house. Practically every window at the back is lighted up an' I can hear the noise of poppin' corks an' laughin' an' talkin' goin' on. This sounds good to me because it looks as if the party was still goin' on nice an' quiet.

Then I turn round again an' start to trot along this path through the trees. I cannot make very good speed because the path is windin' and there are broken branches an' things lyin' all over the place.

It is as dark as hell an' I cannot see a durn thing for a long time, an' I am cursin' an' swearin' good an' hard because the last thing that I want to do at this time is not to connect with this Goyaz mob, who I reckon will start somethin' on their own if I do not show up, because I think that Lottie Frisch is very steamed up with Siegella an' would pay plenty for the pleasure of emptyin' a tommy gun into his guts.

After a bit the trees begin to thin out an' soon I can see the black shadow of the wall ahead an' the place where it is broken down an' the moonlight comin' through.

I get there an' I step through the hole an' I look around but there is no sign at all of Merris. There is nothin' but a big empty field in front of me with some trees over in the distance an' a little light shinin' through them from some cottage way out over the fields.

I do not like this one little bit because I know that Lottie is a great girl for keepin' arrangements, but although I stick around this place until a quarter after one there is no sign at all of this guy Merris.

I reckon that the best thing I can do is to get along to this cottage where the mob is hidin' out an' find out what has held these boys up, an' I start walkin' across the field towards where the light is because I reckon that this must be the cottage as it is the only place where there is any sorta house.

Whilst I am walking across this field, I don't feel so good. I don't like the fact that there is a slip-up somewhere, an' I am wonderin' just how this could have happened.

By this time it is gettin' on for half-past one, an' there ain't a lotta time to be wasted. After a bit I get over to the cottage. It has got a sorta hedge round it an' a little white gate. I go through the gate an' I walk round to the back of the cottage, an' there I see the two cars. They have got their headlights out, but the engines are runnin', so I reckon I have got the right cottage.

I walk up to the back door an' I look through a window just on the right of this door. Inside is a room with a light on, an' I can see that there is a table covered with dirty plates an' glasses, and half empty bottles of whisky, but there is nobody inside.

I try the door an' it is unlocked, an' I go in. I take a look around the ground floor an' there ain't anybody there. Then I go upstairs an' have a look round there. This place is as empty as a second grade clerk's pocket on Friday mornin' an' it looks good an' ominous to me.

All round the place is signs that the mob have been using this place up till a little while ago. The lights are on downstairs an' at one end of the table in the living room there is the stub of a cigar still warm. I reckon that twenty minutes ago the mob was here.

Now I am a pretty tough sorta guy an' it is not my way to get frightened of things, but I'm telling you that I do not feel quite so hot about all this. I go outside the cottage, an' I go over to the cars. I put my hand on the radiators an' I find that these cars are only just beginning to warm up. I reckon they was switched on about twenty to twenty-five minutes before, an' what has happened between the time some guy started these cars an' now, an' what has happened to Merris, Lottie an' the rest of 'em is somethin' that I just don't know, an' I can't guess neither.

I open the car doors an' I look inside. In one of 'em there are guns an' four pineapple bombs. The rest of the bombs is in the other car, but there is one thing missin'; although I look everywhere I cannot see a sign of the tommy gun Willie Bosco said that he and Lottie were takin' down with 'em.

I sit down on the running board of one of these cars, an' I light a cigarette an' I do a bit of thinking. It looks to me as somebody has pulled a remarkably fast one because it looks like somebody—an' I'm layin' six to four that that somebody is Siegella— has got wind of my arrangements for tonight an' crossed me up somehow.

All of a sudden I get an idea—Sadie Greene. I get so steamed up I get on to my feet an' start walkin' up an' down. Supposin' Sadie Greene ain't the little innocent blue-eyed that I thought she was; supposin' she was workin' in with Siegella!

This looks like sense to me because after all I reckon if Siegella wanted to get his hooks on this girl an' make her work for him he'd do it by some means or other, an' he never was particular as to means.

Well it looks like it ain't no good wasting any more time, so I take the bombs outa the second car, an' put 'em in the first one, an' I jump in an' I drive down the car track on to the main road. At first it looks like I oughta get straight back to Branders End in case I have been missed, but on second thoughts I come to the conclusion that I had better get round an' see if Sadie is down at the Hollybush Hotel as arranged, because if she ain't there then I can bet my last red cent that I've been crossed up from the one party that I thought was on the level, an' that I reckon from now on I can look out for myself good an' plenty.

I drive down the road like hell an' I get to this dump at a quarter to two. The whole place is in darkness, but after kickin' on the front door for about fifteen minutes some night guy gets up an' opens the place up.

I was right first time, this guy tells me that there ain't never been anybody like Sadie Greene staying around there. I say O.K. an' give him a half a crown, an' light another cigarette because it looks like that it's goin' to be a showdown for me good an' quick. I get back in the car an' I drive back to the cottage. I think maybe I might find somebody there, but the place is just like I left it.

I turn the lights out, shut the place up, an' I walk across the field back to the broken wall at Branders End. Still there ain't no sign of anybody there. I walk through the little wood an' when I get through it an' on to the edge of the lawn behind the house I get a surprise, because the whole house is in darkness. There ain't a light or a sound comin' from this place. It is as quiet as a morgue an' it looks like one to me.

I stand there for a minute an' then I start to walk across the lawn towards the back of the house. It is not a nice business this walkin' across the lawn, because any moment I am expectin' to get a bullet, but nothin' happens.

I walk round the left hand side of the house round to the front, but everythin' is still quiet, an' when I push the big double doors at the front of the house they open.

I go inside. I light my cigar lighter an' find the electric light switch, an' switch it on. There are the two bars still set up with bottles an' glasses but there is nobody behind the bars an' nobody in front of 'em. I go into the dinin' room an' it is the same. I go upstairs in the drawin' room an' there is not a soul. This Branders End place is deserted an' it looks like there hasn't been a guy in it for years except for the stuff that is lyin' all over the place.

I light myself another cigarette an' I stand there an' I think, although thinkin' is not a lot of good to me because it looks like a lot of my ideas have been wrong. It looks like Siegella has been one too good for me, because he has fixed it so that he makes a quick getaway from this place, an' maybe if I had been around they would have given me the heat too. Perhaps it was lucky I was outside.

I go outa the drawin' room an' I start walkin' along the corridor towards the room where Connie took me to lie down. I look into this room, but there ain't nobody there. Half down this corridor I find another electric light switch an' I switch on the lights. Then I walk down further with my gun in my hand just in case they have left some guy behind to settle up with me.

Right at the end of this passage there is a door an' this door is up two little steps—the sorta thing that you get in these old houses—an' I see somethin' which does not look so good to me, because running under the crack of the door an' down the two little steps is blood.

I try the handle of the door an' I push it open. I stand there with my gun in my hand waitin' for something to break, but nothing breaks. Then I feel round on the left of the door, an' I find the light switch an' I turn it on. This room is a bedroom, an' in the right hand corner opposite me there is a window open, an' lyin' up against the wall in the corner with the tommy gun in her right hand an' shot up to hell is Lottie Frisch, an' whoever has given it to her has given it to her plenty, because I reckon she has been shot in about fourteen different places.

I walk over an' I have a look at her. Then I have a look at the drum on the tommy gun, which like I said has got a silencer on it, an' I can see that Lottie has fired about twenty shots outa this gun before they gave her the heat. Also I can see where her bullets have hit the wall on the other side of the room. I look outa the window an' outside propped against the window ledge I can see a long ladder.

Now I reckon I have got the set-up. It is stickin' out a foot to me that Merris an' the rest of the mob have sold Lottie out to Siegella. Either he got a line on what was goin' on or else they got breezy. I reckon that Lottie overheard them talkin' about it or they gave themselves away somehow, an' she went outa the cottage, grabbed the tommy gun, came up to the house through the hole in the wall an' stuck this ladder against the window an' got up, an' it looks to me like somebody was waiting for her an' as she started shootin' they gave her the heat.

I take the counterpane off the bed an' I throw it over Lottie, because anyway even if she was a bad one she had got some guts, which was a durn sight more than these other guys had.

Then I go downstairs to the hall where I have seen a telephone. I take off the receiver an' I ring the Parkside Hotel London an' I ask for Mr. Schultz, because I reckon that unless somebody tips off Kastlin that Lottie has been bumped, an' that the rest of the Goyaz boys have gone over to Siegella, he is likely to get the heat too. I guess they're not goin' to have him pussyfootin' around London tryin' to find out where Lottie is.

After a minute the reception clerk in the Parkside Hotel comes back to the phone an' tells me that Mr. Schultz has gone, an' when I ask him when he went this guy tells me that a quarter of an hour before there was a long-distance call from Mrs. Schultz asking him to go off an' meet her some place at once, an' that Schultz packed his bag, paid his bill an' scrammed out of it.

I say thanks a lot, an' I hang up. It looks like I am too late, because I reckon that wasn't no long-distance call from Mrs. Schultz, who is lyin' upstairs under a counterpane as full of holes as a nutmeg grater.

I reckon that the phoney Mrs. Schultz was none other than Connie, an' I reckon that when Kastlin gets to the place they've told him he's goin' to get his all right.

I am not feelin' so good. I have flopped on this job all right. They have got Miranda an' the next guy for the bump is me an' don't I know it.

I am feelin' lousy, but that's the way it goes, an' after a bit I slide round the bar an' I mix myself a good one. There is nothin' like whisky when a guy is up against a stiff proposition, and the stiffer the proposition, well I reckon you can always make the drink as stiff.

Another thing is that I am a guy who has gotta lot of ideas about not takin' the count until I can't hear 'em countin'. Just at this moment it looks like Ferdie Siegella has got me tied in knots. It looks like I have been crossed up good and plenty by that lousy Merris an' the rest of 'em.

I reckon that if I had handled this job with Lottie that she an' me could have pulled it, but I wasn't to know that these lousy dogs was goin' to start pullin' fast ones, was I?

At the same time I am sorta takin' myself to task about a whole lotta things I should have noticed an' didn't, an' presently I start thinkin' about Miranda.

I wonder where this dame is an' what is happenin' to her. Between you an' me an' the local bootlegger I am not feelin' so good about that dame. First of all because she has gotta lotta guts an' is liable to spit right in Siegella's eye when he starts doin' his stuff, an' if she does this then that guy is goin' to get good an' tough with the dame, an' although I think that Miranda is a silly jane, yet at the same time she has got guts an' I am liable to go for any dame who has guts.

All of which shows you that the guys who have always said that I was so tough that I used to eat French nails was wrong. Really I am a soft-hearted sorta cuss, only what with one thing an' another I don't sorta remember this fact much—at least not so anybody would notice it.

CHAPTER ELEVEN
THE PINCH

SOME guy said that the postman always knocks twice, an' I reckon this palooka knew his onions.

Standin' there in the hall, with an empty glass in my hand, leanin' against the bar, I started passin' votes of censure so quick that it sounded like a street meetin' at the Ironworkers' strike, but after a minute I reckoned that this line of business ain't any good to me, an' that if I had found myself in the same spots again I calculate I should have used the same tactics. I trusted the Goyaz boys because I had to, an' there wasn't no doubt in my mind that Lottie was on the straight, an' so was Kastlin. They was hot to get one back at Siegella an' they meant to play straight with me, an' it wasn't Lottie's fault that Merris an' the rest of that crowd of yeller rats had sold her out.

It looked like that Merris or one of the others had contacted Siegella some time before Saturday afternoon an' blown the whole works an' the man was just stringin' me along for the rest of the day. The only thing that surprised me was that he didn't try to bump me pronto, but I expect he's got something hot on the grill for me.

I reckoned if I knew anything of Ferdie Siegella he had got something good and hot waitin' for me round the corner an' it looked like I had got to look after myself.

I slip behind the bar an' I mix myself another stiff one an' then I go upstairs an' sorta straighten Lottie out a bit. After this I get around the place tryin' to get a line on somethin' but there ain't nothin' to be lined up. The whole works looks just as if suddenly everybody had packed up an' finished an' gone off just leavin' everything as it was.

Downstairs in the servants' quarters there was white coats an' cooks' hats hangin' up all neat an' orderly. It was just plain that Siegella had the whole thing arranged just so that if anybody thought they was goin' to pull anything he was goin' to spoil it by stoppin' short in the middle of the doings an' makin' a break for some dump that he had got ready-eyed.

An' for all I knew he was on his way over to France or some place else with Miranda in the bag. An' that he'd dispensed with my services was as sure as shootin'.

I reckon that I'd a sneakin' sort of admiration for that clever guy.

I went back to the bar in the hall an' mixed myself another highball an' then sat down on the top of the bar an' started to figure out what the next move was goin' to be.

It was plain that Siegella had been ready-eyed for everything. I reckon that one of the Goyaz crowd—Spegla I should think—had, after we had got the whole bag of tricks planned, scared the others into goin' over to Ferdie Siegella, an' they, like the yeller dogs they were, had fallen for the idea, an' I reckon that Siegella had paid 'em good an' plenty too.

But of course they didn't say anything to Lottie. She had come down expectin' everythin' to go off as arranged, an' I reckon that between the time I crawled out of the bathroom window an' went down to the broken wall to meet Merris an' the time I come back after goin' lookin' for Sadie Greene, Lottie had made up her mind to shoot it out with Ferdie Siegella—I suppose the other guys had just pushed off casual like without sayin' a word, leavin' the motors runnin' in order to give her the idea that everything was goin' through on the schedule.

But Lottie—an' she was a wise jane—had smelt something wrong an' had got out the tommy gun from one of the cars an' come over to Branders End to investigate. Maybe they'd left somebody behind to fix her an' that somebody had certainly given her the heat.

After a bit I got off the bar an' went through the front doors, an' shut 'em an' then started a hike right round Branders End, over to the cottage.

I found this dump in darkness just like I left it, an' I went in and had a good look round just to see if I could pick up any indication at all of what had been goin' on around there.

There just wasn't a thing. Everything was just as the mob had left it, an' there wasn't anything that would give me an idea about a thing.

I went outside an' took the guns outa the cars an' the pineapple bombs. A few yards from the cottage was a pool of water an' I dumped the rods and the pineapples in there. Then I went back an' got in the car an' started off back to Branders End.

I drove straight round to the garage at the back of the house. The door was wide open an' it was empty; when I had been there before I reckon I had seen about thirty to forty cars parked around the place. I reckoned—as it was a dry night an' plenty of dust about—that I might pick up some sorta car tracks that would give some indication as to which way the mob had gone, but there wasn't an earthly chance of this because although there were plenty car tracks runnin' down to the carriage gates, once there they spread all over the place an' it looked as if some of 'em had gone one way and some another. Anyhow I reckon that this is what they would do.

I pulled up by the side of the road an' began to think things out. One thing was durn certain an' that was I wasn't finished with Siegella nor him with me, an' it may sound sorta funny to you just now but it sorta seemed to me that I had somehow got Siegella where I wanted him an' that this time I would get him good an' proper. That he would go out to get me was a stone ginger, but I reckoned that with a bit of luck the letter I had posted to the American Embassy was goin' to be a trump card so far as I was concerned. I was pretty pleased with myself over that bit of business.

I turned the ear an' with a final look at Branders End I started off towards London. I was not drivin' too fast because I was thinkin' hard just what Siegella would do an' what his next move was goin' to be. I was also keepin' my eye open for a telephone box, but the country around there was pretty deserted an' there wasn't a sign of any place to phone from.

Pretty soon I see some guy ridin' towards me on a bicycle, an' as he comes closer I see that this guy is a copper. I pull up an' I wave to him an' he comes over to me an' looks at me through the window of the car.

"Good morning, Sir," he says—ain't it wonderful to hear a copper say "Sir," I reckon I know why England is a great country, guys ain't afraid to say "Sir"—"an' what can I do for you?"

"Just a little thing, officer," I say, "but it might do you a lotta good. You gotta notebook? Right, well, how soon do you get somewhere near a telephone?"

He looks a bit mystified but he tells me that his cottage is about two miles away an' that he has a telephone there.

"O.K." I say. "Well, I want you to do this. Directly you get back to your cottage you put a call through to the American Embassy in London an' you ask for the second secretary an' you tell him that in reference to the note he got yesterday about that guy Lemmy Caution, that this guy is on his way back to his apartment on Jermyn now, an' it might be a good thing if somebody did somethin' about it, otherwise it looks like this guy might get himself spilled all over the place as there is goin' to be a little heavy gun play around London if he ain't corralled quick."

He starts to talk back at me, because he is certainly surprised, but after I have pushed a coupla pound notes into his hand an' told him to get off an' do it an' be a good guy, he says O.K. he will take a chance an' off he goes, an' I only hope he means business because I have got an idea back of my head that Ferdie Siegella is goin' to start a big rubbin' out act with me pretty soon.

When this cop has ridden off I start up again an' I tread on it, an' by four o'clock I am in London.

I leave the car at a garage an' tell them that I will come for it next mornin' an' I walk along to my apartment on Jermyn wonderin' what the hell is goin' to break an' hopin' that it is goin' to break good an' quick, because between you an' me I am beginnin' to feel just a wee bit het-up. Two or three times when I am walkin' along I see some guys standin' in doorways, but I don't take any notice, I just go straight along like I can't see a thing.

I open the front door of the Carfax apartments an' I do a big gum-shoein' act up the stairs because believe it or not I am not goin' to be the slightest bit surprised if I see Yonnie Malas or one of the mob sittin' there waitin' to give it to me, an' I have made up my mind that if anybody is goin' to start any shootin' around this dump it is goin' to be yours truly.

When I get into my own corridor I gum-shoe along an' wait outside my sittin' room door. There ain't any light on in the room an' I can't hear anything so I open up the door an' I go in an' turn the light on.

An' there is Constance, lookin' as large as life an' twice as natural, wearing a big black velvet evenin' cloak with a big fox fur collar an' smokin' a cigarette an' smilin' at me like all the rattlesnakes in hell.

I slip my hand into my armpit for the rod, but she waves a hand at me an' grins.

"You needn't worry, Lemmy," she says. "I ain't come here to bump you because it wouldn't be the thing to do just now, although I'd pay a couple of grand to put some slugs through your yellow guts, you dirty so-and-so. I just come along here to have a few words with you an' then I'm goin' to scram out of it an' I hope I never see your ugly mug again, because this is what you are. . . . ."

Constance then proceeds to tell me just what I am. Well, I have heard some descriptions in my time, but I ain't never heard anything like the stuff that Connie pulled. Was she good or was she good? She called me just about all the things that you could think of an' some that even I had never heard of before. She went into my birth an' my mother's profession an' the manner in which I was born, an' what was goin' to happen to any children I might have some time, an' all sorts of nice an' charmin' things, an' she only stopped when she was almost blue in the face for want of breath.

I go over to the table an' I pour myself out a shot of whisky an' one for her. I hand it to her an' she chucks it in the fireplace.

"Do you think that I'd drink with you, you double-crossin' punk?" she says. "I'd rather take a dive in the lake."

"That suits me, sweetheart," I say, "an' if ever I get the chance I'm goin' to be the guy who pushes you in. Alright, you've spluttered a mouthful, an' now you're goin' to listen to Uncle Pete who is goin' to tell you just where you get off the tram!"

I sit down opposite her an' look at her. I'm tellin' you she looks lovely with her eyes flashin' an' her little white teeth on edge. This dame is as wild as a coupla hell cats.

"Listen, you brown snake," I tell her, "what the hell's the use of your comin' here an' gettin' all steamed up just because I have tried a cross an' it ain't come off? What is the good of your puttin' out all that stuff an' cussin' my head off? Did I ask you to take me into this racket or did I? Did I muscle in or did you do a big sister Ann act on Hay market an' pull me round to the dump on Knightsbridge where Siegella pulls a gun on me an' wishes me in or threatens me with the works. Is that a fact or is it a fact?

"An' what am I supposed to do. I started this Miranda stuff first an' she's my bit of business an' I'm goin' out to get that dame in my own way an' anybody who tries anything on with me is liable to get crossed up just like I tried to cross Siegella."

She laughs.

"You cross up Siegella," she says, "why, you big sissy, you couldn't cross up a Good Friday bun. You're so dumb you oughta be lethalised. You're a heel. You was put in something big an' you wasn't good enough to go through with it, you have to start musclin' around with them Goyaz pikers, an' you have to start doin' your short arm stuff with Sadie Greene who has been stringin' along with us ever since she went to work for the Zelden family!

"Say do you think you got any brains? Because if you have you'll want 'em good an' plenty to get you outa the spot you're in now."

I grin.

"O.K. sister," I say, "an' if that's all you've come to spill you can wish yourself out of this apartment, an' go jump in the lake, an' you can tell Ferdie Siegella that I'll be seein' him back in the States an' I'll let him have a coupla my visiting cards out of the end of a forty-two automatic."

She shakes her head at me.

"Listen, Lemmy," she says, "why won't you stop being a sap? You know as well as I do that Siegella ain't even goin' to let you get back to the States. You don't think he's goin' to let you get around after tonight, do you? You're on the spot an' you know it, an' he's goin' to give it to you good an' quick. By tomorrow night you'll be singin' songs in heaven as full of lead as a shell factory."

"Well, maybe I will an' maybe I won't," I say, "but I'm feelin' a bit tired an' you're beginning to bore me, Connie, so if you've said your piece just bow outa here, will you, an' shut the door quietly because I don't like noise."

She gets up.

"Listen, piker," she says. "Siegella is goin' to give you one chance an' if I was you I wouldn't slip up on it. Tonight in that schemozzle with Lottie Frisch when she got hers that bum stepbrother of hers, Willie Bosco, made a getaway. Now Bosco was in with her, an' he wouldn't come over with the rest of the boys. He was sap enough to think he could play your an' her game against Siegella. Well, he's on the run but it's a stone certainty that he's goin' to try an' contact you, an' it's a stone certainty that he's goin' to come here.

"Well, Siegella says that he's got to be bumped, same as Lottie was, an' he says that you're spotted to do it, an' he says that if you ain't bumped Willie Bosco before tomorrow mornin' then it's all fixed that you're goin' to get yours some time tomorrow afternoon or evenin' an' how do you like that?"

I grin some more.

"So Siegella's afraid of Bosco now," I say. "Hear me laugh. I suppose he is afraid of Bosco tippin' off the cops."

"Don't be a fool," she says. "Bosco can't go to the cops any more than you can. Bosco bumped off Price Gerlan last night when some-body turned the heat on Lottie—he was with her doin' a big gun act—an' Price is deader'n mutton. So how does it look for Bosco to go to the cops?

"You might as well say that you could go to the cops. Maybe you could, only I reckon we got enough evidence that you bumped off Goyaz on the Princess Cristabel to fry you any day of the week an' you know it, so you might as well talk turkey."

"I ain't talkin' anything, Connie," I say, "I'm listenin' an' my ears are hurtin' too. Say listen I'm tellin' you I ain't bumpin' Bosco or anybody else just because Siegella feels that way. I reckon that Bosco was a good kid, at least he stuck to the bargain Lottie made with me instead of goin' over to you yellow-bellied thugs an' standin' by whilst Lottie got ironed out.

"So you can tell your little playmate Ferdie that, an' you can also tell him that I don't like his taste in women neither, an' you can get outa here an' stick out because I reckon that you are lower than a coupla rattlesnakes, Constance, an' it hurts me to look at you."

She picks up the whisky bottle off the table an' she takes a swipe at me with it. I duck an' she misses. I put out my hand an' I grab her an' I put her across my knee an' I give it to her good an' hot. By the time I have finished she is white with rage an' if she had gotta gun she would have tried to iron me out as sure as my name's Lemmy.

She sits on the settee gaspin' an' lookin' at me like I was something that crawled outa the sewer.

"Alright, Lemmy," she says. "You're a big guy, ain't you . . . . so what? You wait till I get through with you I'm goin' to make you look like something that the cat brought in, but just now I ain't losin' my temper with you. I'm just givin' you the straight tip.

"Willie Bosco will be comin' around here. He's got to. He ain't got no friends an' no money because we've taken care of Kastlin an' he ain't goin' to worry nobody no more. An' when Bosco comes here you're goin' to give him the heat an' when you've done it you're goin' to come round to my place at Knightsbridge an' tell me, an' then maybe I'll decide what I'll do with you.

"An' if I don't hear from you by tomorrow night, then I'm goin' to fix that you get the heat good an' quick, an' that's the way it goes."

She pulls her wrap round her an' she gets up.

"Listen, sweetheart," I say, "just before you go let me tell you somethin'. I reckon you're feelin' sore in more ways than one because I certainly smacked you plenty just now, an' I hope it hurt you more than it did me, but I ain't goin' to bump Bosco an' I ain't goin' to do anything else for Ferdie Siegella, an' you can tell him so with my compliments.

"Another thing is he ain't goin' to bump me because he ain't goin' to have a chance, an' I'll tell why."

I then proceed to wise her up to the fact that on Saturday morning I have taken down the fifteen grand that Siegella gave me an' changed it for English dough down at the National Farmers Bank's agents on Pall Mall, an' I then tell her about the letter that I have written to the second secretary at the U.S. Embassy.

Does she look surprised or does she? She stands there like a statue an' I can see her brain workin'. Constance is certainly steamed up for once.

"Alright, honeybunch," I tell her, "an' now what happens. Just this—an' here's where Siegella ain't goin' to get me. I'm just stickin' around this apartment until the English coppers come for me. See?

"Tomorrow mornin' if not sooner these cops are goin' to move. They gotta pull, me in an' they'll pull me in. I'm goin' to tell them a story about that money that sounds as screwy as hell. I'm goin' to sorta suggest that I had a hand in that Arkansas stick-up. The U.S. Embassy will be all steamed up at the idea of gettin' the guy who stuck a bank up for a million an' they'll ask for extradition. An' I won't oppose it, see? I'll let them get their extradition order an' I'll go back to the States under police escort. An' if Siegella wants to iron me out he'll have to shoot his way into a jail here before he'll get me, an' when I go I'll have a coupla cops lookin' after me. An' how do you like that, precious?"

She stands there lookin' as livid as hell. She is so mad she can't even think of anything to say—at least nothin' that would really relieve her feelin's.

"You go and tell your little Ferdie that he's got to get up plenty early in the mornin' to string ahead of Lemmy Caution," I say, "an' you can tell him another thing too. When I get back to the States I can beat the rap. I can prove that I wasn't anywhere near Arkansas when that bank stick-up was pulled, I was in New York an' I can prove it easy. So they gotta let me go, ain't they, an' when they do I'm goin' to get after Siegella so fast that he'll think he's being chased by lightnin' conductors.

"I'll raise every hoodlum in New York an' I'll go after that yellow thug an' I'll shoot seventeen different kinds of hell outa him, that is if I don't decide to burn him alive or something.

"Now you run along an' tell him what I told you, an' scram outa here while the scrammin's good, because if you stick around here much longer I'm goin' to take a rubber belt to you an' give it to you good an' hard because you are a nasty piece of work, Constance, an' I believe that your mother was a chicken-stealer."

"O.K. Lemmy," she says in a cold sorta voice, "I'm goin', but I'm tellin' you that I'm goin' to get you for all this. Maybe you've outsmarted us just for a minute but whether it's when they let you out here, or when they get you back to the States we'll get you just as certain as I'm standin' here an' when we get you, Lemmy, it's goin' to take a long time for you to die."

"Sarsaparilla," I say, bowin' to her. "When you see Siegella tell him I'll take a raspberry ice cream with him some time, an' you get outa here because I'm tired, an' the sight of you makes me think of beef drippin'."

She walks over to the door, an' I go after her, because I think that it would be a good thing to see Connie off the premises.

When we get to the front door I tell her to wait because down the street I can see a taxi-cab comin' along. I signal this cab an' it pulls up.

"Hey, driver," I say, "here's a pretty lady I want you to take home."

He grins at me, an' steps down an' opens the door for Connie. While he is doin' this two guys suddenly come outa the doorway next door. One of 'em grabs me by the arm, an' the other quick as lightnin' gets my gun outa my shoulder holster.

I can see Connie lookin' outa the window at me with her eyes poppin'.

"Are you Lemmy Caution?" says one of these guys, an' when I tell him yes, he goes on. "I'm a police officer an' I am arrestin' you on a warrant chargin' you with possessing and changing notes the property of the Federal Government of the United States of America, knowing those notes to have been the proceeds of robbery under arms. I am chargin' you at the request of that Government for the purposes of extradition an' I must warn you that anything you may say may be used as evidence against you at such extradition proceedings."

Connie is still lookin' out of the cab window, so I look up an' I grin at her.

"Well, baby," I say to her as the cab driver lets in the clutch, "what did I tell you . . . give my love to Miranda, honeybunch, an' don't do anything you wouldn't like your mother to know about."

The cab drives off.

After a minute a police car comes round the corner, an' these two guys bundle me in. An' they are takin' no chances either. I can see that there is another police car behind us.

We certainly speed. It take us about four minutes to get to Scotland Yard.

They stick me in the little police station they have around there, an' I am there about five minutes, then they take me upstairs, an' along a corridor.

They open the door of a room an' I go in.

Sittin' round a table are six guys. Two of 'em I don't know, but the other four are Grant, the Assistant Secretary at the Embassy, Schiedraut—a special agent who worked with me once before—Lintel of the *liaison* department at Washington, an' MacFee's brother, Larry.

The guy who took my gun off me hands it back an' Grant of the Embassy puts out his hand an' introduces me to the guy at the top of the table.

"Commissioner," he says, "this is Lemmy Caution, Special Agent of the Federal Department of Justice, handling the van Zelden case. This," he says to me, "is Colonel Sir William Hodworth, the Commissioner of Police."

I shake hands. The other guys come over an' shake too.

"Well, Lemmy," says Schiedraut, "I reckon we thought you'd got yours this time. How're you makin' out?"

"O.K.," I say, "but tell me, I don't want to appear pressin' but has anybody got a tail on my little friend Connie?"

The Commissioner smiles.

"Don't worry, Mr. Caution," he says, "that cab driver who picked her up just now outside your chambers is looking after that."

"That's fine," I say, "an' by the way, Commissioner, just to sorta cement this international police drag-net arrangement you don't happen to have a little drink around here, do you?"

Schiedraut grins an' goes for his hip pocket where he always has a flask.

"Here you are, Lemmy," he says, grinnin' at the Commissioner. "You ain't acclimatised yet. Don't you know they don't keep it in police headquarters in this country?"

CHAPTER TWELVE
SHYSTER STUFF

NEXT morning when I wake up it takes me about five minutes to remember just where I am, because I am in Brixton jail, an' believe me the few hours' rest in this jail, where they have looked after me very well, has been a great relief to me.

Before I came over here I spent an hour over at Scotland Yard fixing up what we was goin' to do, an' we have got everythin' very nicely scheduled. The fly cop, who was fronting as the taxi-cab driver, who picked up Connie the night before, has taken her back to the flat in Knightsbridge, an' the English dicks are keepin' tabs on this place an' it looks like Connie ain't tryin' to move.

Now I have been thinkin' about this Willie Bosco stuff. First of all I was very surprised to find when I got back to my apartment on Jermyn the night before that there wasn't somebody waitin' for me with a gun, an' when Connie began to do all that talkin' I sorta guessed there was something funny flying about, an' that Siegella an' Miranda was still somewhere around in this country. My idea about this is supported by the fact that Constance is still stickin' around, because I do not believe that Siegella would go off and leave her behind.

But the interestin' thing is this stuff about Willie Bosco. Now it is quite true what Connie has said. Willie Bosco has made a getaway after the shooting on the Saturday night down at Branders End. He has got no money an' no friends, an' therefore it's a stone certainty that he is comin' around to the Jermyn Street dump to contact me. But what are they makin' all this schemozzle about Willie Bosco for?

Connie was right when she said that he couldn't go shootin' his mouth to the cops because his own record wasn't so good, an' if this is so what do they want to make all this excitement about gettin' him bumped off for?

It looks to me that there is one reason, an' that is, somehow Willie Bosco knows something—something that is so important that he has got to be blasted outa the way. It looks like they think that Willie is goin' to come to me an' tell me this thing, an' it looks like that once I know the information that he has got I can still be dangerous so far as Siegella is concerned, an' therefore I think that the information that Willie Bosco has got is where Siegella an' Miranda are.

I reckon that maybe whilst Willie was gum-shoein' around Branders End looking for Lottie just before the shootin' took place, maybe he overheard something. Anyway the English cops have got a dragnet out for Willie an' if they are lucky they reckon they will pull him in within twenty-four hours, an' I hope they do. Because if they don't an' Connie or any of the gang find out where he is then it is goin' to be curtains for Willie.

At eleven o'clock Schiedraut comes in to see me. I get up an' I have some breakfast in the warden's room, an' Schiedraut shows me the mornin' papers where I see that what we arranged last night has been done. On the front page I read a splash report that an American gangster by the name of Lemmy Caution was arrested at his Jermyn Street apartment the night before on a charge of possessing an' changin' the notes which were got in the Arkansas hold-up. Then there is a long splash about the Arkansas hold-up an' how many fellers was killed an' a lot of other stuff.

The report finishes up saying that the arrest was made at the request of the American authorities, who are applyin' for extradition, an' that this Lemmy Caution is being brought up at Bow Street on Tuesday. It goes on to say that Caution denies the charges an' insists on bail, an' that it is expected that bail will be set in a very high figure.

This arrangement looks as if it is goin' to work very well. Because I figure it this way. Supposin' Siegella hasn't got his hooks on to Willie Bosco by the time I get out on this bail thing, all of which is arranged, then the next thing is that he knows that Willie Bosco, who will certainly read the papers, will immediately try to contact me. He also knows that Willie will give me whatever information he has got an' I reckon that Siegella will then try to get the pair of us, after which he is O.K.

Thinkin' it out I have come to the conclusion that Siegella has probably moved to some place in some part of the country where he can easily get abroad, an' another thing I reckon is that he is not using any boat. It looks to me that he threw the Goyaz-Kastlin crowd over in the first place because he changed his plans. I guess he came to the conclusion that he didn't need a boat, an' I reckon therefore that he is stickin' around on some part of the coast an' that he is goin' to get Miranda over on to the Continent by aeroplane, an' he can still do this if he is lucky, because although all the ports and airports are being watched it ain't too difficult to get a plane or a coupla planes to come over at night an' land in a field and pick anybody up, so I reckon we have got to get a move on.

Schiedraut tells me that my case is all framed to come up at Bow Street tomorrow afternoon about three o'clock, so as to give Constance an' the rest of 'em lots of time to read the papers, because I have been gettin' an idea in the back of my head that Constance will put up the bail to get me out an' will she be laughin' at the idea of getting me out of stir when I have taken so much trouble to get into it?

Schiedraut an' I reckon that she will be laughing some more on the other side of her face when she finds out that I am a "G" man, an' the whole bezusus has been laid out for her to walk into.

After a bit Schiedraut goes off because he is acting as contact man between myself an' some guy called Chief Detective Inspector Herrick who is lookin' after the English side of the job. Before he goes he leaves me his hip flask which is a very useful thing because they have not got a bar in this Brixton prison, an' I do not like to keep on sendin' out for whisky, an' he also leaves me all the correspondence in this case between my own chief in the Bureau at Washington an' the English cops.

When he was gone I lay on my bed an' I read this, an' it makes sweet readin'. It is dated eight months before.

"Department of Justice, United States Government, Washington. The Commissioner of the Department of Justice for the United States Government has the honour to present his compliments to

his Britannic Majesty's Secretary of State for Home Affairs, and to thank him for the co-operation which has resulted from his recent request to the Commissioner of Police. It is thought advisable to present hereunder the circumstances leading up to the situation in which this co-operation between the Federal Bureau of Investigation of the U.S. Department of Justice and the detective and police forces operating in Great Britain became necessary.

For the past three years the Federal Bureau of Investigation has been engaged in a long and systematic probe into the well-organised criminal activities extending not only over the nation-wide area of the United States but also into other countries.

The organisation of this international gang was traced to an American citizen of Italian descent—Ferdinando Phillipe d' Enrico Siegella, but owing to the clever and calculated methods of this man it has been entirely impossible to secure sufficient evidence in any State in order to bring and sustain successfully criminal charges against him.

It was known that the kidnapping of the child—Thelma Murray Riboux, successfully carried out near Versailles in France, eighteen months ago, was the work of this criminal organisation, and it will be remembered that, even though a large sum of money was paid as a ransom when demanded, the body of this unfortunate child was found in a packing case in a small town in Missouri some seven months afterwards. Five distinct cases of kidnapping in the United States, three in Germany and one as far afield as Scandinavia, have in turn been investigated by the Federal Department, and in each case there have been indications that the same organisation was responsible.

It was felt that the most drastic steps were necessary in order to obtain sufficient evidence to bring definite and provable charges against the man Siegella. Some months ago a series of bank hold-ups took place over six different States in the United States. Large sums of money were obtained from these hold-ups, and in each case the original gang responsible for the hold-up was either taken over or put out of existence by the Siegella organisation. Yet it was noted that none of the notes or gold certificates obtained by means *of these robberies were put into circulation, and it seemed that this money was being carefully kept as capital for some specific purpose.*

Within a year of this Department becoming possessed of evidence which led them to suspect the man Siegella of being the key-note and leader of this subversive and criminal organisation, steps were taken in order to assist in the investigation. It was known that the majority of special agents operating from this Department were known either to the Siegella gang or to smaller gangs operating under his influence, and for this reason a special agent of the first class—Lemuel Henry Caution—who had been operating as a Secret Service agent in the Philippine Islands for the previous five years, was recalled to America.

Caution, however, did not report back to headquarters. He returned to New York from the Philippines on a stolen passport and once there he gradually implicated himself on the edge of petty criminal activities on the waterfront. He was arrested twice within the first six months, was released the first time on probation after serving a few weeks and the second time completed a two months' sentence. He afterwards proceeded to two or three other States in America where by means of undercover co-operation with special agents of this Department he was arraigned from time to time on different criminal charges.

Eventually he was arrested on a carefully framed charge of shooting a police officer and was sentenced to twenty years' imprisonment, his escape being carefully arranged so as to appear as a cleverly planned escape plot some two months afterwards.

By this time Special Agent Caution had secured for himself a reputation of a mobster of the worst description, and was contacting more closely with subversive influences which were slowly but surely bringing him into touch with the Siegella organisation.

Soon after this it was discovered that the Siegella organisation had planned a coup on a grand scale. This was nothing less than the kidnapping of Miss Miranda van Zelden, the only daughter of Gustav van Zelden, who is probably one of the richest men in the United States.

Mr. Caution was able to inform this Department that this kidnapping would take on a definitely international aspect, as having regard to the tightening up of the legal system in the United States and the intensive war which was being waged by this Department on crime of all descriptions, Siegella had decided that the kidnapping of Miss van Zelden would take place outside the United States.

Unfortunately the character and temperament of Miss van Zelden made this plot more easy to carry out. This young lady, who is of a headstrong and wilful disposition, was in the habit of proceeding to different countries at a moment's notice, and under the impression that she was studying life, making the acquaintance of all sorts of underworld denizens in her search for new excitement and thrills.

Mr. Caution believes, and it is the considered opinion of this Department, that the Siegella organisation intend to carry out their kidnapping plot against Miss van Zelden on the occasion of her next visit to England. This is extremely probable as kidnapping plots have already been successfully carried out in France and Germany, and it will probably be considered that a plot carried out on English soil with the transportation of the victim within a few days to some other country on the Continent, would enable the extortion of a huge ransom to be successfully made against Mr. van Zelden.

This Department has therefore two very definite angles of action:

1. It considers that this Siegella organisation should be encouraged—if such a word may be used—to carry out this kidnapping as soon as possible in order that a definite provable and coherent series of charges may be brought against the man Siegella and all members of this international criminal organisation taking part in the plot, and

2. That the co-operation of the British police well in advance of such activity should be secured.

It is therefore confirmed that the conversations on this matter previously held between the Hon. Derek C. Washburn of this Department, the representative of His Britannic Majesty's Home Office, and the Chief Commissioner of Police in London, in which conversations the organisation for combating any criminal attempt on Miss van Zelden within Great Britain was planned, should be put into effect on the lines laid down in those conversations.

The general routine to obtain is confirmed as follows:

*During the interim period between the writing of this document
and the next visit of Miss van Zelden to Great Britain, Mr. Caution,
in his capacity as a gangster whose services are at the disposal of
any one who will pay for them, will obviously make endeavours
to contact and obtain the acquaintanceship of Miss van Zelden. It
is felt that this process will bring him to the notice of the Siegella
organisation, which will conclude that Caution the gangster has
himself designs on Miss van Zelden.*

*On Miss van Zelden's planning to leave the United States for
Great Britain and applying for her passport for that purpose,
Caution will himself apply under a false name for a U.S. passport
to proceed to London. This application will be refused officially,
and Caution will proceed to follow Miss van Zelden to England on
a passport which he will obtain by some illegal method.*

*These careful steps are being taken in order to ensure that
throughout all his activities Mr. Caution maintains his character, which he has successfully held up for the past two years, as a
gangster.*

*On the same boat Special Agent James W. MacFee, travelling
on a United States passport as a Special Agent of the Department
of Justice, will come to England unofficially to act as under-cover
assistant to Caution, and should his identity be discovered at any
time to act as a Special Agent of this Department in pursuit of the
gangster Caution who broke gaol a year before.*

*On the arrival in England of Miss van Zelden and Caution the
latter must be left to make his own arrangements and to keep contact
so far as is possible through Special Agent MacFee.*

*If Siegella is desirous of putting his kidnap scheme into operation
the obvious presence in London of the presumed gangster Caution
will inspire him with the idea that Caution is himself planning
some coup, and it is confidentially expected that Siegella follow-
ing his usual procedure on occasions when he expects to meet with
opposition will find the means to contact Caution and will, in all
probability, offer him a considerable inducement to join forces.*

*This is the situation desired and from this point should this situ-
ation obtain Caution will endeavour to discover the exact modus
operandi to be used by the Siegella organisation, and will, in co-oper-*

ation with MacFee and the British police, make such arrangements as may be necessary for the protection of Miss van Zelden and the apprehension of Siegella and his associates.

Unfortunately it will probably be necessary to allow Siegella to actually obtain possession and custody of Miss van Zelden in order that the charges against him may be pressed fully. If this situation can be organised through the activities of Special Agent Caution then the United States Government will ask for extradition of Siegella and his associates in order that the many other charges which have, through bribery or some other subversive methods, been shelved on previous occasions, may also be pressed, and this criminal organisation broken permanently.

There was a lot more of this stuff an' there was the minutes of the conversations between our boys and these English cops, an' it all looked very swell to me except that I was a bit worried about this van Zelden dame.

By now, you have got a pretty good idea of this Ferdie Siegella. I reckon that his own life didn't mean very much more to him than anybody else's, and it looked a certainty to me that if he thought that the law was goin' to get him he would most certainly bump off Miranda an' shoot it out with the cops afterwards.

That is why I am backin' this bail idea to get me in touch with the mob again. I reckon that Siegella will think I am not so pleased at bein' in the big house here; that he will certainly think that I think he has scrammed outa this country an' that once I get out he will get his hooks on me an' will certainly clean up the pair of us.

I take it easy all day and just hang around smoking an' drinkin' Schiedraut's applejack an' playin' draughts with some prison guard—jailers they call 'em here—who is certainly a scream an' who makes me laugh considerable because he talks English so funny, an' when I read the evenin' editions I see a lot more stuff all about me an' how I am comin' up before the magistrate at Bow Street next day an' a lot more punk.

But at seven o'clock I get one big thrill.

Schiedraut comes in an' says that some English lawyer who has been briefed by some friend of mine is already gettin' busy an' is goin' to make a big play to get me out on bail next day, an' that he is sayin' that the cops have got no right to pull me in here at all, an' that I am the victim of circumstances, an' that the courts here have got no right to take any criminal record I may have in America as evidence in an English court, an' that therefore if somebody puts down the dough they will certainly have to spring me tomorrow.

At about eight o'clock the warden comes along an' tells me that some guy wants to see me an' gives me a card. I read this card an' on it is "Alphone Kranz, representing Soners, Schiem and Hyften, Attorneys at Law, State of New York, an' I say O.K. I will see this guy.

They rush me back to a cell an' lock me in an' after a bit in comes this guy Kranz. He is a shifty lookin' cuss an' it don't take me two guesses to reckon that these Soners, Schiem and Hyften, who are a very hot firm of shyster lawyers in New York are workin' in with the Siegella mob an' are now preparin' to pull a fast one on me if they can.

Kranz starts tellin' me a lotta stuff an' eventually it comes out that he has been instructed by Mrs. Constance Gallertzin—an' this was the first time that I knew Connie was a Mrs. or that her name was Gallertzin—to instruct a firm of English lawyers to act for me an' to get me out on bail.

I say that's O.K. but maybe I don't want to get out on bail at all, an' this guy then proceeds to pull a lotta stuff about there being a lot of misunderstandin' between Mrs. Gallertzin an' myself, but that I can take it from him that everything is okey doke an' that if I am a good boy an' do my stuff Constance an' her friends—an' I reckon that this means Siegella—are all for me an' that when they get me out we are all goin' to be boys together once more an' all that sorta business.

After a lot of persuadin' I say all right an' this guy tells me that next day when I come up before the magistrate that there will be a very good lawyer lookin' after me an' that Constance is goin' to put up the bail if they will take it an' that I will be sprung by tomorrow night.

He then goes off an' I proceed to do some more thinkin'.

First of all it looks to me that it is a swell idea of Constance to spring me outa this jail into which she thinks I have got myself with a lotta trouble an' pay good money for bail just in order to bump me off when they get me out, but I am thinkin' that there is a durn sight more in it than that, an' it looks to me as if Siegella is off some place an' that Constance is runnin' things on her own and gettin' good and het-up about what Willie Bosco might do, that is supposin'—as I believe—that he knows a helluva lot about something that he ought not to know an' that if he starts shootin' his mouth it ain't goin' to do the Siegella bunch any good at all.

As a matter of fact I have come to the conclusion that that big scene that Connie put up in my apartment on Jermyn is just pure bluff. I reckon in fact that neither Siegella nor Connie want to bump me. I am still too useful. They want me for something else first, and the threatening act that Connie put on was just so as to get me in the right frame of mind.

It is eleven o'clock an' I am playin' patience in the warden's office when Schiedraut busts in an' says that the cops have picked up Willie Bosco. Willie is bein' held at some station house out at Hampstead an' he has been pinched on a charge of bein' a suspected person an' is shoutin' for these coppers to ring me up at the Jermyn Street place an' tell 'em that he is an honest to goodness travelling salesman or something like that, by which I conclude that Willie Bosco has been so busy running around that he has not seen the papers saying I have myself been pinched, which is just as well because otherwise he would probably have been too scared to ask for me.

I reckon this is great news. After a few minutes this Chief Detective Inspector Herrick, who is a nice guy an' seems to have a whole lotta brains, Schiedraut and myself get in a police car an' go over to the Hampstead Police Station.

We go downstairs an' we see Willie Bosco in a cell. Willie don't look so good, I'm telling you. He has got a two days' growth of beard an' he looks like he has spent a whole lotta time runnin' backwards through hedges, an' is he glad to see me?

"Say, listen, Lemmy," he says, "these guys have pulled me in on some frame-up. They say I am a suspected person or somethin', an' I don't know what they mean. Anyway, I ain't talking, an' if you will get me a lawyer or—"

"Skip it, Bosco," I say.

I put my hand in my pocket an' I show him my badge.

"I am a Special Agent of the Federal Department of Justice U.S., Willie," I say, "an' I am co-operatin' with Chief Detective Inspector

Herrick of the English Police in wiping up this Siegella mob. Now listen!"

Willie's eyes pop, his mouth sags open an' some beads of sweat start to stand out across his forehead.

"Jeez," he whimpers, "you—Lemmy Caution—a fly cop. Well I'll be . . .!"

"That's fine, Willie," I say. "Now we'll do a little quiet talkin'. You can take it from me that the game is shot to pieces. You can take it from me that in about three days we are goin' to have Siegella where we want him. In the meantime things don't look too good for you, do they, baby? Because what is goin' to happen? It's a stone certainty that within the next two three weeks you're goin' to be brought up here for extradition. That's even supposin' the English police don't want to bring charges against you here for any illegal stuff you've pulled over in this country.

"Now I reckon Inspector Herrick here will support me when I say this. If you're a good kid an' come clean, I'll get the Federal Department to ask the English police to waive any charges they've got against you. We'll get you extradited, an' you'll stand trial in a Federal Court in the States as an accessory to attempted kidnappin'. But if you do your stuff now then I reckon I'm goin' to have a special plea put in for you that you rendered assistance to the Department in cleaning up the Siegella mob, and if you behave yourself, I'll get you off with a two three years' sentence. Otherwise, baby, I have got enough on you to get you fried maybe. Well, are you talking?"

He don't wait a minute.

"Well, of all the—" he says, "just fancy you a cop! Well, after that I don't know anythin' at all. I'm talking, Lemmy."

"O.K.," I say. "Now listen. First of all I want a know what happened to you down at Branders End, an' how Lottie got hers."

"I'll tell you," he says. "Lottie an' I went down on Saturday night. We took the T. gun with us in the car. We got down to the cottage about eleven o'clock. We drove the last two or three miles down there with no lights on an' we came up to the cottage across those fields at the back so as nobody would see us. We parked the car outside with the other car, an' we go in.

"The mob is there. We stick around an' have a drink, an' at a quarter past twelve Merris says he reckons he'd better be gettin' across to meet you as arranged. He goes off. He's back at the cottage at twenty to one, an' he tells us that he has seen you an' that the boys are to go across with him an' hide out at the back of that wood behind the house so as to be ready when you want 'em.

"I reckon this was all hooey, they was just framing us, but it looked as if it was right because it was what we had arranged. Lottie an' me is goin' along, but Merris says no, that you have said that she an' me are to stay behind in the cottage and to wait fifteen minutes an' then start the cars up so that they'll be nice and warm for us to make a getaway. So we stay behind.

"We wait fifteen minutes an' then we go outside an' start up the cars, an' then Lottie gets an idea that somethin' is screwy, because she finds that the mob has not taken the T. gun, the extra rods we left in the cars or the pineapple bombs. Lottie tells me that she don't like the look of this, that she reckons she's goin' to take a walk across the field and see what the boys are at. She goes off.

I stick around for a bit but Lottie don't come back, an' I can't make out what's goin' on. Everythin' seems sorta screwy, so I take the T. gun outa the car an' I scram across the fields, keepin' in the shadow, an' I get to the broken wall. I don't find a sign of Lottie or anybody, so I start goin' through that little wood at the back of the house, an' just when I get to the edge of it I see Lottie hiding behind a bush. The back of the house is in darkness except for some room on the second floor, where there's a light, an' the window open.

Alongside the wall on the right of the house we see a long ladder an' Lottie an' me put this ladder up against the window quietly, an' she takes the T. gun off me an' she tells me to wait, she's goin' to have a look round. So she goes up the ladder an' I see her gettin' across the window-sill. Then she gets inside the room. A minute after this I hear a shot, just one. Then I hear Lottie firin' a burst of about ten outa the T. gun.

I reckon I have gotta take a hand in this, so I yank out my rod and climb up the ladder. Just as am gettin' to the top I see Lottie at the window. She's hit bad because the whole front of her dress is covered with blood, but she has still got the T. gun an' she has also got a big document wallet. She chucks this out to me, an' says, "Willie, scram outa this." Then she turns round an' fires another burst, then I hear some more single shootin' an' I hear Lottie give a sorta squawk. I reckon I can't do anythin' else. I scram down the ladder an' through the wood, an' up to the broken wall, but I am too clever to go back to the cottage for one of the cars because it looks to me like Merris an' the rest of the boys have ratted on us, so I turn right and run along towards London in the fields.

"Pretty soon I get a lift and that's how it is. This evenin' the cops picked me up."

"O.K., Willie," I say, "now that explains a lot to me. Do you know what's in that document case you've got, an' where is it?"

"It's under the floor boards in the room I got near King's Cross," he says, "the cops never even searched the place."

"What was in it, Willie?" I say.

He grins.

"A whole bunch of stuff," he says. "I reckon there's enough stuff in that wallet to fry Siegella an' the rest of his mob about two hundred times over."

"O.K., Willie," I say, "you be a good boy and take it easy, an' maybe I'll look after you like I said."

Herrick an' Schiedraut an' me get back in the car an' drive back to Brixton. We are feelin' pretty good. The whole thing is now clear to me. I know why it is that Constance is so keen to get me out an' I know why it is she wants me to get Willie Bosco, she wants those documents. It looks to me like it is a nice situation, it looks to me like Siegella, the mob an' Miranda, are parked somewhere in the country, an' Connie is behind lookin' after the job of gettin' these papers back.

I reckon the idea is to get me out, because Willie Bosco has got to come back an' find me, because not knowing I am a cop he thinks I am the only friend he's got.

Connie knows he will give me the documents because he reckons I will be able to do a trade with Siegella for him an' for me.

And there you are. A sweet set-up!

CHAPTER THIRTEEN
APPLE SAUCE

HERRICK, Schiedraut an' me take a fond farewell of Willie Bosco, who by this time ain't quite sure whether he's standin' on his ear or his elbow. The fact that I am a fly cop seems to have knocked him for a home run.

We get back into the car an' we streak across to this dump in King's Cross that Bosco has told us about. This place is a dirty roomin' house at the back of some street near the King's Cross depot an' sure enough, there, under the floorboards, is this leather document case.

We don't waste any time goin' through this, an' it looks like Bosco was doin' a spot of exaggeratin' when he says that there is stuff here to fry the Siegella mob, because it looks to me that the best part of the papers are in some sorta code.

However, there is a lotta weather forecasts and wind directional reports—the sorta stuff used for flyin'—an' there is also some night flyin' charts. The weather forecasts are over the period of a week ahead of us an' it looks to me like I thought that Siegella never intended to use a boat but is goin' to take Miranda wherever she's goin' by plane.

Herrick says that the fact that these documents are in code don't matter any because they have got guys round at Scotland Yard who can work these things out in no time, so we scram back there good an' quick an' he hands these papers over to the right department to get this job done.

When we get there we have another meetin' an' I have to tell Larry MacFee that his brother is bumped an' Larry don't like this very much, an' gets a bit keen to get out after somebody an' get some of his own back. I tell him not to worry, that we will clean these guys good an' proper before we are through.

We also get some interestin' reports from the Chief Commissioner who has just got a wireless from New York. This shows that Siegella is goin' through with the job as planned. By this message it looks like that Siegella had started makin' other arrangements about some guy in New York to contact old van Zelden over the ransom money good an' early on Saturday mornin' so I am right when I think that the rat Merris went over an' sold Lottie out very late Friday night, an hour or so after our meetin' at the Parkside Hotel. This decoded message says:

FEDERAL BUREAU INVESTIGATION U.S. DEPARTMENT OF JUSTICE TO F.B. OPERATIVE ATTACHED AMERICAN EMBASSY LONDON ENGLAND STOP ADVISE CAUTION AND ENGLISH CO-OPERATION TELEPHONE CALL RECEIVED GUSTAV VAN ZELDEN THAT HIS DAUGHTER MIRANDA KIDNAPPED RANSOM OF THREE MILLION DOLLARS PAYABLE DUTCH BANK ROTTERDAM WITHIN TEN DAYS IN BEARER SECURITIES INTERNATIONALLY INTERCHANGEABLE UNLESS IMMEDI-ATE ASSENT BY TELEPHONE TO UNKNOWN AGENT IN NEW YORK ONE OF VICTIM'S TEETH WILL BE DESPATCHED EACH DAY BY REGISTERED AIR MAIL UNTIL ASSENT RECEIVED ANY ATTEMPT POLICE INTERFERENCE WILL RESULT IN TORTURE OF VICTIM STOP ASSENT HAS BEEN DULY MADE AND ARRANGEMENTS FOR RANSOM TO BE DEPOSITED AFTER FOUR DAYS' INTERVAL STOP YOU HAVE FOUR DAYS EFFECT RESCUE OF VICTIM OTHERWISE VAN ZELDEN INSISTS RANSOM BE PAID STOP HE REFUSES TO CREDIT DEPARTMENTS' ASSUR-ANCE THAT IN ANY EVENT VICTIM WILL BE MURDERED STOP

ACKNOWLEDGING YOUR PREVIOUS MESSAGE RECORDS DEPARTMENT HERE SHOWS WOMAN CONSTANCE TO BE MRS. CONSTANCE GALLERTZIN ORIGINALLY WIFE OF UNION SICILIONE MOBSTER PATRICK SCARZZI NOW COMMON LAW 'WIFE OF SIEGELLA MOBSTER YONNIE MALAS STOP SHE IS WANTED FOR MURDER AND ESCAPE IN TWO STATES STOP DIRECTOR FEDERAL BUREAU OF INVESTIGATIONS ON BEHALF U.S. GOVERNMENT EXTENDS THANKS FOR BRITISH CO-OPER-ATION STOP PLEASE INFORM CAUTION BUREAU EXTENDS BEST WISHES FOR SUCCESS STOP

By this time we are all pretty tired an' Herrick, Schiedraut, MacFee an' me go back to Brixton an' we teach Herrick to play poker. This guy thought that he knew how to play it before but we showed him something. After this I have some more of Schiedraut's applejack an' I go to bed.

The next mornin' the fun begins to start good an' proper. At eight o'clock Schiedraut and Larry MacFee come bustin' in with the transcript of the Siegella papers that the decodin' department have been handlin'. An' was this stuff sweet? In these papers an' lists was the name of practically every Siegella operative in three countries an' my idea about the aeroplane thing was right because there was arrangements about aero transit hangar accommodation and a lotta stuff like that, an' it looks like that Siegella has got two three planes operating for him between England, France an' Italy, which will account for the mysterious night plane stuff that was appearin' in the English press about a year ago, when a lotta guys said that they had heard aeroplanes dronin' overhead at night but nobody knew who they was. It also looks like that this French kid Riboux was snatched by plane an' taken to Germany an' shipped over to the States from there.

Siegella has made the one big mistake that every big mobster has to make when he gets big enough. He has gotta start puttin' things down on paper. Practically every big shot pinched by the Federal Bureau durin' the last coupla years has slipped up because he has been checked either through the Income Tax people or the State revenue officers.

When he is a little mobster it don't matter. He don't have to worry any about accounts, but directly he gets big he's gotta know where the money is comin' from and where it is goin' to. Mobsters who muscle in on the liquor racket, gaming houses, vice houses, an' all that sorta stuff are doin' business in such a big way that they even have to put their own accountants in. These guys have got to make reports and directly you get papers you get trouble because in the long run somebody always pinches 'em or gets hold of 'em somehow, just like Bosco did.

There is only one thing that ain't in these documents, an' that is where Siegella an' Miranda is just now, an' it looks to me like we've got to find out pretty quick, because I know that guy, an' if he says he's goin' to send one of Miranda's teeth to her old man every day if he don't get the ransom you can betcha sweet an' holy life he'll do it, an' maybe he'll throw in a finger or two for luck.

I told you before that this guy Siegella was responsible for nailin' a feller to a tree up in Toledo. One of our agents who was up there workin' with a mob told me that he heard that the guy stuck around an' watched this guy die.

Now although I reckon that Miranda needs a lesson all right to stop her gallivanting around the places like a big kid, I reckon she has got one by now, an' the idea of them pretty white teeth of hers being yanked out by some thug like Yonnie Malas don't please me any, in fact I am a little bit worried about what has happened to her up to now. But already I have got a pretty good idea as to how I can get next to this racket providin' everything goes all right, although I am a little bit windy about it because it might not be so good for me.

Sittin' there in the warden's office at Brixton with the Siegella papers in front of me, I start thinkin' of the marble tablet that is let into the wall in the main hall of the Federal Bureau of Investigation at Washington. There is a long list of names on that tablet. It is a record of special agents of the Bureau of Investigation who have got bumped whilst in the line of duty, an' I can sorta see my name stickin' at the bottom an' it don't make me feel good any, because although I have very nearly been bumped quite a lotta times it has always been for somethin' that might have been worth it, an' the idea of gettin' ironed out just because this silly hell cat Miranda likes to go rushin' about the place doin' her stuff with a lot of punk mobsters an' generally behavin' like a two-by-four idiot, don't give me any real satisfaction, at least not so you'd notice it.

Now I get rid of this grief on the application of a little of Schiedraut's applejack, after which the world appears to be a better an' a brighter place. I stick around an' have a good lunch an' after lunch we put on the big act. Some guy sticks a pair of handcuffs on me an' they stick me in a patrol wagon that they call the Black Maria, an' they take me round to Bow Street. I am taken downstairs an' presently a copper comes up to me an' grabs me by the arm an' takes me up some stairs an' shoves me in the dock.

There is plenty people in this Court because it looks like the inhabitants of London are keen to get a look at this mobster they have heard so much about in the papers. Down in the well of this Court I can see Herrick, Schiedraut an' Larry MacFee lookin' very stern. I also see the legal expert to the Embassy sittin' around there.

I look at these fellers with great contempt just like real mobsters do on the pictures, only I don't spit.

Then they start movin'. Some guy gets up an' starts tellin' a long spiel about me by which it looks like I am about the worst guy that ever happened. By the time this guy has finished talking about me everybody is thinkin' that I am the guy who taught Al Capone his business originally, an' the people in the Court are lookin' at each other an' wondering if I am goin' to produce a tommy gun outa my ear.

The magistrate, which is what they call this judge, is just sittin' listening with his head on one side, but everythin' is nice an' quiet an' there ain't no wisecrackin' from the people around like you get in the States an' nobody has to bang with a gavel for order.

Presently this feller sits down an' after this the two guys who pinched me on Jermyn Street give evidence on the arrest an' the fact that I was carryin' a gun when I was arrested. When this is over, some nice-lookin' guy of about forty-five who is sittin' next to Kranz who is workin' for Connie, gets up an' I must say this guy puts up the marvellous act on my behalf.

He says first of all that the fifteen grand that I changed down at the bank was done quite openly an' that if I had known this money was pinched I would have changed it some place else, an' not down at a bank. He also says that I am not a mobster at all, that I am the victim of circumstances an' that although things may look very black against me I am a well-known Kansas City business man. That I am over here for my health an' the fact that I am carryin' a gun don't mean a thing because as everybody has read in the papers a lotta guys carry guns in the States. He also says that although I have not got it with me I have been granted a permit to carry a gun in the States owing to threats which have been made against my life.

He then says that I am not opposin' being extradited in the slightest degree an' he makes out that my one idea is to be sent back to the States so as I can answer any charges which are brought against me.

The magistrate is still noddin' his head an' lookin' very stern, and having regard to the fact that the whole of this business is a frame-up I think he is playing his part very well.

This guy who is doin' the talking then says that there is no reason so far as I am concerned why the normal extradition proceedings should not take place, but that I should be allowed five or six days to complete my business affairs in this country, an' that friends of mine are quite willin' to find any reasonable security or bail for me, an' that during this period pending extradition I am quite prepared to report to the police every day.

This magistrate guy then asks Herrick whether he has any objection to me being let out on bail an' Herrick says that providin' the amount of bail is big enough he ain't got any objection. The magistrate guy then says that he will allow bail in two securities of £5,000 each, an' up gets Kranz's pal an' says that is O.K. by him an' that it will be fixed immediately.

Everything looks okey doke, but Herrick now gets up on his feet again an' refers the magistrate to a second charge against me which is bein' in possession of a Luger automatic an' ammunition without a licence.

Now I think this is very clever of Herrick because it makes this thing look good, an' there is a lot more palooka about this gun an' eventually I am fined forty shillings on this charge an' the gun is to be surrendered to the police.

They then let me out of this dock an' I go to some office where there is a lotta papers an' things signed, an' after a bit Herrick comes up to me very stern an' says that I have got to report every evenin' at Cannon Row, an' that if I don't, an' I don't behave myself good an' proper then the ten thousand will be pinched and that I will be pinched too, an' that it won't be so hot for me.

I say thank you very much an' I go outside. Down at the bottom of the steps leading from this Court I see Connie's roadster an' inside it is Connie. She waves to me an' grins outa the window. I go over to her.

"Well, Lemmy," she says, "get inside. I reckon you've been a whole lot of trouble to us one way an' another, but it ain't no good you thinkin' you can get away."

I laugh.

"Well, it's cost you ten thousand to get me out, Connie," I say, "an' at the moment I would like a drink. Another thing I have got no money because these guys have taken everythin' I have got an' I shall not get it back till to-morrow."

"O.K., Lemmy," she says, "I guess we'll look after you. In the meantime I think we'll get outa here."

She starts up the car, an' we drive to some restaurant in Piccadilly where we have tea. On the way there Connie don't say very much, but lookin' at her sideways I think she has got a very nice an' kind expression for a dame who is wanted for murder an' escape an' who is anyway the common law wife of Yonnie Malas.

When we have finished tea, durin' which time I wise-crack about anythin' I can think of, Connie gets down to cases.

"Now listen here, Lemmy," she says, "I've been havin' a long talk with Siegella on the phone about you, an' although you may think he is a tough guy, he is sometimes very understandin' an' I reckon he knew just how you felt about this business. After all, what you said was right, you was in on this Miranda thing on your own an' we brought you into it whether you wanted to or not. Well, you tried to cross him up an' you fell down on the job, but he ain't bearin' any hard feeling. We've got Miranda an' old man van Zelden is goin' to pay that money an' he is goin' to pay it quick.

"We're sittin' pretty. Now you know as well as I do that you oughta be bumped, an' you know that if it was anybody else except you Siegella would do it without thinkin' about it. But he reckons you're a great guy, you've brains an' you've got a whole lotta guts an' he says that it is stickin' out a foot that you two guys should be workin' together, an' that between the pair of you once we've got this Miranda thing fixed up you can do pretty well what you like."

"Listen, Connie," I say, "do you mind turnin' off that soft music dope, because it's givin' me a pain right behind the left ear. Are you tellin' me that that guy has gone to all that trouble to get me outa stir for nothing, an' believe me he's gone to plenty trouble to do it, an' you can betcha sweet an' holy life that it's cost him the forty thousand dollars bail because I'm goin' to skip just as soon as I can. They ain't stickin' me in any more prisons about here. I don't like it an' I don't like the food, neither."

"Well, you put yourself there, Lemmy," she said, "an' one time it didn't look as if we was goin' to get you out, but you're right about one thing, Siegella does want you to do somethin' an' I reckon you've got to do it for your own sake just as much as for his."

She then tells me the story about the documents an' by what she is sayin', allowin' for a few lies which she slips in here an' there, it looks like that when Lottie Frisch was gettin' up that ladder Siegella was sittin' in that room talking to Yonnie Malas an' a few more of the boys about what they was to do, an' generally givin' them instructions, an' he has got all those papers on the table in front of him.

Then when he's finished he puts the papers back in the document case an' everybody walks across the room an' goes outa the door. Yonnie Malas, Connie an' Siegella are the last, an' as they get to the door they turn round an' they see Lottie get through the window on the other side of the room.

As they turn round Lottie brings the T. gun into action, but her shootin' is bad an' she fires a burst into the wall. This was the shootin' that Willie Bosco heard while he was waitin' down on the ground. But Yonnie, who is very quick with a gun, drops to the floor, pulls his rod an' shoots Lottie through the lung twice, but Lottie manages to get to the table an' chucks the document case outa the window. I expect she guessed that these papers was the works an' that it would get Siegella pretty mad if Bosco got 'em. This don't take a second, an' then she falls on the floor, but she makes another go to use the T. gun an' she manages to fire a few more shots, but by this time she ain't feelin' so good, an' she don't hit anything. While she is doin' this Yonnie lets her have some more an' by the time he is finished shootin' she is very dead. By the time they get the other guys lookin' for Bosco he was well away.

"Well, that's the way it is," says Connie, an' those papers are pretty incriminatin', an' another thing, Lemmy," she says, lookin' across at me with an arch look, "is that your name is amongst them papers. It won't be so hot for you if anybody finds 'em."

I nod.

"So what?" I say.

"Well, now, Lemmy, be your age," she says. "Ain't it stickin' out a foot? You bet wherever Willie Bosco's hiding, he's in London, an' you bet that when he reads in the papers that you've been let out on bail he's coming round to see you, because he ain't got any money an' he ain't got any place to go, but he's got those papers an' he knows durn well that if you had 'em you could do a deal with Siegella; that he'll pay plenty money to get those papers back, an' you an' Willie would be sittin' pretty."

I nod.

"That sounds like sense to me," I say, "so then what?"

She takes a cigarette outa my case which is lying on the table an' she lights it, an' she looks at me through the smoke.

"Listen, big boy," she says. "We got to get outa here, all of us. The whole thing's planned out and ready-eyed. It's easy! But before we go we've got to have those papers an' we have got to get Willie. Now here's the way it is. You go back to your apartment on Jermyn, it's a certainty that some time today Willie Bosco is goin' to come through to you on the telephone. You tell him to come round late tonight. He'll come an' he'll bring those papers with him. Well, then it's easy, when you know the time he's comin' you telephone me—I'll give you my number—an' when he gets up to your place you give him the heat, grab the papers, an' I will be waitin' for you with a car some place near. By next morning, big boy, you an' me, Miranda an' the whole works will be coolin' our heels in a nice little place in Corsica, an' everythin' will be hunky dory, an' not only that, but if you're a good boy," she says smilin', "an' you do your stuff properly this time, you're on one million; Siegella says so."

I pick up my cup of tea, an' I look at it, then I drink it an' I put out my hand.

"Say, Connie," I say, "it's a deal."

Pretty soon after this I said goodbye to Connie an' went round to the Jermyn Street place. Before I left her she gave me a Knightsbridge telephone number which I reckon was the number at the flat where she'd been all the time.

When I got to Jermyn Street there was a package waitin' for me. I opened it an' inside was my gun an' a note from Herrick. He was a thoughtful guy, this Herrick. He didn't talk much, but he was pretty good. In the note he told me that in the bathroom I would find a direct private line through to his office at Scotland Yard—an' I call that very quick nice work—an' that he would be waitin' in to talk to me.

I got through right away an' I told him about my meetin' with Connie, an' what the idea was. Then we fixed this.

Willie Bosco was to be released. He was to be given the document case with the papers inside, an' he was to go over to a telephone an' ring me up at Jermyn Street. Then when he came through I was goin' to tell him to come around an' see me about eleven o'clock that night. We didn't want him to come till it was dark because of one or two other little things we had in mind. When he got round to my place it was arranged that I would give him further instructions.

I then fixed up with Herrick what we were goin' to do afterwards, because the way I figured things out if we slipped up anywhere it wasn't goin' to be so good for me or Miranda, in fact it looked like it would be curtains for the pair of us. But Herrick told me I needn't worry about his end of the job because it looks like these guys in England have got a very smart radio system workin' in conjunction with their police cars—the Flying Squad is what they call it—an' Herrick said that this end of the job would be O.K.

Schiedraut an' Larry MacFee would be stringin' along with him. After we got this all fixed up I take a shower an' finish Schiedraut's flask of applejack which was very good stuff, an' just as I am doin' this Willie Bosco comes through on the telephone.

This guy starts shootin' off his mouth an' askin' a lot of questions, but I tell him to shut up an' do what he's told, otherwise he will very likely finish up in the morgue before another day is out. I tell him that he is to come round to my place on Jermyn Street at eleven o'clock sharp an' he is to walk down Shaftesbury an' right across Piccadilly Circus, so that if anybody is keeping tail on him they can see that he is comin' my way.

He will have the document case under his arm, an' that when he gets to my apartment he will be shown straight up. He says O.K. an' I then go to bed because what with one thing an' another I reckon I am goin' to have a very busy night.

At nine o'clock I ring up Connie an' she is certainly sweet on the telephone, in fact if I did not know that this dame was a hot potato I would think that butter wouldn't melt in her mouth. I told her that Willie Bosco has been through to me on the telephone an' that he is comin' round to me at eleven o'clock an' that he is bringin' the papers with him. I tell her that Willie has got a very swelled head about having these papers and that he reckons that Siegella has gone

outa the country, an' his idea is that we should get in touch with a
friend of Siegella's in New York on the telephone an' tell him that
we wanted plenty money to be sent over to England or else we were
goin' to walk round to the American Embassy with these papers.

I tell Connie that I have told Willie that this is a good idea, an' we
have got Siegella in the bag, an' that Willie is very pleased with himself.
I also tell her that when Willie comes round I will look after him all
right, but that I am relyin' on her to fix that I make a quick getaway.

"Listen, Lemmy," she says, "don't you worry about that, all you've
got to do is to fix Willie, an' get along with those papers. Now listen,
what time will you have the job done?"

I tell her that what I am aimin' to do to Willie will not take me
very long. Maybe about five seconds, an' that therefore I oughta be
available for her at the outside at a quarter past eleven. She tells me
that at a quarter past eleven she will be in a tourin' car which will
start drivin' up Lower Regent Street from the Pall Mall end very slow,
an' she calculates that this car will be passin' the Regent Street end
of Jermyn at a quarter past, an' if I am not waitin' on the corner by
that time she will turn right at Piccadilly Circus, go down Haymarket,
turn right again an' up Lower Regent Street. She has also cased the
traffic controls an' she tells me that there is a traffic stop at the junc-
tion of Regent Street an' Piccadilly Circus. The chances are that the
car will be held up in a traffic block an' I can slip into it. This car is
goin' to be a dark green Ford V.8 with black wings.

I say O.K. an' that I reckon I will be standin' on the end of Jermyn
Street at fifteen minutes past eleven. When she has rung off I go into
the bathroom an' I get on to Herrick again an' I give him a description of the car. After which I go to bed some more because I have
told you before I am very fond of bed.

I get up at a quarter past ten an' I get the valet to bring me a
man's size steak. I then dress an' put on my shoulder holster with
the Luger in it, although I have got an idea that this gun is not goin'
to be much use to me.

At five minutes past eleven Willie Bosco shows up. He has got
the document case, an' inside is Siegella's papers which have been
photographed. I give him a shot of whisky, an' I tell him that he will
stick around at the apartment until such time as the cops come an'

pick him up. I also tell him that I have spoken to Schiedraut about him an' in case anything not so nice should happen to me Schiedraut will see that when he is sent back to the States he gets a break, an' that if he is lucky he will get away with a two-three years' sentence.

Willie says thanks very much for the whisky. I stick around till it is sixteen minutes past eleven, an' then I take out my safety razor blade, an' I cut the top of Willie Bosco's finger. I then arrange some blood spots on my left hand shirt cuff. After this I say so long to Bosco an' tell him not to drink all the liquor, an' I pick up the case an' I go out.

As I am walkin' down Jermyn Street towards Regent Street I am not feelin' quite so hot, because it looks to me like this is goin' to be a very near thing, but I don't see any other way of handlin' this job because if someone had been able to show me some other way I would have took it.

At the end of Jermyn Street I stand on the corner an' after two to three minutes I see comin' up very slowly a dark green Ford V.8, an' I can see that Constance is drivin' it. I cannot see anybody in the back of the car. Connie pulls over in front of an omnibus, slows down an' leans over an' opens the door. The car is by this time goin' at walkin' pace. I get in an' sit down beside her, an' as I do so the traffic cop at the top signals go. Connie puts her foot down an' we slide round into Piccadilly.

"Well, Lemmy," she says, an' I see her lookin' at the blood spots on my right shirt cuff; because Connie has got very quick eyes. "I see you got the papers. Did you have any trouble with Bosco?"

"Not a bit, Connie," I say, "not the way I fixed it. When I'd finished with him I folded him up an' stuck him in my steamer trunk, an' I reckon they won't find him for days. So that's that, an' now where are we goin'?" I ask her, because it looks to me that we are goin' in the direction of the Knightsbridge flat.

She looks round at me an' she smiles.

"We're goin' to see Miranda," she says. "She's not far from Oxford. Siegella an' ten of the boys are down there an' we're leavin' tonight by aeroplane."

Chapter Fourteen

SHOWDOWN

WE SLIP through Kensington an' we do a quick streak down the Western Avenue, an' it looks to me by the way Connie handles things that she has made this journey plenty times before.

I don't say anything much except to make a lotta casual remarks about this an' that, but I am keepin' my eyes pretty well skinned an' I start to acquire some admiration for the way these coppers work over here.

Down Knightsbridge we was tailed by a little two seater sports car with two young guys in sporting coats in it, an' this outfit dropped us near Kensington an' we was picked up by a florist's delivery van. The guys drivin' this faded at the Western Avenue, but when we had done about two miles a fellow an' a girl in a sports car come out of a side turnin' an' run with us for about a mile an' then we go on for a bit on our own because I suppose these cops are wirelessin' ahead all the time an' gettin' us picked up just where it suits 'em.

But I am hopin' good an' strong that the wireless is goin' to work alright because if they are expectin' us to keep on goin', an' the cars that are goin' to pick us up an' tail us are goin' to be too far ahead, an' if we turn off suddenly, up some side road we are goin' to be ditched— at least I am—an' I am not lookin' forward to any little meetin's with Siegella, that is unless I am at the right end of the gun, because I reckon that there is goin' to be a showdown pretty soon, an' when the time comes I want to have all my friends around me otherwise I am not goin' to be worth my keep to any guy.

About ten miles on the other side of High Wycombe we come to a sorta track leadin' up a hill on the left hand side of the road. Connie has a look around but there ain't anybody about an' we turn up this track an' at the top we run into a sorta drive that goes through some trees an' at the end of this drive is a house.

I cannot see anybody around an' no cars an' it looks like what I was afraid of has come off, an' that the next police car is too far ahead. Anyhow there it is an' it ain't any good cryin' about it.

I notice that on the left of this house is a very big flat field that looks like it might make a first class runaway ground for an aeroplane to land or take off from, an' this idea is probably right because at each corner of this field I can see a sorta shed place an' I reckon that there is a lighting system of some sort worked from these sheds to signal the landing ground to planes at night.

It is pretty plain to me that Siegella has got this thing darn well organised, an' I reckon that if I was a gangster I would certainly like to work for a guy like him because he has got brains although he has also got a tough way of usin' 'em.

Connie runs the car into a garage at the back of the house. There are two three other cars in this place an' I make a note of this for future reference. Then we walk around an' go in the front door which somebody opens from inside, an' standin' in the hallway grinnin' is Siegella.

He looks pretty pleased with himself an' he is holdin' a glass in one hand an' a bottle in the other, an' as I go through the door he pours out a stiff one an' hands it to me.

"Listen, Lemmy," he says, while I am drinkin' this bourbon—an' it was nice stuff too—" don't let's have any hard feelin's between you an' me, maybe we have both pulled a fast one an' now we're quits."

"That suits me," I say. "I reckon that we gotta let bygones be bygones and start off fresh. But there's one thing has got me burned up an' that is leavin' forty grand with these cops for the bail which we will certainly have to lose unless we axe goin' to try an' hold up the Treasury here."

He laughs some more.

"You should worry," he says. "Why in a week or so we're goin' to be worth over a million each, an' then we can start operatin' properly."

He leads the way an' me an' Connie follow him into some sittin' room that is there on the ground floor. I am carryin' the document case under my arm but up to now he ain't asked for it, an' I just throw it down on some chair.

Connie sits down an' helps herself to a drink and Siegella goes over to a window an' looks out at the moonlight. I see that most of the windows in this place have got iron bars across 'em outside an' shutters inside.

I light myself a cigarette.

"How's Miranda?" I ask him.

He turns round an' grins.

"She's fine," he says. "Mind you, I wouldn't say that she was pleased with things, air she's been behavin' a bit high-hat, but she's alright. I guess we'll teach her a little bit of reason within a few days."

I laugh.

"I suppose she wouldn't come across with the usual agony column stuff for old van Zelden," I say. "Don't you usually get 'em to write a letter?"

"You're right, Lemmy," he says, helpin' himself to a cigar out of a big box an' lightin' up. "She just told us to go jump in the lake, but that's alright, I rather like 'em that way. However, when we get the lady outa this country I reckon we'll talk to her in a different language."

He walks across to me holdin' the cigar under his nose so that he can smell the aroma.

"Howd'ya like to up an' talk to her, Lemmy?" he says. "What about tryin' out that sex-appeal stuff of yours on the little lady? Take him up, Constance, an' let Miranda take a crack at him."

"O.K.," says Connie, "but that dame makes me sick. An' why you stand for all that stuff instead of smackin' her down when she opens her mouth too wide I don't know. I know what I'd like to do to her. I'd like to do what I did to Lottie Frisch round at Knightsbridge."

"There'll be plenty time for that," he says.

Connie gets up an' I go after her. We go up two flights of stairs an' along a corridor, an' there is a guy standin' outside a door smokin'. Connie takes a key off him an' opens the door an' we go in.

Miranda is standin' over against the other wall, lookin' out of the window which is barred like the others. The room is nice and comfortable, an' well furnished. Her hands are tied with manilla rope.

She is lookin' O.K. except that she is a bit pale, an' she looks at me like I was a large beer stain.

"Well, here she is, Lemmy," says Constance, "take a look at the millionaire girl. She wanted to know the gangsters, an'," Connie goes on with a grin, "she knows 'em . . . so there you are!"

She hands me the key.

"Lock the door when you come down, Lemmy," she says. "I'm goin' to wash up, an' if you want to get gay with her go ahead. She can't do nothin' to you. She's just gotta to be a good girl, ain't she?"

She gives me one of them looks an' she goes out.

I listen till her footsteps die away an' then I take out my case an' offer Miranda a cigarette.

She says yes, an' I put it in her mouth an' light it for her.

"Well, Lemmy," she says. "I suppose I asked for it an' I got it, but I was disappointed about you. I don't know why but I somehow didn't think you was in on this sorta stuff."

I look at her an' I can see she has been cryin' a helluva lot.

"All that friendly stuff you put on was just applesauce, I suppose," she goes on, "you were just playin' me along so that I would walk into this, an' now I suppose you're laughing your head off."

"Why not," I say, "you knew I was a mobster, didn't you? What did you think was goin' to happen, anyway?"

"I don't know," she says. "I expect I've been a fool, and I suppose if you go on being a fool long enough something does happen—this kind of thing."

"Right first time, Miranda," I crack back, "an' why shouldn't it happen? People who play with hot coals get burned, an' the devil of it is that sometimes they get other guys burned too."

"Meanin' what?" she says.

"Meanin' nothin'." I get out my safety razor blade, an' I start work cuttin' the rope round her wrists.

"Now you keep your head shut an' don't start askin' a lotta fool questions," I say. "You do as you're told an' we might have a dog's chance, because the way things look around here if anything goes wrong then I reckon we are both booked for slabs down at the local morgue wherever that may be.

"First of all don't you believe that you are goin' to get outa this job easy, anyhow. Even if your old man was to pay that ransom six times over he wouldn't see his little ewe-lamb daughter no more, because Siegella is all set to bump you directly the ransom money's paid, that is after he an' any of the others who fancy you get through with you, an' I don't reckon that you'd have a good time neither, because these guys are not at all nice, an' they didn't learn manners on Park Avenue. What they wouldn't put you through before they finally gave you the heat would be nobody's business."

She looks at me sorta frightened, an' I guess this was the first time I ever saw her look that way.

"Just what do you mean .by that, Lemmy Caution?" she says.

By this time I have got the cord cut an' she is rubbin' her wrists which look pretty numb to me.

"I don't understand, Lemmy," she starts . . . but I butt in.

"You don't have to," I say, "all you gotta do is shut up an' listen before I start gettin' really rough with you. I had to come down here just to find out where you were, otherwise I'd have paid plenty to stay away from this death house, because that's what it can be an' darned easy too.

"Now get this. I like livin' an' I'm goin' to do the best I can to go on livin'. An' it only wants a false move an' we're both for Lead Alley."

I then tell her that I am a Federal cop an' that I reckon by this time the English dicks will have started to concentrate around this house. I tell her that they cannot start anything until they get some sorta indication from me because they know durn well that one false move means curtains for both of us.

Then she starts to cry. Which is the sorta thing that dames do just when you don't want 'em to. After a bit she eases up an' looks at me like I was the Leaning Tower of Pisa or somethin' screwy, an' she starts to do a big act.

"You just can that, sister," I tell her, "because it makes me laugh. I'm doin' this because I get paid for it, an' it burns me up that I should have to get around lookin' after a fool dame like you just because you ain't got enough sense to come in outa the rain."

She shuts up then an' starts dryin' her eyes with a little handker-chief about as big as a stamp. While she is doin' this I am indulgin' in some heavy thinkin' because I do not know where we go from here.

Just whether Schiedraut, Herrick an' the rest of the boys are wise to just where this house is, an' whether they actually had a tail on us all the way I don't know, but in any case this house is a darned hard place to get near because it looks as if Siegella will certainly have his usual lookout guys, an' it is a marvellous night just because I don't want it to be an' the way this house is fixed standing on its own it is difficult for anybody to get up to it without bein' seen.

By this time Miranda is finished with the eye dabbing act an' I take out my gun an' stick it under the mattress of the bed which is in the corner of the room. We have been talkin' pretty quiet in case the guy who is standin' outside in the corridor has got big ears, an' I walk over to the door an' have a look out. I see that this guy has wandered down the corridor a bit an' is lookin' through a window out over the fields, an' I reckon that this fellow is doin' double duty— keepin' an eye on Miranda an' keepin' a lookout along the path that Connie an' me drove up.

"Now," I say to Miranda, "just you get a load of this: Under that mattress is a gun an' it's the only one I've got. Don't you use it unless you have to, but if you gotta shoot anybody shoot 'em good so that they're goin' to stay dead, because if we get as far as that it is goin' to be serious business.

"I'm goin' to go downstairs an' see Siegella. I'm goin' to tell him that you are bein' a good girl, an' that you're goin' to do what you're told, an' then I am goin' to take a walk around on some excuse that I gotta think up. If I can see some of these cops around here then I will start something if it looks like we can pull it off quick, an' if you hear any shootin', then you grab that gun an' just shoot your way outa here if you can, because it will mean that something has happened to me an' I can't get along.

"Once you get outa here just keep down the path over this hill place until you get on to the main road an' somebody or other'll pick you up alright because if anything ain't gone wrong this part of the world oughta be lousy with coppers."

"Alright, Lemmy," she says. "I reckon it isn't much good my saying anything now, but I think you're a great man, an' if ever I get out of here I'm goin' to find some way to make that plain to you."

"O.K.," I tell her, "that's alright by me an' if you like you can get old man van Zelden to build me a coupla monuments like Nelson's column somewhere around forty-second street where the boys know me."

An' with this crack I get out.

When I get out into the passage I turn around an' shut the door an' pretend to lock it. I am holdin' in my hand a yale key that I have taken off my own key ring, an' I then walk down the corridor an' hand this key—one that won't open Miranda's door—to the fellow who is lookin' outa the window. He is a nasty lookin' piece of work an' I am wonderin' where I have seen his ugly mug before.

Then I go downstairs an' I go into the sittin' room. Siegella is there at the table smokin' his cigar an' goin' through a lotta papers. Connie is sittin' in the corner of the room readin' the photogravure section of some dames' paper an' there are a coupla tough eggs hanging around just doin' nothin'.

Siegella looks up.

"Well, how's the dame, Lemmy?" he says. "Is she listenin' to reason?"

I grin.

"She's all right," I tell him. "She's just a bit worked up that's all, an' wouldn't you be if you was snatched? I talked to her an' she listened all right, an' she says she's goin' to be a good girl an' string along because I told her that's the way she has to be if she wants to see the old home town some more."

He nods.

"Like hell," he says. "Only whatever she does she won't see nothin' of the old home town."

He starts grinnin' again, an' I think I would like to smack that grin off him with a baseball bat.

"I reckon that when we have got this ransom money an' everything is hunky dory, that I know a guy in the Argentine who will pay a little money to take Miranda over," he says, "an' that is the easiest way outa the job, because then when she don't show up no more we can tell her old man that she decided to go to Buenos Ayres an' we couldn't stop her goin'. An' we will fix it so that we can prove she went there, an' if they like to get busy an' find out what has happened to her, well, I reckon that's their business."

I take one of his cigars out of the box an' I light it.

"Do you reckon that that is necessary?" I say. "What's the matter with lettin' the dame go when we get the money. There'll only be a lotta trouble if she don't show up."

"Be your age, Lemmy," he says. "Do you think that I'm goin' to have this dame kickin' around shootin' off her mouth about us? She knows who we are an' all about it, an' I personally ain't goin' to get myself in any spot where I can be identified by some dame that I have snatched. Sendin' her to the Argentine is better than bumpin' her because I reckon that when she's been there a week or so she'll be durn glad to bump herself off. The guy she's goin' to has got medals for makin' women wanta commit suicide."

I get up.

"Alright," I say, "you're the boss. Well, I reckon I am goin' to get a little air, because these cells in this Brixton dump of theirs ain't so airy, although they are better than one or two I been in way back home."

"O.K.," says Siegella, "You get around, Lemmy, but if you're a wise guy you won't go far. I have got guys all around here in the woods an' shrubberies keepin' an eye open, because when it gets a bit later we're goin' to put on a light or two so's the plane can see where to come down. I reckon we'll be outa here in about an hour's time an' then it's goodbye England for us."

I walk out an' I cross the hall an' open the front door an' I go out. It is a grand night an' so light that you can see fine. I take a walk around the house an' I can't see nothin', except in two-three places I see guys hangin' about, an' then I start to wander down the path that Connie an' me drove up when we arrived—the one that leads down to the main road.

This path is a sorta cart track an' on one side is a wood an' the other is just plain fields with hedges. Away on the right, formin' a sorta table top on the hill is the place where the planes are goin' to land an' take off, an' believe me Siegella has certainly picked a spot for it, because this place is as lonely as a desert, an' if we had not got tapes on it the way we have I reckon that he would have got away with this business as easy as easy.

An' I am not quite certain that he is not goin' to get away with it now.

I am peerin' about all over the place, an' although from where I am standin' against a tree at the side of the track I can see the main road, way down in the distance, I cannot see a sign of a car or any cops or anything, an' I am beginnin' to think that this does not look so good an' that maybe the wireless stunt has gone wrong like I have known it to slip up before an' that Herrick an' his cops have gone some place else.

While I am standin' there I see, all of a sudden, comin' up the road from the High Wycombe direction a car, an' believe me it is goin' some. I think for a minute that maybe this is the first Flyin' Squad car, but I am wrong because when it gets to the place where we turned off it shoots round an' after a minute or two I see it comin' up the hill, an' it is stickin' out a foot that it is goin' to pass me an' go right on up to the house.

An' whoever is drivin' that car is either drunk or silly because it is swayin' and shootin' all over the road.

I stand by the side of the road, outa the way, an' in a few seconds the car comes up towards me.

It is goin' pretty slow now an' I can see that it is a racin' sports car an' that it is bein' driven by Yonnie Malas.

He has gotta cap pulled down over his head, but underneath the cap I can see that he has got his head tied up an' the blood is runnin' down one side of his face.

I jump out an' wave to him an' he stops the car, an' I go over.

"Hell, Yonnie," I say, "what's the matter. Are you hit bad? Let's have a look at you."

He is breathin' hard an' it is durned easy to see that he is hit bad.

"Come here, Lemmy," he says, "I gotta tell you somethin'."

I lean over the car an' he shoots his head out and he catches me by the coat collar, an' I can see that in his other mitt is a gun. He is lookin' at me like all the devils in hell an' I can see the little trickle of blood runnin' down his neck from where he has been shot somewhere in the head.

"So I got you," he says, "you double-crossin' rotten cop, an' I'm goin' to give you yours, an' right now."

"Say listen, Yonnie," I say, "what the hell are you talkin' about. Are you bats or screwy or what?"

"You bumped Bosco, did you, you yeller liar?" he says. "Well, let me tell you somethin', we ain't so darned dumb as you thought we was, an' I stuck around after you'd left your place in Jermyn an' I saw them cops come an' take Willie Bosco outa that dump of yours, an'

I shot the dirty so-an-so just as they was gettin' him into a car, just the same way as I'm goin' to give it to you, you lousy double-crosser."

"Don't be a fool, Yonnie," I say, "Look, here they come!"

He does what I want him to. He turns his head for a minute an' I smack him across the face with a dragged punch, an' get my hand on the gun. He makes a bit of a struggle but he is pretty weak, an' I pull the gun outa his hand.

Like a mug I think I am on top of the situation an' I step back an' as I do this he steps on the accelerator an' the car shoots forward.

I take aim for one of the back wheels an' fire, an' while I am doin' this Yonnie who has got another gun in the car turns around at the wheel an' lets me have a couple.

One of 'em gets me. Right across the top of the shoulder where the nerve is, an' I give a squeal an' drop because that nerve hurts plenty when hot lead hits it, an' by the time I have changed my gun to the other hand an' got up again Yonnie is a good way up the hill.

I fire four more shots at him an' I hope to cripes that I have got him, an' I then start to run up this hill like hell, because I reckon that the game is well bust open now, an' that if Yonnie arrives with the good news then they will iron out Miranda pronto.

My only chance—an' I am backin' on this—is that I have hit this guy an' that what with the other wound he has got he will not last out until he gets to the house.

An' when I get up to the top of the hill that is the way it looks because ahead of me I can see the car is goin' very slow an' snakin' all over the place, an' I can see Yonnie doubled up over the wheel an' it looks like he is certainly handin' in his dinner pail good an' fast.

I run like hell, because I reckon I gotta get to that house, an' good an' quick, but he evidently knows I am comin' along, because he makes an effort an' puts his foot on the gas.

The car shoots forward just as I am almost up with it, an' Yonnie drives clean up the front steps of the house an' smacks through the open double doors, an' right into the hall, an' the car smashes into the wall on the left.

I think I can still make it, an' I put on a spurt an' get into the hall just as Siegella an' Connie an' some more thugs get outa the sittin' room.

Yonnie pulls himself up over the wheel. His face is covered with blood an' I can see where I have hit him again through the neck.

He points to me.

"We're crossed up," he gasps. "That dirty . . . the cops . . . I the cops . . . !"

CHAPTER FIFTEEN
CONNIE PULLS ONE

I YANK up my rod an' am just about to start a little fireworks when I realise that the gun is empty, an' before I can do anything about half a dozen guys are on top of me an' they are not bein' particularly gentle.

Eventually when I get on to my feet, I can see Siegella bendin' over Yonnie, an' then he straightens up an' looks at me with his usual grin.

"Shut the doors, boys," he says, "an' fix it so they won't open."

Then he looks at me.

"So you did it again, you rat, did you?" he says. "So you shot your mouth to the cops, did you? Alright, well, you see what we're goin' to do to you."

I straighten up. From up the stairs an' outa the other rooms a whole lotta guys have streamed in. There are about fifteen of these toughs an' they are all hardboiled as hell.

"Listen, Siegella," I say. "Get this straight. I ain't been shootin' off my mouth to the cops, because I *am* a cop, see, an' I'm takin' you an' the rest of this bunch."

He starts to laugh.

"So you're takin' us, are you, Mr. G man?" he says. "Listen to me laughin'. We ain't goin' to be taken by nobody an' I reckon I'm goin' to give you a paraffin bath, an' Constance here will light it for you."

I stall for time.

"Listen," I say. "Here's how it is. You ain't got a dog's chance, an' this place is lousy with cops. They'll be here in a minute anyhow, an' you can see for yourself. Now why don't you be your age an' not make it any worse for yourself than it's goin' to be?"

"Nuts," says Siegella. "You an' your tin badge make me sick. Just like your little frame-up with Miranda upstairs made me sick. Connie just got that gun off her when she tried to do a big wild west act with it, an' we're goin' to give it to her too, an' . . . ."

Just then some guy busts down the stairs.

"Boss," he croaks, "they're all round the place. They're in the signal huts on the other side of the field . . . . they're comin' across now."

"O.K.," says Siegella, an' he starts to laugh.

"Here's the showdown, boys," he says. "Close the place up—pull the shutters an' get two Tommy guns on the roof. It's them or us an' if they take us we'll die anyhow, because there ain't a guy here would get away anything so easy as fifty years."

He signals to Ritzkin.

"Take him upstairs an' chuck him in that room with little Miranda," he says, "an' then get some guy to sneak out the back way round to the garage an' get half a dozen tins of petrol. Say boys, you remember what we did to that guy at Joplin—the one who crossed us up there—well, we'll repeat the dose."

He turns to me.

"Lemmy," he says. "I reckon I finish here, an' I'm goin' to see that you get yours. In about five minutes we're goin' to give you a nice little bath, an' Miranda can watch you take it before we give her the heat. Take him up, Tony."

The place is bristlin' with guns as Ritzkin takes me up the stairs. I am feelin' pretty lousy because this wound I have got in my shoulder is not so good.

Ritzkin takes me along to the room where I left Miranda, an' some other guy who is with us ties up my wrists an' they chuck me in the room an' lock the door. I can see Miranda is tied to the bedposts an' is tryin' hard to smile.

Just then there is a burst of fire from somewhere above us, an' I reckon that somebody has opened fire on the cops from the roof with a Tommy gun. I can hear shootin' from all around the house.

I flop down on the floor an' lean up against the wall, because it looks like to me this was the end of the story so far as I am concerned an' it don't look so good for Miranda either.

Presently she starts talkin'.

"What will they do to us, Lemmy?" she asks.

I try to grin.

"Why ask me?" I say. "What do you think?"

I don't allow that they're goin' to give us the freedom of the city. I reckon that this is where we get the heat good an' proper. It's curtains for two, Miranda, an' if you've got religion or anything like that in your system, I'd get down an' say my prayers nice an' quick, just so's you don't get interrupted."

While I am talkin' the door opens an' I can see it is Connie. The shootin' has died away a bit, although there is an occasional rattle from upstairs as the guy on the roof starts to play tunes with the Tommy gun.

There is a light in the passage outside an' behind Connie I can see a guy with a lotta tins of petrol on his way. Down the passage I can hear 'em emptyin' this stuff into a bath.

Now an' then a fierce beam of light comes in through the window, an' I reckon the cops outside have got a searchlight from somewhere playin' on the house, but I don't know that it is goin' to do me any good, because I reckon that they cannot rush this place an' are goin' to take their time about it, because I suppose that they believe that after this waitin' about Miranda an' me are already ironed out.

At this moment I am wishin' more than anything else that I had a cigarette.

Just then Connie opens the door wide an' comes in. She walks over to me an' she puts a cigarette in my mouth an' she lights it, an' then she does the same to Miranda.

From the roof above there comes another burst of firin', an' downstairs somebody gives a howl as he gets some hot lead.

"Listen, Lemmy," says Connie, "I wanta talk to yon."

I look up at her. She has shut the door behind her but the moon is now shinin' through the window an' I can see her pretty plain. She has got an automatic gun in one hand an' a cigarette in the other, an' she is sorta smilin' a faraway smile like the look on the face of your favourite film star when she does a close-up—all teeth an' what have you got.

Anyhow I know that Constance is as screwy as hell, an' I would just as soon believe anything she said as I would listen to a travellin' salesman, but I reckon that she is goin' to pull some act, an' when she gets that faraway look in her eyes I know that she is goin' to talk about love or something else just as screwy.

I can see Miranda lookin' at her, an' then at me an' she looks like a tiger. I reckon that if Miranda an' Connie got down to it good an' proper an' no stallin' they would just about tear each other to pieces, because these two dames were just opposites. Miranda was a thrill-seekin' sportin' young woman who had been brought up to believe that she was entitled to anything she wanted, an' Connie, like the rest of her sort, had brought herself up to know what she wanted an' go out an' get it.

Anyhow Connie comes over to where I am, an' she stands there lookin' down at me, an' I can see that she has sure got swell feet an' ankles, an' it's durn funny, but even fixed as I was there with darn little hope, I got comparin' Connie's ankles with Miranda's which just goes to show what mugs some guys can be, don't it?

Then Connie starts to talk:

"Listen, big boy," she says, "I gotta talk quick an' you gotta listen an' think quick. I don't know why it is, but you know, Lemmy, I've always had a soft spot for you, an' I suppose that underneath everything I'm a woman same as any other one."

"I wouldn't know that, Connie," I say, "I ain't looked, but I'm prepared to take your word for it. So what?"

"Well," she says, "What about you an' me doin' a deal? I reckon that if I can get you two guys outa here, then you ought to give me a break. You ain't got anything on me anyhow, except this kidnappin' business, an' if I get Miranda outa this then I reckon I've squared the book."

"Ain't you marvellous, Connie?" I say, an' I am hopin' that Miranda will kill that look of hope that is comin' over her face—" but you gotta remember that you been an accessory right the way through, an' all I could do for you would be to prove that you did your best to get us outa here when you knew the game was up, an' that we had got Siegella in the bag, but if you're content to do that then it's O.K. with me."

"Alright," she says. "Well, here I got another proposition. I gotta car parked near here. I had it for two days hidden in a dump in the bushes down the road. If I spring you two guys outa here an' we three get off together, will you give me a break an' let me get away in that

car, an' see if I can beat the cops to it. I reckon that's fair enough .
. . . . if they get me they get me, an' if I am smart enough to make a
getaway I reckon I've given you a fair deal."

"It sounds good," I say, "an' what is Siegella doin' while all this
is goin' on."

She smiles.

"Don't you realise that I'm for you, Lemmy?" she says. "I reckon
that I've always been stuck on you, an' I just can't bear the idea of
your dyin' the way Siegella has fixed for you. Can't you see I'm tryin'
to give you a break an' this silly jane too?"

I start breathin' again because it looks to me as if Constance means
what she says an' am I tickled at the idea of even gettin' a chance to
get outa this hell-broth that I am sittin' in.

"O.K.," I say, "but the first thing you can do is to cut my hands
an' give me a gun, an' then I'm agreein' an' not before."

She don't say anything. She just comes over an' takes my safety
razor blade outa my pocket where I tell her an' cuts the cord around
my wrists; then she does the same for Miranda, an' then she hands
me the automatic.

"I can't do much fairer than that, can I, Lemmy?" she says sorta
piteous, an' when I look at her I see tears in her eyes.

"Now listen," she goes on. "In a minute Siegella is goin' into one
of the back rooms downstairs to burn some papers he don't want the
cops to get their hooks on. I'm goin' to get myself another gun an'
when he's in there I'm goin' to let him have it. I reckon I gotta choose
between him an' you, Lemmy, an' I'm choosin' you."

"That's swell, Connie," I say, "but there's just one thing that I
wanta make certain of an' that is that the guy does get his, an' I don't
mean maybe."

"Don't you trust me, Lemmy?" she says.

"You bet I don't," I tell her. "I been listenin' to people like you for
a long time, Connie," I go on, "ever since I first started gettin' around
with the mobs an' it don't get me no place."

I walk over to her.

"Listen, baby," I say, "I'm for Siegella gettin' his quick, first of
all it saves a whole lot of trouble an' secondly, that is supposin' they
extradite him when they get him, that he don't pull any of his usual

stunts with the jury. You gotta remember that this guy can pull a lot over the other side that he wouldn't be able to pull here. But if these cops get him then I reckon that Uncle Sam is goin' to ask to try him first an' there's just a chance that he might pull a very fast one an' get away with it, so I'm all for execution on the spot, an' I don't know anybody who's better suited to do it than you, an' if you do it then I'll believe you're tryin' to play straight with me."

She looks at me sorta piteous again.

"I'll fix him, Lemmy," she says. "I gotta make you believe in me. I gotta show you I'm trying to make out. Just stick around for a minute an' I'll fix him."

"Okey doke," I say, "but I didn't sorta reckon that you would take a run-out^ powder on Siegella, Connie. Ain't this a bit sudden?"

She is almost at the door an' she spins around.

"Ain't you got any sense, Lemmy," she says, "or are you dead from the neck up? The cops are all around us. They're closing in from the runaway side of the field. They're down on the road, an' it's just a matter of an hour or so before they'll get us.

"Well, ain't I entitled to a chance? What has Siegella done for me anyhow? I reckon I hate that punk, an' I allow that here's where I give him his, an' what's more I'm goin' to like doin' it."

"O.K., sister," I say, "only mind he don't see you comin'. Otherwise he might iron you out first an' what would we do without our little Constance."

While I am speakin' there is a grunt from outside the door. The guy who has been standin' at the window in the corridor has got his. Some cop has registered on this guy's neck an' he slides down to the floor in a lump and dies. Connie goes over to him an' she takes the rod out of his fist an' she sorta looks wise at me over her shoulder an' she goes off.

Miranda comes up for some more air.

"Oh, it's wonderful, Lemmy," she says. "We're goin' to get out of here. I didn't think we had a chance. . . . . ."

"Pipe down, gorgeous," I say, "an' don't start countin' any chickens yet."

I walk over to the window an' standin' with my back to Miranda I pull the ammunition clip out of the automatic that Connie has just given me. It is empty. There ain't a shell in it, which just goes to show you what a sweet little four-flushin' twicer this dame Constance is. I tell you the dame is so screwy that she would make a corkscrew look like a West Point flagpole.

"Listen, Miranda," I say to this jane, who is still rubbing her wrists, "if you think that you're outa this jam—come again. You ain't an' you might never be. This Connie bit has just handed me out an empty gun an' I don't like it, an' if I know anything of her she's goin' to pull a fast one in a minute so watch your step, Miranda, otherwise some guy will probably have you on a catsmeat stand next week."

After a minute or two we hear Connie comin' back. She comes in an' she is very white about the mouth, an' she is cryin' like smoke.

"I done it, Lemmy," she says. "I bumped him. He was in the back room an' I gave it to him. He fell over the desk sorta lookin' at me an' it made me feel like hell. Now come on an' let's get outa here!"

She leads the way down the passage, an' we go through a room at the end an' down a stairway, an' we cross the room at the bottom an' go along some balcony an' into a sorta loft and from here we drop down into the garage.

Connie is leadin' the way an' she has got her handbag under her arm, an' just when she gets to the doors of the garage I pull the handbag away from her an' I open it.

"Now, don't get excited, sweetheart," I crack, "because upstairs you issued me with a gun that ain't got any lead, in it an' when I use a gun I like one that shoots."

I take the gun she has got in the handbag an' put the empty automatic in its place. She don't say nothin', she just leads the way out of the garage an' we start to make for the path leadin' down to the road.

From away over at the right I can hear a lotta shootin' an' I reckon that the cops are closin' in on the house from that side, an' they are not worryin' much about this side because they have got plenty people down on the road, an' they reckon that nobody can make a getaway from this direction.

When we have got about one hundred yards down the track Connie takes a path leadin' off to the left an' we go down this for a bit an' away at the bottom I can see a clearin' an' on the other side of it is a roadster standin' there with the moonlight shinin' on it.

An' my nose tells me that a whole lot about this business is screwy so I let Connie go well in advance of me, with Miranda bringing up the rear, an' I am just waitin' for something to happen, an' as we walk into the clearin' it happens.

Siegella gets up from behind the car where he has been hidin'. He is grinnin' like a coupla hyenas. He has got a rod in his hand and he don't seem to be worryin' about the one I've got. I get a sorta sickenin' feelin' that there is something wrong about this rod too.

Connie suddenly springs ahead an' runs round the car to Siegella. I jerk up my gun, an' she starts laughin'.

"Be your age, Lemmy," she says. "That gun ain't loaded either. I thought that you might get clever about the first one an' pull mine off me so I took the shells out. Well, how d'ya like it?"

"Nice work, Connie," I say, "but one of these fine days somebody is goin' to give you yours an' it won't feel so good."

Siegella laughs. He is pointin' the gun at me, an' it looks like he is enjoyin' himself.

"Well, sucker," he says. "I'm goin' to give you two the heat an' then we're scrammin' outa here. I reckon that you fell for that little story of Connie's pretty good, didn't you! Maybe we'll get away with it, and maybe we won't but we'll make a certainty of you two first. So if you believe in Santa Claus you can get down an' say a few prayers, Mr. G man, because I'm goin' to blast you an' I'm goin' to give it to you in the guts."

Miranda has been standin' behind me, an' I feel her move. She walks round to my side.

"Just one minute, Mr. Siegella," she says. "I think that you're forgettin' something." She takes a coupla paces forward so naturally that he don't do anything an' then, quick as a knife, she throws her shoe straight at him. While she was standin' behind me she had been slippin' it off.

He fires, but his aim is deflected an' he gets me through the top of the shoulder—which is the second one that night. I reckon that there ain't anything to it but a showdown an' I go straight for him, an' I am lucky because the next time he fires the automatic jams which is a very nice thing to happen when some guy is shootin' at you.

I jump straight for the car an' out the other side as he is backin' away. I go straight at him an' I hit him with my head as I arrive which is an old trick I learned in the Philippines.

The guy is no fool at infightin' an' he lets me have it in the stomach with his knee an' I feel that I have been kicked by a squad of racehorses, but I grab him again, an' we roll down a bank into a sorta dip beneath.

We do everything we know, an' the man is fightin' like he never fought in his life. I am not feelin' so very good myself, because my shoulder is givin' me hell, but I am pullin' a lot of dirty tricks that I have learned since I have been gettin' around with the mobs an' by the time I have got my thumbs in one of his eyes an' am screwin' his head round with my leg an' kickin' him in the face every time his head jerks back he is not feelin' so good either.

But I know that I am gettin' weaker every minute because I can feel that I am bleedin' from my shoulder an' this guy is in good condition an' I reckon that I have gotta pull a fast one on him otherwise it is goin' to be curtains for Lemmy.

So all of a sudden I go sorta limp, as if I was finished. I let go with my hands, an' I relax with a grunt, an' the sucker falls for it. For just a split second he lets go, an', as he does so, I shoot out my two legs, scissor him an' throw him flat, then, before he can move, I get a leg lock round his neck an' after a minute I get a first-class Japanese neck hold on him.

This neck hold is a daisy. It was shown me by some Japanese judo merchant that I once got out of a hole, an' it's something like a half Nelson only a durn sight worse, an' it hurts good and hard.

By this time I have got him turned over on his face, an' he strugglin' and workin' against my right arm which is under his neck, an' tryin' to move my left arm because he knows I am hurt at that shoulder, but I am buttressin' my left arm with my left leg an' he can't do a thing.

He tries to throw me, but I hit him a flat one across the back of the neck with my leg an' I tighten my grip with my arms.

"Listen," I tell him, "An' you ought to listen because you ain't goin' to hear any more after this. I'm goin' to make a certainty of you. I'm goin' to finish you like the lousy rat you are. Have you got that?"

He groans.

"Listen, Lemmy," he pants, "I can give you plenty dough. I can make you a big shot. I can—"

I smack him another one across the neck.

"You can't do a thing," I told him. "An' you ain't never goin' to anything after today, sweetheart, except push up flowers wherever they stick your bum carcass. But before I give you the works you gotta listen to this.

"For a coupla years an' some months I been stringin' along with your lousy friends an' your cheap mobsters. I just had to do it because that's the way Uncle Sam's workin' these days, an' I had to like it.

"You an' your sort ain't worth two shakes in hell. You're lousy and you're yellow. You'd walk out on your own mother just like you an' your lady friend Connie have taken a run-out powder on the mob that you've left up there in the house. Them guys are rotten too, but they was decent enough to stick to you an' you ratted on them like you'd rat on anybody.

"An' you was goin' to sell the Miranda woman to your pal in the Argentine when you'd got the ransom money, huh? an' you reckoned that that was funny because you never thought she'd last the life that she'd get out there for a month. She'd have killed herself an' you was countin' on that.

"Listen, baby. We know you was the guy who kidnapped that kid in France an' let her die in a packin' case after the ransom money had been paid. We know that you was the guy who snatched the two Grotzner girls last year an' I'm the dick who found them in a vice house in Bakersfield where you sent 'em when you was through with 'em.

"Well, I reckon that there's some rotten rats in the mobs, but the two worst ones that I know was you an' Goyaz. I gave Goyaz his. I gave him five. Two for MacFee, an' two for Gallat—a poor guy that didn't have enough sense to know that he was alive, an' one for me an' I'm goin' to give you yours.

"You ain't goin' to get no chance to get extradition an' try to pack a jury or frame anybody. You're through with bribin' officials because there ain't goin' to be no officials except me. I guess I'm the judge, the jury an' the court, an' I'm sentencin' you, Siegella, an' here it comes!"

I put the leverage on my right arm, an' I force my left arm down, an' I press with my leg over the two arms, an' it works.

His neck snaps like a rotten twig.

I get up an' I look at him. He is lyin' all huddled up like the cheap punk that he was.

I climb up the bank an' at the top I find Miranda who has been chasin' around trying to find where I have been. Constance has made a getaway, but I am not worryin' about this dame because I know she will not get far.

My shoulder is aching pretty bad an' I sit down an' lean against a tree. Away to my right through the bushes I can hear the cops workin' up towards the house. The shootin' is dyin' down an' I see Schiedraut drinkin' applejack out of his flask.

Now this seems a good idea so I send Miranda over to borrow this flask before he has given it the works, an' I watch her walkin' between the trees an' I see that this dame Miranda has got a swell walk—you know what I mean, one of them walks that give you a whole lot of ideas that ain't in the training manual, an' I get a big idea that I could go for this Miranda in a big way, an' I don't mean maybe, an' I think that when I get

all this business cleaned up may be I will think about this.

An' what would you have done, anyway?

THE END

Lightning Source UK Ltd.
Milton Keynes UK
UKHW012001030322
399530UK00001B/145

9 781914 150852